The
Wartime
Vet

BOOKS BY ELLIE CURZON

ELLIE CURZON

The Wartime Vet

bookouture

Published by Bookouture in 2024

An imprint of Storyfire Ltd.
Carmelite House
50 Victoria Embankment
London EC4Y 0DZ

www.bookouture.com

ISBN: 978-1-83790-969-8
eBook ISBN: 978-1-83790-968-1

To the people who fought on the home front... and the animals who relied on them.

PROLOGUE
SPRING 1941

Laura's journey down to Bramble Heath from Coventry had been a long and tiring one, as the train had to take the long way round to avoid bombed-out tracks. The carriages jostled with young men in uniform, carrying their kitbags and gas masks, whose chirpiness didn't match the shadows around their eyes. The war had scoured the country, leaving devastation everywhere, and Laura hadn't felt safe on the train, always alert for the dreaded sound of aeroplane engines and sirens.

Guilt had tugged at Laura as she'd left Coventry, a city so damaged by Nazi bombs. She'd stayed through such unimaginable horrors, but she knew that in Bramble Heath she could really help the country get through this terrible war. She'd grown up on a farm and had followed the vet around whenever he'd visited, fascinated by his skills and knowledge and the affinity he had with the animals. She'd been proud to take her first job in Coventry after qualifying as a vet herself, caring for much-loved cats and dogs. But now she would be able to do her bit for the war effort, working with farmers to keep their livestock fit and healthy; to keep the nation fed in its darkest hours.

She wasn't running away from danger by coming to

Bramble Heath, she knew that. With a busy airbase just outside it, the village wasn't as safe as other places in the countryside. But she had a job to do, just as much as the brave airmen who took to the skies to fight the enemy, never knowing if that flight would be their last.

The train steamed past rolling fields of sheep and cows, the spring sunshine chasing shadows through the clouds. Old stone farmhouses dotted the hills, and tufts of woodland stood about here and there. Finally the train came to a stop and, although the station sign had been removed, there was a warm sensation in her chest, almost as if she had come home. Was this Bramble Heath?

'All passengers for Bramble Heath!' came the announcement, and Laura's heart skipped with excitement. This was it; her home for the foreseeable future.

Laura smoothed down her tweed skirt and patted the waves of her light brown hair into place beneath her simple felt hat. She collected her things, then stepped down from the train, steam spilling from the shiny black engine and clouding the platform. As it began to clear, Laura could see the station's small, red-brick Victorian building, decorated with posters demanding IS YOUR JOURNEY REALLY NECESSARY? and advising passengers that CARELESS TALK COSTS LIVES. It certainly would here, Laura knew, with the air force base on the edge of the village. Two airmen in RAF blue were climbing onto the train, the stationmaster respectfully touching his hat brim to them as the pilots waved back.

Those young men risked their lives every day for the war effort, and, now that Laura was going to work as a veterinary surgeon at the farms around Bramble Heath, she would be doing her bit too. She would be a vital cog in the machine that would keep the country fed.

AN ARMY MARCHES ON ITS STOMACH, declared another poster, showing a farmer standing in a field full of wheat. He was flanked by a cow and a pig while he brandished a fistful of carrots, and Laura smiled, her blue eyes sparkling with joy, because she would be working with farmers just like him to keep the nation's stomachs filled.

Laura left the station, her long legs carrying her along the avenue that led to the village. She loosened her coat as the welcome spring sunshine broke through a gap in the clouds. Cottages peered out between the old oaks and sycamores, and eventually the lane widened and Laura found herself in the village's main street. There was a row of shops, a post office, a pub, an ancient church and a tea room. Even though it was impossible to forget there was a war on, with windows criss-crossed with tape and arrows pointing to public air raid shelters, the village still felt cheerful and cared-for.

A grey-haired woman approached, carrying her shopping. Laura felt her curious gaze take in her suitcase and her vet bag, before the woman nodded hello and said warmly, 'Afternoon! You must be the new vet. Iris told us you'd be coming.'

Laura beamed. She'd been in Bramble Heath mere minutes and she'd already had a warm welcome. Mrs Pearson, her land-lady – Iris – had evidently spread the news about her imminent arrival.

'Yes, that's me,' Laura replied. 'It's wonderful to be here!'

Moments later, after some helpful directions, Laura found herself outside Mrs Pearson's cottage. It was built from mellow Sussex stone, and the small front garden was busy with daffodils and crocuses.

Her heart racing with anticipation, Laura knocked on the door. After a few seconds it was opened by a very smiley young housewife, who was wearing an apron covered in a cheerful print of flowers.

'Miss Fellgate, hello! Come in!' she said, her cheeks dimpling. 'I'm Mrs Pearson, but you must call me Iris.'

'Hello Iris!' Laura replied. 'Then you must call me Laura.'

Iris stood aside so that Laura could come into the hallway, with its prints of rural scenes on the walls, and wellington boots and shoes near the door.

'You must be exhausted after your journey,' Iris said, going to open the door that led off the hallway. 'Put down your things and come and have a cup of tea.'

'That would be very welcome, but first of all, I must give you my ration b—' Laura's words froze.

Because the moment Iris opened the door, a cheer went up.

She stood in the doorway, staring into Iris's lounge. It was crammed with people she had never met before. But every one of them, from the little blonde girl who looked like a cherub to the policeman in his uniform, were all smiling broadly at her.

'Gosh,' Laura said awkwardly. 'This *is* a surprise!'

'When I told them that the new vet was going to be my lodger, news went round the village like wildfire!' Iris explained, bringing Laura into the room. 'And they all wanted to come and meet you!'

Laura was overwhelmed by their show of welcome. Iris bustled her around the room, introducing her to Annie the nurse, and her father Henry, the local policeman; Betty from the post office; and so many other people that Laura's mind spun. They were all full of smiles, and after her long, tiring journey it was a tonic to be surrounded by so much kindness.

Laura had never dreamed of such a warm, friendly welcome. Even with all the challenges that doubtless lay ahead, doing such a difficult job during wartime, she knew that it would be so much easier in a village full of people who had welcomed her like a long-lost friend.

ONE

SPRING 1942

The telephone was already ringing as Laura stepped through the front door of the veterinary practice. The sound echoed harshly off the tiles in the hallway as she hurried to answer it, but Charles Morgan strode out of his living room, the *Telegraph* under his arm, and got there first. Laura's employer was never a particularly welcoming figure, but faced with a ringing telephone he was more glowering than ever.

Morgan snatched up the receiver of the Bakelite telephone, his eyebrow arched at Laura. She wasn't late, but he seemed annoyed with her already and the day had barely started.

'Bramble Heath Veterinary Surgery, Morgan speaking,' he snapped. It was his practice, but he seemed to resent lifting so much as a single finger.

Laura took off her raincoat and hung it on the antique wooden coat stand. The paintings of racehorses and gundogs that lined the panelled hallway peered down at her from their burnished frames.

Morgan nodded as he listened to whoever was on the other end.

'Harsh, rapid breathing... frothing at the mouth...' He

frowned. Laura lingered in the hallway, curious. It didn't sound good at all. 'Muscle tremors...'

Laura should've gone straight to the cluttered little room they used as the pharmacy, as she usually did first thing every morning to prepare the medications, but she was frozen on the spot. She recognised those symptoms and, if she was right, something was very, very wrong. This was not going to be an ordinary call-out.

'In that case, Miss Fellgate will be with you presently. Goodbye.' Morgan banged the receiver down and ended the call. 'Miss Fellgate, you're to go to the Goslings' farm right away. I'd go, but the place is overrun with Land Girls, and I *cannot* work with all their nonsense and giggling.'

There wasn't a farm in the area that didn't have Land Girls now, the young women who'd taken up farm work when the war started. But Morgan hadn't taken to them and, despite claiming that large-animal vet work was a job for men, he did what he could to avoid them; and ever since Laura had arrived, a year before, he usually sent her in his place instead.

'Of course, I'll go up there at once,' Laura replied as she took her coat from the rack again. 'It sounds serious.'

'I doubt very much it is,' Morgan retorted. 'Those classes you've been giving them have been more trouble than they're worth. You've been putting daft ideas into the silly heads of those impressionable girls. That was Nicola on the telephone – she said she's sure two of the Goslings' cows have been poisoned.'

Laura fumbled as she hurried to put on her coat.

Poisoned? That's exactly what I feared.

TWO

The gearbox of the rusty old Clyno groaned as Laura turned off the lane. She didn't notice the near-cloudless sky or the fluffy white hawthorn blossom starting to open in the hedgerows. Her thoughts were fixed entirely on getting to the Goslings' farm as fast as possible and trying to find out what on earth was going on.

A van was heading towards her, and it pulled aside into a passing place. Laura recognised Joan at the wheel, who took deliveries to the farms around Bramble Heath, and waved hello as she drove by.

She didn't have far to go. There were figures in the top field nearest the road wearing the Land Girl uniform of dark green jumpers and breeches, similar to how Laura had come to dress since arriving in Bramble Heath. The field was full of cows, which some of the Land Girls were guiding away, while near the hedge Laura saw two cows struggling to stay on their feet.

Laura pulled up, grabbed her leather vet bag and ran across the field. Her brogue shoes were sinking in the soft earth, but she didn't care. She wasn't going to waste valuable time changing into her boots.

'Are these the patients?' Laura called.

'Aye!' Nicola replied, hurrying to meet her, her hair escaping from the loose bun she always wore. Her face was darkened with concern for the cattle she and her companions were entrusted with. 'I came out into the fields to check on our girls and found Agnes and Nora proper out of fettle, bless them. Will you give these lasses the once-over, veterinary? It's not like my girls.'

People like Morgan wouldn't have believed the care that the Land Girls had for the cattle they looked after. Instead they complained that, on their evenings off, the girls liked to drink pints with airmen in the George and Dragon pub.

Laura approached the first cow, who was struggling for air, lips garlanded in white froth. The animal's pulse was fast, and Laura carefully opened the mouth a little further to see inside, and immediately spotted the dark red colour. She couldn't smell the scent of bitter almonds, but that meant – Laura hoped – that the dose was small.

'You think it's poisoning, don't you, Nicola?' Laura said. She trusted the sturdy Nicola, who had eagerly thrown herself into Land Girl work. With her rolled-up sleeves and rosy cheeks, she already looked like a farmer. 'I agree with you. This cow is displaying clear symptoms of cyanide poisoning. I'll give her a stimulant, it'll ease her breathing.'

It wasn't guaranteed to work, and Laura was very concerned that the Goslings could lose some of their livestock. With the war raging and shortages worsening by the day, they really couldn't afford to lose any of the animals. Lives depended on it. Laura had seen first-hand the hellish bombing raids on Coventry, and the sight of queues at the soup kitchens, set up to feed the people who'd lost everything short of the own lives, still haunted her.

Laura took out a bottle and filled the syringe. 'Hold her steady, girls,' she said.

Nicola reached out her hand to the beast and gently stroked its head, murmuring softly as though comforting a baby. She scratched the cow behind the ears and said, 'Come on then, Agnes, pet, let the doc sort you out.' Then she gave her friends a nod and they flanked the struggling creature protectively, holding Agnes steady as Nicola put her arm round the cow's broad, brown neck. As she did, she looked to the other cow and said gently, 'You'll be next, Nora, don't fret now.'

Laura stroked Agnes's neck before giving her the stimulant injection. 'Come on, girl, you'll be all right.' *I hope to heaven I've got here in time*, she thought, before examining Nora. Her symptoms were the same, and she prepared to give her the injection while Nicola stroked her gently.

Her voice subdued, Nicola said, 'We've some new girls on the farm.'

Laura glanced up at Nicola. 'I wonder... do you think they've made a mistake with the fodder? It's the only way I can think of for the cows to get cyanide poisoning – if the linseed cake sits in cold water, cyanide leaches out.'

The farmers got the linseed from flax that they grew in their fields. It was a vital crop; the flax was sold to make linen and parachute straps, while the seed could be used for oil and animal feed, so long as it was carefully prepared.

'Aye,' Nicola murmured, her concern for the animal clear in her usually cheery expression. 'That's what I reckon's happened. I'll be giving them all a fresh lesson in how important it is to get the linseed cake properly boiled up and mashed. I'm not having my lovely lasses getting poorly because folks don't do the job they're here to do.'

'That's the spirit,' Laura replied. If only Morgan could hear Nicola right now. 'They could've got poisoned from eating cherry laurel leaves, but there's none growing anywhere near here. It must be the fodder, I'm afraid.'

Laura checked her patients again. The cows were a little steadier on their feet now, their breathing improved.

Nicola chewed her lip, looking between the two ailing cows with all the concern of a worried mother. Whatever Morgan might think, the Land Girls worked hard and knew their stuff. They'd given up the lives they'd known to travel across the country for the war effort, not just to chase airmen and annoy the likes of him. Nicola had been right to call her in as soon as she saw how sickly the cows were; someone with nothing but air between their ears wouldn't have acted as quickly as she did. She could only hope they'd been able to treat the cows in time.

If they died, the farm's milk production would be hit, and people would go hungry. Farmer Gosling would need to find another farm willing to sell some of its cattle – if he could get the money together to buy them. And the blame would fall on the Land Girls, because Laura was sure it wouldn't just be Morgan who'd be complaining about them. Everyone needed to pull together, not point fingers and accuse, otherwise the evil in Germany would be even harder to hold back. Laura shuddered, picturing again the soup kitchen queue winding through the ruins where people's homes had once stood. She'd seen all too well what the war could do.

The girls who had shepherded the cows away down the field were coming over. Laura didn't recognise them, and realised they must be the new girls. They looked ashen-faced with worry.

'Are they going to be all right?' one of them asked, a girl with large, frightened eyes.

'Hopefully,' Laura replied.

'I've never seen a cow fall ill before,' she admitted. 'But Nicola knew what to do.'

'It took a bit of learning, but that's why we're lucky having Laura as the vet in the village.' Nicola was still stroking the cow's soft head. 'She taught us what to look out for when the girls aren't feeling canny. Laura, this is Martha and Lottie, they're our new Land Girls. They mixed up the feed for the girls.'

And Laura knew what that meant. If the linseed cake *was* to blame, and it looked like it might be, it was Martha and Lottie who'd be getting a lesson in preparing feed for the cattle on the Goslings' farm.

'W-we did, me and my sister.' Lottie swallowed uncomfortably, and Laura got the distinct impression that the new Land Girls were also worried that they were to blame.

'How did you prepare it?' Laura asked her, looking from one girl to the other and noting the family resemblance between them; the same large, blue eyes and dark blonde hair.

'Just how we were told,' Martha replied, glancing to her sister for support. 'Boil it up in the copper, that's what Nicola said.'

'And you're sure it was boiled?' Laura asked them. But if they had made a mistake, would they admit it? She couldn't help but feel sorry for them – what a shame, to accidentally poison two cows when they'd only just arrived at the farm. One mistake like this could kill, and would mean that the villagers would lose their trust in the girls who'd come to Bramble Heath to do such a vital job. And what if it put off other girls from joining the Land Army? How would the nation's farms function without them? How would the nation's stomachs be filled?

'Yes, I'm sure.' Lottie nodded so vehemently her hat almost fell off.

Nicola didn't say anything for a long moment. Instead, she simply nodded, before finally telling the sisters, 'Well, we'll do it together later just to be sure. It's an easy enough thing to get wrong and let it sit in the cold water for too long, but it's the worse for my girls if we make mistakes.'

'Gosh, I'm so sorry. I was sure we followed what you said.'

Lottie bit her lip. 'But... yes, let's do it together, then we can make absolutely sure not to get it wrong... again.'

Poor girl. It's not a good start.

'What's up with the girls?' asked a young voice.

Laura turned to see Sarah, a girl who had been evacuated to Bramble Heath. She was fascinated by the farms around the village, and often popped up when Laura was on her rounds.

'Morning, Sarah!' Laura replied, taking in Sarah's tousled appearance. One sock was up, the other fallen down, her coat was undone and sliding off one shoulder. Her bobbed brown hair had been combed and parted, but the tortoiseshell clip keeping it off her face had slid down, and strands of her hair were falling into her eyes. But it never seemed to bother Sarah; she was too busy having adventures to care. 'They've eaten something that disagreed with them. But I've given them their injections and they're slowly getting better. And how is the youngest Land Girl in Bramble Heath today?'

'I'm all right,' Sarah murmured as she clambered over the fence into the field, but she was obviously worried at the sight of the patients. She ran across the mud towards them and reached up her hand to stroke Nora's nose, then crossed to Agnes to do the same.

'Let's get them off the field and into the cattle shed,' Laura said. 'They're steadier on their feet now. I'll need a couple of you to keep an eye on them during the day – and if the symptoms come back, get on the telephone right away and I'll be here as fast as I can.'

'They're looking a lot more canny now!' Nicola told the girls with obvious relief, and Laura could certainly understand why. In wartime every animal was precious, and Agnes and Nora's herd were an essential part of the milk supply not only for the village of Bramble Heath, but for people further afield too. In a time of rationing, every drop counted. 'All right, girls, help us

get the herd into their shed and we'll refill the troughs while
they rest.'

The cows wouldn't be pleased to be moved inside, away
from the fresh spring grass and soft spring sunshine, but they
couldn't stay outside and risk eating fodder that could kill them.
So Laura and Sarah helped the Land Girls to shepherd the
cattle off the field, heading down the lane towards the Goslings'
farm buildings, built in stone and wood over the generations,
looking for all the world as if they had grown from the hillside.

A cockerel who stood sentinel on the gatepost near the
farmhouse announced the unexpected arrivals with a loud
crow, and everyone chuckled. Even Martha and Lottie, who had
looked so worried before.

'Someone's pleased to see us!' Laura joked, glad that something had lifted the mood.

Once the Land Girls had settled the cows, Laura patted
Nicola's shoulder. 'You saved the day, Nicola. If it hadn't been
for you, Agnes and Nora wouldn't—' Laura shook her head. She
didn't want to finish her sentence.

Nicola nodded. She understood.

'I know,' she replied. 'Thanks for coming out to my girls,
Laura. And I'll make sure the new lasses know what they're
doing. I'm not having this again on this farm.'

Laura smiled. She admired how much responsibility Nicola
was willing to shoulder. 'I wish more people were as conscientious as you are. Now, I'd better get back to the village.'

She looked around for Sarah. The girl was going between
the cows, looking them all over as though to satisfy herself that
there weren't going to be any further casualties. Laura could see
something of herself in the ten-year-old who had left London
behind for the country air, and who had thrown herself into life
on the farm as readily as if she'd been born to it. Every day as
soon as school finished, she'd race up the road from Bramble
Heath and her hosts, the Hubbard family, and join the Land

Girls in the fields. Every weekend she was there too, toiling alongside them and taking lessons from them in how to care for the animals in their charge. It was a long way from Stepney, but Sarah had settled in perfectly. It was a long way too, from the Blitz that had rained down terror over London as the girl watched, the world she had once known disappearing into rubble day by day.

Sarah reminded Laura of the children in Coventry who had stayed at home with their parents. It chilled her to think that there were more girls like Sarah, who had lived for adventures and fun, and were now lying in a mass grave, their lives cut short by the vicious onslaught of one terrible night. She had never told Sarah this; it wasn't right that children were losing their innocence. It was bad enough that Sarah must worry about her family back at home. That every bombing raid that flew overhead to London could mean that she might become an orphan. All Laura could do was to protect her, make a fuss of her, and hope against hope that Sarah would never know the pain of losing her family.

'Sarah?' Laura called. 'I'm going back to the village now. Would you like a lift?'

'Not really. I'd rather stay here,' Sarah admitted. 'But I said I'd help Ma Hubbard sort out the garden, so I'd better go. She said I can come back later, though!'

'If you come back later, maybe you can help get the cows back into the field again?' Laura suggested as they headed back along the lane, towards her haphazardly parked car. 'You were a great help today, Sarah. Did you see how much the cows enjoyed the water you brought them?'

Sarah beamed proudly. 'Just doing my bit!'

'Do you know, when I was a little girl growing up on my parents' farm, I wished and wished that I could go to London,' Laura admitted, thinking of her childhood in the Cotswolds. 'But for you it's the other way round!'

They'd reached the car, but Laura glanced back into the field and saw one of the troughs that the cows had been eating from. She decided to take a quick look and went back into the field, swishing through the new grass. Once she reached the trough, she couldn't see anything untoward – it contained linseed mash, as she had expected.

But just as she stepped back from the trough, she felt something crunch under her foot in the otherwise soft soil.

Curious, Laura peered down and saw some feed that hadn't quite made it to the trough, as if it had spilled when it was poured in. But it wasn't mash, it was dry feed.

'What's up?' asked Sarah as she climbed up and leaned over the fence.

'I'm not sure. It's probably nothing,' Laura replied. Slipping on a glove, she scooped up the small amount of spilt feed and put it in a wrap of paper in her pocket. She didn't want the Land Girls to miss it when they came back to clean and refill the troughs. 'But just to be on the safe side... Right, let's head home, shall we? That was a good morning's work!'

I'll have to report this, Laura thought to herself, her mind racing. *Could someone really have poisoned the cows on purpose? But how could anyone do such a thing, just when the home front is more important than ever?*

THREE

Laura dropped Sarah off outside the Hubbards' thatch-roofed cottage. It always reminded her of the nursery rhyme about the old woman who lived in a shoe; as well as taking on Sarah, the Hubbards already had four children of their own, and whenever Laura came by it seemed that twice as many again had come round to play. But the couple didn't seem to mind; they always managed to find space for more, and clearly loved their busy home.

Two of the Hubbards' brood were running about in the front garden, and hurtled over to the gate as soon as they saw their friend Sarah arrive.

'Take care, Sarah, and I'll see you again soon!' Laura said.

'See you later, Laura!' Sarah beamed. 'We saved them cows today, didn't we?'

'We did.' Laura grinned at her. She loved to see Sarah's enthusiasm. She'd get the bug to become a vet herself, Laura was sure of it. 'Bye!'

'Bye!' Sarah called as she clambered down out of the car and greeted her friends with a wave. Then, with a glance back at Laura, she turned to the Hubbard children and told them,

'Wait until you hear what I've been doing today!' And with that, she ran towards the garden and left Laura to go on her way.

Laura drove on, passing the ancient stone church that seemed as old as time itself, where the white-haired Reverend Ellis stooped before the parish noticeboard, talking to an airman. Rose, dressed as always in her neat black dress and white apron, a snowy white cap on her dark hair, was looking out through the window of the teashop she ran, a tray in her hands. Betty Farthing, such a glamorous young woman and one of the first people Laura had met in Bramble Heath, headed through the door of the village post office where she worked, her blonde hair fashionable but practical in a crocheted snood. Fruit and vegetables were piled up outside Knapps' greengrocer's, a more plentiful amount than Laura used to see in Coventry, while Ernie stood in the doorway to his butcher's shop, wearing his spotless striped apron. As she rounded the corner, Constable Henry Russell, the village's resident bobby and Annie's father, gave her a very smart salute. The cheery smile that accompanied it made the gesture feel anything but formal, though.

Laura waved to Constable Russell. She'd had several adventures with him, chasing cattle that had got loose or tracking down the owners of lost dogs. He was never anything but affable and full of good cheer.

Bramble Heath was a lovely place to live, even if the airbase nearby meant they saw more of the war than they would do otherwise in the countryside. The locals had all made her feel welcome, from the many farmers she visited to the Polish people who lived in the hamlet and the airmen at the base. The village was used to welcoming incomers.

Although Charles Morgan hadn't been quite as welcoming. His son had joined up, leaving the family practice in Bramble Heath for the Royal Army Veterinary Corps. He always talked with great pride about his son and his endeavours, but Laura knew he must be worried about him, and it was obvious he'd been frustrated to lose manpower just as the farmers were needed even more. And with so many other vets – male ones, at least – joining up to do their bit, Morgan had reluctantly hired Laura. She had grown up on a farm and it seemed that had made the bitter pill of taking on a female vet easier for him to swallow.

The veterinary practice was at the end of the high street, on the edge of the village, a rather smart Georgian house with pillars on either side of the door. Two brass plaques were in pride of place, shiny against the red brick of the house; one for Morgan and one for his son. Laura wasn't expecting to see her own name on a plaque there soon, if ever.

She drove round to the back of the house to park the car, then let herself in at the back door. Her shoes were filthy from the muddy field, but the floors of a country veterinary practice were never without mud for long.

'Mr Morgan?' Laura called. 'Are you with a patient?' He might be in the consulting room, or perhaps in his favourite armchair reading the paper.

'I am doing my paperwork!' came the barked reply from Mr Morgan's sitting room. Laura knew what that meant: he was studying the racing form and would have no time for what he would undoubtedly dismiss as girlish concerns. 'When we have concluded our cases, we do our administration.' Mr Morgan appeared in the doorway of the hallway that led to his living quarters. He peered at Laura over the top of his half-moon spectacles and asked pointedly, 'Have we done our administration, Miss Fellgate?'

I've only just parked the car! Laura swallowed down her retort. 'Not yet – I'm about to. I thought you should know, I'm sure it was a cyanide case—'

'A linseed cake case.' Morgan cut her off sharply and reached for the stubby pencil that was tucked behind his ear.

'And once again, girls who know more about Hollywood actors than the business of farming place our agricultural output at risk!'

I was right about the racing form, then, she thought, as Morgan hid the telltale pencil in his jacket pocket.

'Yes, it was most likely the linseed cake,' Laura replied. It was best to begin by agreeing with him. 'But Nicola – oh, she's a *canny lass*, as she'd say. She suspected it at once, got on the telephone to us right away, cleared the cows who weren't showing symptoms to the other side of the field... and her care for those animals, Mr Morgan. When I first came here, you told me that the welfare of the animals should always be our main concern, and Nicola more than lives up to that. She really cares for those cows, Mr Morgan.'

'I'm sure Farmer Gosling will be delighted to hear it when he receives the bill.' Morgan sniffed. 'An expense that could easily have been avoided if the young ladies had prepared the fodder appropriately in the first place. Am I not correct?'

Laura really didn't want to agree, but she couldn't deny what he'd said. Avoidable bills from the vet weren't something that any farmer welcomed and she worried that, if word got about, the farmers might end up resenting the Land Girls being in the village. But those young women were just as vital to the war effort as anyone else. 'Yes, but they're new girls, and they're terribly keen to learn. It won't happen again.' But there was something in Morgan's words that was nagging at the back of Laura's mind. He'd known it was linseed cake straight away. 'Have you had another cyanide case recently?'

'Several,' was his curt reply. 'What Hitler's bombs failed to achieve, our so-called Women's Land Army should ably complete. At the very least, they shall bankrupt the farmers of this parish!'

Laura blinked at him in surprise. 'Doesn't this strike you as rather odd? It's not as if the Land Girls only arrived last week.

They've been working on the farms since the war began. Do you see what I'm driving at?' she asked carefully. She didn't want to overstep the mark, but it had to be said. 'If all of this *is* really down to the Land Girls, then why are we only seeing these cases now?'

'But we have had a significant number of new Land Girls, have we not?' he suggested. 'Mrs Morgan has reported a veritable influx of giggling silliness in the tea rooms of the district, as though the safety of our nation is naught but a playground game!'

'We have, yes...' Laura agreed, trying not to sigh at his rudeness. Why was he so convinced that Land Girls were hopeless? 'But even so, I'm not the only vet who gives the Land Girls classes on how to look after the animals. How to milk them, how to look for disease, all of that. They pay attention, they ask excellent questions. They're conscientious and want to do their bit, just as much as anyone else does. This just doesn't feel right to me, Mr Morgan.'

Morgan heaved a sigh, then took his gold pocket watch from his waistcoat and examined it for a moment. 'Out with it, Miss Fellgate. What revelation are you so awkwardly groping your way towards?'

'Could we not be looking at foul play?' Laura ventured. She drew the wad of paper from her pocket and carefully unfolded it, revealing the few pieces of dry feed. 'Look what I found on the ground, near the trough.'

'That is generally where one would find food that has escaped the trough, is it not?' He peered down at the feed Laura was holding in her palm. 'Not quite the startling conclusion one might have been expecting. Miss Christie, I feel, has nothing to fear.'

'But don't you see?' Laura insisted, even though Morgan evidently thought she was ridiculous. Even *more* ridiculous than he'd already decided. 'The Land Girls had put mash in the trough, not dry food. If it'd been put out a few days ago, it'd be soggy by now in the mud. But it's not – it's dry. What if someone else, *not* a Land Girl, put it there? What if someone is poisoning the cows on purpose?'

But who would do such a thing? Could someone really resent the presence of the Land Girls to such a degree that they would deliberately poison the cattle so that they would get the blame? The very idea was shocking, when everyone in the country relied on the nation's farms, which were now staffed by so many girls just like Nicola, Lottie and Martha.

Morgan shook his head. 'I shall speak to Gosling and make him aware that his girls need watching,' was his only suggestion. 'Nobody is poisoning cows, Miss Fellgate. This is not the picture house nor the wireless drama, this is simply poor practice and ill-prepared young fillies. Now, paperwork, if you please. This is a business, not an amateur theatrical!'

Laura returned the feed to her pocket. If only Morgan could see round his incredibly unfair views about the Land Girls, then surely he'd agree that something very suspicious was going on here?

But that wasn't going to happen. It was a wonder he'd ever hired her, and Laura knew that if he'd had the chance to employ a man instead of her he would've done, in the blink of an eye.

'All right, I'll go and do my paperwork,' she replied in a small voice, the one she used when she knew that, for the moment, she was defeated.

She went down the hallway, intending to go to the practice's small office, but the thought of the dry feed in her pocket wouldn't go away. Instead, knowing that Morgan had gone back to his racing form, she went into the pharmacy.

She took a textbook down from the shelf and flicked through the pages until she found what she was after.

A test for cyanide, that's what I need.

She carefully set up her experiment, and, within a matter of minutes, Laura knew without a doubt that she was right. The dry feed she'd found contained cyanide.

The world seemed to stop for a moment as she stared at the test tube. Her worst fears had been confirmed.

It's in the dry feed. Someone's poisoned it and put it in the trough on purpose.

But there was no point at all in telling Morgan. He clearly wasn't interested, convinced as he was that the Land Girls' carelessness was solely to blame. Laura just couldn't agree with him. It seemed clear to her that there really was a saboteur in the area, deliberately poisoning the cattle.

Something had to be done.

She tidied away the apparatus, then went into the practice office. Taking a seat at the old wooden bureau, she took out a piece of paper and dipped her pen in the ink.

But she wasn't doing her paperwork: Laura was writing to the Ministry of Agriculture.

They'll know what to do. I just hope someone will listen.

FOUR

After she had filled out her paperwork, Laura hurried out to the post office with her letter.

'I'm just going to send off an order,' she called to her boss as she closed the door behind her. He left admin jobs like that to her, and today it came in handy.

It was a bright spring day, still not warm, but there was the promise of summer in the blue sky and the gentle sunlight. Laura had lived in Bramble Heath for nearly a year and had quickly settled in. She'd grown up on a farm on the edge of a village rather like Bramble Heath, and so in some ways it was a home from home. But she missed her parents and, because travel was so difficult because of the war, she hadn't seen them, or her home, for some time. They understood, though, after what she had survived in Coventry, after the night she'd spent in the basement at the veterinary practice, comforting the pets left in her care as hell rained down outside. Somehow, she'd been spared. And now she needed to do her bit, even if she didn't get on all that well with her boss. Veterinary surgeons were a crucial part of the system that would keep the nation fed.

And someone in Bramble Heath seemed determined to

disrupt it. Laura held her letter tighter. She wasn't going to let them.

Outside the post office, she saw a motorbike parked up. It belonged to Annie Russell, the local nurse. Some young boys were standing around admiring it, and Laura recognised Jamie, Betty Farthing's brother.

The boys turned to wave at Laura.

'Our Barney's doing really well!' one of the boys, Tommy, told her. 'Whatever you did to his hoof, he's back on his feet again and munching carrots!'

'That's what I like to hear!' Laura recalled her visit to the gentle donkey with a sore hoof. He had placidly let Laura treat him, not complaining once. For all that the poisonings had shaken her, cases like Barney's reminded Laura of the joy she found in her work.

'The car's sounding a bit creaky,' Jamie called to Laura. 'If you want me to give her a quick tune-up, drop her round the back whenever you've got time. I need all the practice I can get if the RAF are going to let me work on their Spits when I'm old enough!'

'Thanks, Jamie, that's really kind of you,' Laura replied. 'I may well take you up on your offer. It's a wonder that car still runs at all. I'm sure it's only held together with pieces of string!'

Laura went into the post office and the bell jangled above the door. Betty and her mother were behind the counter, but the post office didn't have any customers except for Annie in her crisp nurse's uniform, who was speaking in hushed, worried tones.

Government war information posters were tacked up on the walls, and shortages meant that the shelves and racks of the shop weren't well-stocked. But the place always felt friendly, a hub of village life, thanks to Betty and her mother.

The letter to the Ministry felt heavy in Laura's hand. *This* was the Bramble Heath she loved, and she hated to think of there being a bad apple, hell-bent on disrupting this village that had welcomed her, and so many others, with such warmth and kindness.

'Hello!' Laura said, taking her place at the counter next to Annie. 'How is everyone?'

'Setting the world to rights.' Mrs Farthing chuckled. 'You must've heard about the campfires, out and about on the farms? Joan just called in and says somebody lit another one last night.'

Laura shook her head. 'Campfires? No, I haven't heard anything about them.'

'Well...' Mrs Farthing leaned across the counter, evidently keen to impart the news. 'They say that the evacuees have been lighting campfires in the woods!'

Laura shook her head. That didn't sound very sensible of them. 'Surely not in the blackout? And with the airbase close by too...'

She closed her eyes for a moment, holding back a memory of that terrible night in Coventry; the relentless onslaught of noise, the stench of smoke and fear.

Annie stepped in. 'Dad knows all about it. He went up to check. There was a campfire there, all right. Someone must've lit it. I can't get over how reckless it is, how stupid. It's like setting up a beacon to help the Nazi bombers find Bramble Heath. But I really hope it's not the evacuees. Dad's going to knock on some doors and offer some friendly fire-safety advice.'

'I've already spoken to Jamie,' Mrs Farthing said. 'He swears blind he knows nothing about it. I'm sure he wasn't telling a fib either. He's promised to make sure the kids know not to light campfires.'

'That's very decent of him,' Laura replied. Betty and Mrs Farthing smiled proudly at her words.

'Now, anyway, what can I do for you, Laura?' Mrs Farthing asked, steepling her fingers.

Laura's hand trembled as she slid the envelope across the counter to Mrs Farthing. 'I need to send this letter, please.'

I just hope they reply. They have to.

After she'd posted the letter, Laura said her goodbyes and went out into the street. Henry, the local bobby, was talking to Jamie and his friends, no doubt about the campfires. Laura waved to him, and Henry came over.

'Ah, Laura, how d'you do?' he asked.

'Not so bad. I hope you're all right,' Laura replied. A tiny frown appeared on Henry's brow, and she realised he could sense that something wasn't quite right. Laura lowered her voice.

'Henry, I think you should know there's been some cyanide cases on the farms,' she told him. 'No one's lost any livestock yet, but... I'm not sure what we can do, but I've just sent a letter to the Ministry of Agriculture.'

'Sounds sensible.' Henry nodded slowly as he absorbed Laura's news. 'Cyanide, you say? Something's poisoning the cattle?'

'Not some*thing*,' Laura whispered apprehensively. 'I think it could be some*one*.'

FIVE

That evening, Laura headed back to her lodgings. The blackout curtains were already drawn, which made the cottage feel cosy. It was nice to have a place to come home to. Her landlady was about to put her three-year-old twins to bed. She carried Sam in her arms, and Tom gripped the hem of her dress.

'Goodness me, you look washed out,' Iris told her lodger. 'I'll put supper on just as soon as I've got these two down.'

Laura realised that her worries were showing on her face. She shook her head. 'Nonsense, let me help. I'll carry Tom for you.'

Tom blinked at Laura, then let go of Iris's dress to hold his arms up to her. Laura picked up the round-cheeked little boy and hugged him.

Iris and Laura headed up the stairs with the two toddlers. Sam was almost asleep, while Tom was showing Laura his teddy. The toy was still wearing a sling that Tom had insisted Laura put on the bear for him, even after Laura had explained that she'd never had a bear as a patient before.

The floorboards of the cottage creaked as they went into the boys' bedroom under the sloping roof. Their father watched over them from his photograph on the mantelpiece. It had been taken at a studio, lit as if he was a film star in his army uniform. The boys always said goodnight to him via the photograph, and on his last leave Bertie had told them he always said goodnight to the photograph he had of the twins back in barracks.

'I just hope they don't forget him,' Iris fretted as she wriggled her sons into their pyjamas. 'A few months can be a long old time at their age.'

'I'm sure they won't,' Laura said gently, as she always did when Iris spoke her fears aloud. She knew that Iris found the separation difficult too, and Laura wondered what it was like to love someone as Iris clearly loved her husband.

I'm not sure I'll ever know.

As Laura helped to tuck the boys into bed, she thought of all those years of study it'd taken her to become a veterinary surgeon. She had started to look for a post as soon as she'd graduated, but her boyfriend had told her that they should get married – and that she really didn't need to worry any more about her hobby.

Hobby? My career isn't a hobby!

The heartbreaking fallout had inevitably been the ending of their relationship. Six months later, her now-former boyfriend married his best friend's sister.

Laura knew his view wasn't unusual. What man would want to be married to a vet, working long hours, coming home with straw and mud in her hair? It was hardly a ladylike profession. She knew her parents were proud of her, but she sensed their disappointment that, after all her studying, she had insisted on taking a job that wouldn't help her find a husband. She had made no attempt to find a new boyfriend. Even if Bramble Heath was full of dashing pilots in their RAF blue, Laura was certain that none of them would be interested in her.

She was happy to be Auntie Laura to Iris's twins, reading

their favourite Beatrix Potter stories to them as they drifted off to sleep.

As usual when the animals of Bramble Heath didn't need Laura's help, she had supper with Iris, and afterwards they sat together in the lounge listening to music on the radio. Iris's knitting needles clacked as she worked on some socks for Bertie, and Laura tried to relax.

But her mind kept going back to the cows struggling to breathe, and the test tube that had proved her worst fears. She'd done what she could – she had told Henry, and she'd reported it to the Ministry of Agriculture too. But she couldn't settle. Someone was intent on doing harm in Bramble Heath, poisoning the livestock, destroying the reputation of the Land Girls and leading Nazi bombers to the village and its airbase. Laura knew she wouldn't relax.

Not until she'd stopped them.

SIX

Each day, Laura hoped for a reply from the Ministry. Maybe she was hoping for too much. They were very busy with the war causing so much disruption – but surely they'd see the seriousness of what she had reported? Someone had deliberately left out poisoned feed, and it wasn't an isolated incident either; it had affected several farms. Fortunately all the animals had recovered, but if it happened again there was a terrible risk that Laura might be too late. And she had overheard gossip in the village, that *those blasted Land Girls don't know what they're doing*. They didn't deserve that, and it was an attitude that would send them back home. Who would work the farms then?

How could someone do such a thing, not only intentionally harming the farm animals but wilfully putting the nation's food supply at risk? The ships bringing wheat and other supplies across the Atlantic were targeted by submarines, so there was little to go round as it was. Whoever was leaving out the poison was no better than the men who launched torpedoes at those ships; they were all attempts to starve the country into submission.

Laura was ready to leave for work. She stuck her head

round Iris's kitchen door. As usual, she was busy. She kept her kitchen glisteningly clean, despite the best efforts of her boys.

'I'm off to work now,' Laura told her. 'If you see any post for me...?'

'Oh, yes – this came for you,' Iris told her, holding out a letter.

It must be from the Ministry!

But Laura recognised her mother's handwriting on the envelope. She tucked it into her coat, so she could read it later. And carrying it in her pocket meant a little piece of her parents was with her.

Would she ever receive a reply from the Ministry?

She headed off to work and began checking stocks in the pharmacy, trying to keep herself busy as she listened for the telephone, her worries building inside her. What if there was another case today? Why wouldn't Morgan listen?

Once she'd finished her tasks, she went to see her boss.

'Mr Morgan?' she asked, knocking on the living room door. 'I've finished in the pharmacy.'

'Thank you, Miss Fellgate,' Morgan replied as he opened the door. He had his newspaper tucked under one arm and a cup of tea held in one ruddy hand. 'When I've completed my paperwork I have an appointment at the Bishop farm. A once-over of the new foal.'

And of course Mr Morgan would give himself that particular job, because it meant plentiful tea, scones and racing talk. All in return for ten minutes of very light consulting over a robustly healthy new arrival.

That's being the practice owner for you.

Suddenly, the air was split by a frantic hammering on the door. Whoever it was, it must be an emergency for them to arrive so early, before the practice had even unlocked for the day.

'They'll wake the dead,' Mrs Morgan tutted as she bustled

past, wiping the flour from her hands on the pristine white apron she was wearing.

As soon as Laura had arrived at the practice, she had realised that Mrs Morgan was its unpaid member of staff, without whom the entire place would cease to function. She answered the telephone and the doorbell, chased farmers for invoices, passed on messages to her husband, and somehow found time to cook and keep the house immaculate. She never seemed to rest. Laura had hoped she might find an ally in her, but it seemed that Mrs Morgan was too busy to make friends with the new vet. And the first time she had seen Laura in trousers, she had pursed her lips and walked away in stony silence.

Mrs Morgan disappeared along the hallway, leaving her husband to say with a superior air, 'Perhaps someone else has been poisoned, eh, Miss Fellgate?' He chuckled indulgently. 'Poison hath residence and medicine power, as the bard did say.'

'Just a min—' As Mrs Morgan called out, Sarah came hurtling along the passage. Laura took one look at her and knew that something was amiss.

'Up on Bryant's farm!' Sarah stopped to catch her breath, then reached into her pocket and thrust out a little paper bag, the sort that might contain sweets from the post office. 'I was up there to help the girls turn out the cows and I spotted this in the trough, just like the stuff you found on the ground at the Goslings'. A couple of the cows had already started eating, but I told the girls to stop them!'

Laura was astonished, but she had to admire the girl's quick thinking. 'Well done. Let me have a look at that.' She took the paper bag from Sarah and peered inside.

It looks exactly the same as the dry feed I found at the Goslings' farm.

Laura put it in her pocket, then went to retrieve her coat. She could run a test on the feed later, but first she had to check the cows. She couldn't risk any deaths. 'Sarah, are the cows all right? You saw them at Goslings' farm – does it look like the same thing to you? I'll go up there at once.'

'Miss Fellgate, we cannot be summoned by city children to country farms!' Mr Morgan shouted as he followed her, casting a furious glance at Sarah. 'How on earth are we to place this on an account? Will this child pay for our time and expertise, because I am very sure that Mr Bryant shall not!'

Sarah must have heard his complaints, but she gave no sign of it. Instead she darted past his ambling bulk to join Laura at the door.

'They only got a couple of mouthfuls, so I hope they'll be all right,' she said fretfully. 'But you'd better come up and see them. You never know, they're greedy girls!'

'If Mr Bryant has a concern, Mr Bryant will telephone!' Morgan chastised them. 'I forbid you—'

At this, Sarah finally turned to the older vet. 'Mr Bryant's out at the cattle sale,' she said. 'And his wife says one of you two's to come out to the farm!'

'That settles it,' Laura said as she picked up her bag. 'I'll go, seeing as Mr Morgan has a prior engagement.' Not that Morgan would give up his far-from-taxing morning appointment for cows and Land Girls anyway.

Laura strode out of the house with Sarah, before Morgan could say anything else. She opened the passenger door of the car and, once Sarah had climbed in, gave the girl her bag to hold.

'Hold tight, we don't want it getting bumped about, do we?' Laura knew Sarah would enjoy the responsibility. Then she got behind the wheel and headed off for the Bryants' farm, the gearbox complaining as usual.

'Mrs Hubbard don't know I've come out,' Sarah admitted, but Laura wasn't entirely surprised by that revelation. 'But I know if she wasn't out getting her rations, she would've told me to fetch you. So it wasn't really a lie.'

'Ah, I see...' Laura nodded. She had to admire her. 'That was very resourceful of you. I'm sorry about my boss. He doesn't view these cases in the same light as I do.'

I'm not sure anyone does, apart from Sarah and the Land Girls.

The Clyno protested as Laura took the car into the lanes, but she didn't care. She had to get to the farm. She had to—

What on earth is that man doing?

Up ahead in the narrow lane, Laura could see the figure of a man. He clearly wasn't a farm worker, and she couldn't understand what he was doing walking alone out here. He was tall, and tidily dressed, with a neat moustache. Just under his homburg hat, Laura could see silver streaking his hair. His overcoat was draped over his arm, and he carried a suitcase in one hand, and in his other—

'Sarah, look, that odd man's carrying a kitten!'

The little tortoiseshell kitten was curled in the crook of his arm, nestled happily against the dark grey suit he wore. Laura had never seen anything quite like it, even in Bramble Heath.

Although she had to get to the farm as quickly as she could, there was something wrong about the besuited man carrying a kitten. Her duty was to all animals, and she stopped the car with a screech, then reversed a few feet along the lane to catch up with the man.

Once she was level with him, she opened the window. 'Excuse me, sir, is there a problem with the kitten?'

'The problem with the kitten is that there *is* a kitten,' he replied in polite, though not overly plummy, tones. His accent had a hint of the north, Laura realised, so he wasn't a local in any respect. 'Is this the road to Bramble Heath?'

'Yes, yes, it is,' Laura replied briskly. But she couldn't drive off. The man was a puzzle; no one like him arrived in

Bramble Heath on foot. Where on earth had he materialised from? '*Why* is there a kitten? Forgive me for asking. I don't mean to appear rude, but I'm a veterinary surgeon, you see. Is it hurt?'

Laura *did* sound rude, she knew that. But if a life was at stake, she needed to know.

'The train stopped a mile or so along the line. Sheep on the line,' the man explained. 'I was the only person travelling to Bramble Heath, so the guard put me off and told me to walk. That's where the kitten comes in.'

Laura blinked at him. 'Well, I suppose that makes sense.' *In a way.* 'And the kitten?'

She looked down at the tiny cat lying so incongruously in the man's arms. She couldn't see anything obviously wrong, but it was hard to be entirely sure without a proper examination. It was clearly very young.

'The kitten was in the middle of the road, crying,' he told her. 'I spent half an hour looking for the mother or an owner and found neither. Since my first call is at the village's veterinary surgery, I had no choice but to bring the animal too.'

The only veterinary surgery in Bramble Heath was Laura's.

Maybe he's a pharmaceutical rep? He'll get plenty of orders from us if he's selling antidotes for poisons.

Yet he didn't really look like a travelling salesman. Especially wandering the lanes with a kitten. And there was something about him, something Laura couldn't quite put her finger on. Something official.

'That's where I work,' Laura replied. 'Are you going to see Mr Morgan?'

'You're not Fellgate, by any chance?' the stranger asked, much to Laura's surprise. Sarah leaned right over to get a better look at him as he stooped to the car window.

'I'm *Miss* Fellgate,' Laura answered, surprised by his rudeness. If he wasn't a travelling salesman, he could be from the

Ministry. But she daren't get her hopes up. Would they really send someone out so soon? 'And you are...?'

'Commander Alastair Seaton, Ministry.' He put down the suitcase he was carrying and held out his hand to the open window. 'Your letter landed on my pile.'

Relief flooded through her. So much for Morgan; the Ministry of Agriculture was taking her seriously even if her own boss didn't believe her. Bombs were falling from the sky, shortages got worse every day, and a dot in the clouds could turn into an enemy plane primed to kill. And death didn't only come from the sky; there was someone on the ground, attacking the farms and the nation's food supply at a time when everyone had little enough in their ration books anyway.

'You're from the Ministry of Agriculture?' Laura asked him hopefully.

'There are several Ministries,' Commander Seaton replied curtly. 'I am from one of them.'

Maybe he wasn't here to help at all? She quailed inside at the thought. It would hardly surprise her if the commander had been sent out to put her in her place and abandon what Morgan thought of as her silly ideas about poisoners. Another man telling her she was wrong, hysterical, and everything else that she had grown up hearing. A man of rank too, a *commander*, to really send the message home.

That's all I need.

But maybe she could change the commander's mind? Laura thrust out her hand and shook Seaton's. 'That's the best news I've heard all week! Hop in, Commander, we've just had another case come in. That's where I'm off to now.'

'I'm Sarah, I'm Laura's assistant,' said the little evacuee. 'That's why I have to sit in the front.'

'Pass me the kitten, Sarah will look after it,' Laura said, reaching through the window for the cat.

He handed it to her with obvious care, murmuring to the

little kitten as it opened its amber eyes and blinked up at Laura. She had learned to be careful of fiery torties over her years in the profession, but this one seemed entirely mellow at being passed from person to person. Perhaps it knew that they were helping it.

Laura gave the kitten a quick look-over. She couldn't immediately see anything wrong with it.

Sarah took the kitten from Laura and cuddled it in her arms. 'I'll look after you,' she whispered. Then she told Seaton knowledgeably, 'You've got to watch these sorts of cats, you know. They've got a right temper!'

'My mother has three.' Seaton winced, as though remembering past scratches. Then he picked up his suitcase again, opened the car door and climbed into the back seat, along with whatever pieces of straw and hay he might find in there, because it had been a long time since the rickety little vehicle had seen a proper clean.

'I've never met a commander before,' Sarah observed, twisting in her seat to look at the tall figure currently wedging himself into the compact space behind Laura's seat. 'What do you command?'

At Sarah's question, Commander Seaton flicked his gaze up to the rear-view mirror, where it met Laura's for the briefest of seconds. Then he said, 'Nothing. Perhaps that will change in Bramble Heath.'

Well, don't think you can turn up in our village and order us around, Commander Seaton.

Once he was settled, Laura started the car and they drove off.

SEVEN

The stone buildings of the Bryants' farm lay just ahead. Iris's husband, a cousin of the Bryants, had worked on the farm as a ploughman before signing up. Laura had heard lots of funny stories about the place on Bertie's last leave, but there was no cause for mirth today.

The pasture, usually full of cows, was empty, and Laura was sure she knew why.

'Sarah, did they take the cows back inside when you found the feed?' Laura asked. She hoped Seaton would realise that the Land Girls knew how to deal with the risks they were faced with; they weren't the silly girls Morgan dismissed them as.

Sarah nodded. 'Yeah,' she replied. As she listened, Laura was acutely aware of her passenger taking all of this in, making whatever judgements he was making. And what was a man with a naval rank doing at the Ministry of Agriculture, anyway? 'Like I say, a couple of the herd got a few mouthfuls in, but they didn't get a chance to proper dig in.'

'The same thing happened at Goslings' farm.' Laura caught Seaton's gaze in the rear-view mirror before turning her attention to the bumpy, single-track lane that led up to the farm. 'The cows were taken out to the fields first thing and ate the poisoned feed. It must be left out overnight, that's what I think. Someone up to no good in the blackout.'

But it's not what Morgan thinks, and I suppose you won't agree with me either.

'Well, we shall wait and see.' Yes, he looked the type to wait and see. Which Laura knew from her training and her career so far meant, *wait and see what another learned gentleman thinks.* Seaton's reflected gaze matched hers, unblinking.

'We've got a wrong 'un,' Sarah said as she nuzzled a kiss to the kitten's head. 'Sickly cows in Bramble Heath? That ain't life round these parts!'

'We'll see,' he reiterated, thoughtful. Laura wasn't sure what to make of him, but he didn't seem exactly effusive... and he definitely wasn't what she'd call dynamic either. But why would he be? He was a civil servant who'd been bundled out to the middle of nowhere to poke through cow fodder.

Laura pulled up in the yard, where she saw a group of Land Girls looking anxiously towards the cowshed.

I hope I'm not too late.

'If you'd like to follow me, Commander Seaton,' she said, getting out of the car. She opened his door for him.

'Should I leave Winnie in the car?' asked Sarah as Seaton climbed awkwardly out of the back seat and brushed the straw from his suit. 'That's my new cat's name. She's Winnie.'

'Leave Winnie just now, and we'll ask the Land Girls for a box to put her in,' Laura replied. There was of course the risk that, while they were gone, Winnie would run riot in the car and shred the upholstery to pieces, but the car couldn't look much worse than it already did.

Jennifer, one of the Land Girls, came over to see them. 'Laura, I'm so glad you've come. And...?' She glanced at Seaton, taken aback. He didn't really look very at home on the farm in his tidy city ensemble.

'This is Commander Seaton, he's from the Ministry of Agriculture,' Laura explained, and Jennifer quickly adjusted her Land Girl hat.

'I don't think I've ever met a commander before,' Jennifer said, eyeing Seaton with even more surprise. He met her interest with a polite raise of his hat. Polite, but entirely professional. This wasn't a man who was planning on staying in Bramble Heath a moment longer than was necessary.

'Have you got a battleship?' Sarah asked him mischievously. Then she addressed Jennifer, more seriously this time. 'How're the girls? Are they all all right?'

'They came over a bit peaky and were gasping,' Jennifer explained, her large, dark eyes full of concern. Laura gripped the handle of her bag tightly. Her heart plummeted. *I'm too late.* 'But they recovered. They're a little tired now, but we're keeping an eye out.'

'I'll check them over anyway,' Laura said. It sounded like a mild case, fortunately. 'They must've only had a tiny amount, which is a relief.'

'This one—' Jennifer proudly slipped her arm round Sarah and hugged her. 'This one spotted the feed and swooped in just in time.'

Sarah beamed. 'I didn't know for sure,' she explained. 'But I know Laura here didn't look very happy when she found that stuff last weekend. So better to keep the girls waiting than risk them getting poorly.'

From the farm building, Mr Bryant came hurrying towards the little gathering, hobbling as fast as he could on the stick he was never without.

'What's to do here?' he asked. 'I'm not back longer than five minutes and I'm told we're taking orders from a London evacuee? Cows in the barn, cows out of the barn... they should be feeding!'

'Mr Bryant, good morning.' Laura stepped forward to speak

to him. She'd have to explain and hope he'd realise how serious it was. 'I don't know if you've heard about what's happened over at the Goslings'? And at quite a few other farms too. There's been several cases of cyanide poisoning, and I think it's from the dry feed.'

Bryant looked Seaton up and down through his pebble glasses and said, 'And who's this?' He took his pipe from between his lips. 'I said to the missus, there's a bloody London suit in the farmyard with the veterinary!'

'But a Yorkshireman at heart.' Commander Seaton held out his hand to Mr Bryant. The farmer took it in his own grimy grip and shook firmly. 'Commander Alastair Seaton. I'm from the Ministry.'

And at his words, Laura saw the farmer visibly tense.

'Hey now,' he warned, 'I'm not doing anything I shouldn't. We're all in order here, I'm not backhanding anybody milk and chops!'

'I'm simply here to observe,' said Alastair calmly. 'Entirely routine.'

'Commander Seaton's here because of what's happened at the other farms,' Laura explained. She saw Mrs Bryant peering through the kitchen window at them, clearly curious about the stranger who was standing in her yard. 'And it seems like it might've happened here too. By the way, I don't suppose you've got a box to hand, do you? We've managed to acquire a kitten.'

Laura glanced at Alastair, whose expression gave nothing away. She couldn't help but grin at him, though, seeing as *he* was the one who had brought the kitten along. His gaze met hers and he gave the very slightest hint of a smile. He might not want Laura to see it, but she did.

'Get off into the kitchen and see the missus,' Bryant told Sarah. 'She'll sort you out.' Then he clamped the pipe between his teeth again. 'Now then, come on! Let's go and look at these cows.' He looked Alastair up and down. 'Good luck with them there London shoes, Mr Commander.'

Laura looked over at Alastair's sensible, neatly polished lace-ups. *Oh, dear*.

'I'm sure I can find you some wellingtons later,' she said, as they headed across to the cowshed.

The smell of dung and straw and warm animals wafted out to greet them, but it wasn't a scent that made Laura recoil. Far from it – it reminded her of home.

The cows welcomed the visitors with a chorus of moos and rustled through the straw to poke their heads over the fencing. They all looked in good shape.

'The three cows that ate the feed are down the end here,' Jennifer told them, pointing to a pen created from fencing where three of the herd were lying down.

Laura let herself into the pen. The cows looked tired, but they were breathing normally. She approached the nearest one, and nodded Alastair over.

'Commander, I want you to hold this cow's head steady for me while I examine her mouth,' Laura said. *Let's see how the man from the Ministry handles* that!

Farmer Bryant gave a croaky laugh and murmured, 'Not in that suit... eh, Admiral?'

'Commander,' Alastair corrected as he took off his suit jacket and hat and laid them on a bale of hay, then ably climbed over the fence to join Laura in the pen. If she had been expecting the neatly turned-out man from the Ministry to quail at the thought of a cow pen, he seemed anything but reluctant. Instead, to Laura's surprise, he immediately dropped to one knee beside the cow and unfastened first one cuff then the other, before rolling his sleeves to the elbow. 'The cows at the other farm were in a worse condition than this?'

As Alastair asked his question, he wrapped his arm round

one of the animal's necks and gently steadied it, murmuring, 'There now, it's all right...'

Laura hadn't expected the ease with which he took on her challenge, and his arms were as toned as any farm worker's. But when did they ever learn how to look after cows in the navy? The light caught the gold ring on his wedding finger, and Laura wondered what his wife had made of him being sent to the Sussex countryside.

A ring of Land Girls had circled the pen and were watching. Sarah pushed her way through them and stood at the front, chewing her thumbnail anxiously as she awaited the verdict.

'They were very poorly at the Goslings',' Laura said. 'Struggling for breath, frothy mouths, quick pulse... I administered a stimulant. They rallied, but they must've had more of the cyanide than these three girls have. Let's see...'

Laura carefully opened the cow's mouth. It was a little redder than the healthy pink she would normally have seen, but it wasn't dangerous.

'Yes, it looks like she might have consumed a small amount of cyanide,' Laura explained. 'See that slight redness, Commander? It's the cyanide affecting the blood. I'll give them charcoal, to stop them from absorbing any more of it if it's still in their system, but they don't require an injection. Girls, I need three buckets of water, please.'

Two of the Land Girls nodded and went off to fetch the water.

'Bloody hell...' Bryant sighed, shaking his head. Then he turned to look at the Land Girls. 'Right, which one of you fine fillies made a right royal mess of preparing the linseed cake? Speak up!'

The girls looked from one to the other. A short girl with her blonde hair in a crocheted snood blushed. 'I made it, Mr Bryant, but I followed the instructions.'

'Matilda's always made the linseed cake,' Jennifer said, defending her. 'Why would she make a mistake now?'

'Nobody's wandering around Bramble Heath knocking off bloody cows!' said Bryant. 'I'm not happy about this, ladies. Not a bit!'

Alastair told Laura in a whisper, 'I don't think it's a feed preparation issue. Do you?'

Laura was stunned. She'd been convinced he'd be on Morgan's side and that he'd think she had an overactive imagination.

He believes me. Good heavens, he actually believes me.

'I don't either,' Laura whispered in reply. Then she said to Bryant, 'This has suddenly started happening in farms all across the area. Why? Yes, we've had some new Land Girls recently, but this has happened on farms where experienced, trustworthy girls have been making up the linseed cake.'

Matilda blushed even more, but she was smiling now at Laura's words of praise.

'And the other reason I know it's not the linseed cake is because it's dry feed that's to blame,' Laura went on. She took the paper bag that Sarah had given her from her pocket and carefully opened it to show Bryant and Alastair. Was she imagining it or could she smell a very slight scent of bitter almonds? Did someone have a vendetta against Bramble Heath? But why would anyone want to harm the home front at such a crucial time? 'This isn't linseed cake, Mr Bryant. If your Land Girls haven't been putting it in the troughs, then who has?'

EIGHT

Once they were back in the village, Laura dropped Sarah home with Winnie safely in her box. The kitten was meowing heartily.

'I'll come round tomorrow and check on her,' Laura promised. She glanced at her watch: midday, and nearly time for lunch. 'Are you sure Mrs Hubbard won't mind you bringing a cat home with you?'

Sarah shook her head. 'Nothing bothers Ma H, not with four kids of her own and me too! She'll love Winnie just as much as I do.' She tightened her arms around the box as Alastair climbed out of the back of the car and came round to open Sarah's door, a gesture that surprised Laura with its chivalry. 'Ta, mister! You might not have a battleship, but you did well to find this little mite. She wouldn't have stood much of a chance out on her own.'

Alastair gave another of those barely-there smiles and said, 'You have the sheep on the line to thank. Any objection to me taking your seat since you'll no longer be needing it?'

The girl scrambled down from the car and replied, 'It's all yours. Have a good day, Laura!'

With a polite raise of his hat, Alastair finally climbed into the passenger seat.

'And you too!' Laura waved. She felt a lightness she hadn't known since the first poisoning case at the Goslings'. Thank goodness Alastair believed her. 'And take good care of Winnie!'

She tooted the horn on the old car, which sounded more like a wheeze, and set off again.

'She's a good girl. She was evacuated down here from London,' Laura explained. Alastair was no doubt puzzled by her schoolgirl assistant, but he didn't seem to object. 'I hope she'll make a fine vet one day.'

'She's an East Ender if ever I heard one,' he replied. 'Settled in nicely, eh?'

Laura chuckled. 'She is! But she's definitely part of Bramble Heath now. This is the main part of the village, by the way,' she explained as they drove slowly past the shops, the tea room and the George and Dragon pub. She felt rather like a tour guide.

'I believe the Ministry has me billeted at the pub. I had some business at the airbase last year, but didn't get to the village,' Alastair said. Once again, Laura found her quiet passenger was more than capable of surprising her. What business could the Ministry of Agriculture have had with Heath Place?

'It's a nice pub. Very popular with airmen and Land Girls,' she told him. 'Gosh, I wouldn't have thought the Ministry of Agriculture would be involved with the airbase. Unless the planes were upsetting the sheep! Well, I hope you enjoy your first visit to the village. It's a lovely place, but just now it seems as if someone's out to harm it, and I have no idea why. There's even rogue camp fires being lit. People say it's the evacuees, but I'm not so sure.'

'I hope your suspicions are mistaken,' said Alastair. 'Because if you're not, it's not just Bramble Heath that's at risk. Someone in this lovely village is trying to sabotage our nation's food supply.'

If only I was mistaken, thought Laura. *But I'm sure I'm not. And the thought that someone – someone I might even know – could do something so horrifying? It terrifies me. First they poison the cows... maybe they even start those fires blamed on the evacuees... what will they do next?*

NINE

Laura parked the car outside the veterinary surgery. Mrs Morgan was outside in the sunshine, busily buffing up the shiny plaque that bore her husband's name. She stood back to admire her handiwork, then leaned forward to breathe onto the plaque that displayed her absent son's name and buffed that too, darting her duster back and forth.

'Hopefully Mr Morgan's back by now,' Laura said, although in some respects she hoped he wasn't. She couldn't see him taking Alastair's appearance very well. 'He went over to see a new foal earlier.'

'And left his employee to deal with the crisis,' Alastair observed as he took in the house. 'At least the plaques are shiny.'

'I don't have one,' Laura whispered. 'Or even a piece of paper tacked onto the door!'

'I used to have a destroyer, but even I never had a plaque,' Alastair replied. 'I'm sure your day will come. Shall we?'

Laura tried to hide her surprise. A destroyer? This man had been in command of a huge battleship bristling with guns? And now he was in Bramble Heath. What on earth had happened for his circumstances to change so much? She glanced at him, wondering if he'd been injured somehow as he sailed in his destroyer across the sea.

As they climbed out of the car, Alastair looked over at the Georgian house with its long sash windows. Only a few stubs remained of the metal railings that had once fenced off the house from the street. They had been taken down for the war effort, to be melted down and turned into the planes that flew from Bramble Heath.

'Miss Fellgate,' Mrs Morgan greeted her. 'And...?' She looked Alastair up and down, clearly assessing the stranger.

'Commander Seaton,' Laura replied. 'And Commander, this is Mrs Morgan, she's Mr Morgan's wife.'

'The practice owner,' Mrs Morgan added quickly, with a nod towards the plaques she'd just polished. 'I see you've already met Miss Fellgate, my husband's assistant. She's helping out while our son is at war. He's in the Royal Army Veterinary Corps,' she said proudly.

Assistant? Helping out? It's nice to know I'm valued around here.

'Yes, I've already told him that I'm a qualified veterinary surgeon,' Laura said, her face heating with embarrassment at being spoken about like that in front of Alastair.

'I'm from the Ministry, Mrs Morgan,' Alastair said as he lifted his hat. 'I'm here to see your husband. Miss Fellgate will come too.'

Mrs Morgan pursed her lips. She wasn't used to being spoken to like that. Most of the locals tugged their forelocks to the Morgans, as the residents of *the big house on the high street*.

Laura led the way into the house as Mrs Morgan bustled ahead. Morgan's tweed coat was hanging on the stand by the door, and her stomach clenched with trepidation. He was here, and so was Alastair, and...

Why am I so nervous? I had to do something. Mr Morgan wouldn't, so I have!

Mrs Morgan knocked on the sitting room door and announced their visitor, but in a rather pinched tone. 'Mr Morgan, there is a gentleman to see you. A Commander Seaton, from—'

The sitting room door was wrenched wide open and Mr Morgan stood on the threshold, bristling with excitement at the obvious import of the unexpected visitor.

'A gentleman of the Royal Navy!' he exclaimed as he looked Alastair up and down. Clearly liking what he saw, a smile spread across his reddened face. Laura swallowed uneasily. Morgan had obviously identified Alastair as one of the boys. 'And a commander, no less! Good morning, sir, good morning! How on earth may this humble gentleman of medicine be of service to you?'

Laura cringed inwardly. Mr Morgan was evidently the sort of person who thrilled to rank and title, trying to become the instant friend of anyone who might move in elevated social circles.

Alastair opened his mouth to speak as Mr Morgan darted out one hand and snatched the hat from his visitor's hand. 'Mrs Morgan, tea for the commander!' Then he looked to Laura with barely concealed annoyance at her presence. 'Don't stand there and gape, girl, go and fill in your paperwork! Even a wild goose chase must be recorded!' He shook his head and told Alastair in a conspiratorial tone, 'Young ladies are always bowled over by a title, Commander.'

And red-faced vets too.

Mrs Morgan went off to the kitchen, but Laura didn't move.

'Mr Morgan, I'm with the Ministry.' And as Alastair said those words, Laura saw her employer deflate like a punctured balloon. 'I've been asked to pay a visit to Bramble Heath and speak to you about some animals in your care.'

Mr Morgan's mouth set into a line and this time when he looked Laura's way she saw annoyance in his gaze.

'Then you had better come in and sit down,' he said, stepping back into the room so Alastair could enter. 'Miss Fellgate, I won't tell you again. Commander Seaton wishes to speak to the organ grinder of this organisation.'

But Alastair shook his head. 'On the contrary, Miss Fellgate is the person who alerted the Ministry to a possible concern.' He offered Laura a nod. 'I'd like you to join us.'

'Thank you, Commander,' Laura replied, glad that he wasn't sending her away as her boss had tried to do. She knew Morgan wasn't going to be pleased that she had contacted the Ministry without his knowledge. But what else could she do? Allow the poisoner to carry on unchecked, and have people starve? 'Of course I will.'

'Sit down, sit down,' Mr Morgan said to Alastair, moving a pile of *Sporting Life* and veterinary journals from the armchair next to his own. 'I received no notification of your visit. Whatever you need to see, accounts, what-have-you, we're always on top of our paperwork here.'

'Thank you.' Alastair sat down neatly. 'There was no time to send word.'

Laura perched awkwardly on the edge of the sofa, knowing that her boss didn't want her there. But she was not going to leave, not with so much at stake. In Coventry she'd only been able to wait out that dreadful night, but in Bramble Heath she could actually *do* something.

Morgan's gaze slid from his visitor to Laura as she twisted her hands together.

'I'm sure there's no need to detain Miss Fellgate unnecessarily,' he said. 'I am the owner of this practice. My assistant is simply that. *My assistant.*'

She was being dismissed again, and belittled too. But Laura didn't go.

'I have already said, Mr Morgan, that she should stay,' Alastair told Morgan, a steeliness in his voice that Laura knew would take Morgan aback. 'Miss Fellgate wrote to the Ministry of Agriculture about a spate of possible cyanide cases in herds around Bramble Heath. I'm here to investigate. The home front relies on our farmers for its food.'

Morgan shook his head at Laura, chuckling like an indulgent uncle. 'Oh, Miss Fellgate and her ideas! There's nothing unusual about such cases, Commander. Nothing at all. It's merely the carelessness of the Land Girls. Naive young flighty types, escaping the bombs in the cities to plague the countryside with their ham-fisted inexperience. It's poorly prepared linseed cake that's to blame, mark my words. Ladies do fuss and panic so, but to inconvenience a gentleman from the Ministry with such nonsense... I can but apologise, sir.'

He was smiling, but it didn't quite reach his eyes. Laura knew that this joviality was an act for Alastair, and a sensation of panic began to creep through her.

Oh heck, I've landed myself in it now.

'Then that's what my investigation will show,' Alastair told Morgan. 'But nevertheless, it must be undertaken.'

'Investigation?' Morgan said slowly. 'Oh, no, Commander, we can't have you *investigating*. The farmers will get very suspicious. You must realise how much trouble we had getting the farmers to sign up to the tuberculosis scheme. They won't be at all happy to have a man from the Ministry of Agriculture poking about in their business on top of that.'

'The farmers will be considerably more unhappy if their livestock die, their buildings burn and they lose their livelihoods,' Alastair replied crisply. 'And the people whose ration coupons can't be fulfilled won't be impressed either. Hence my investigation, *sir*. You have a duty to the people of the district and to the nation to ensure the livelihood of the animals in your care.'

He clearly wasn't going to bend to Morgan, and Laura's worry about her boss's reaction had now taken on an edge of amusement. Finally, someone who stood up to him. Of course, Alastair might end up agreeing with Morgan and decide that Laura was just a hysterical woman like Morgan thought. Alastair was a closed shop, and Laura wasn't yet sure if he was an ally.

'Well, then I can but assume the Ministry is not overburdened with other concerns,' Morgan retorted coolly. 'Well, I oughtn't keep you from your investigations, Commander. The sooner you realise it's just ill-prepared food, the better. I shan't expect an apology; you're not a gentleman of the land, after all.'

But after seeing Alastair's confidence at the farm, Laura wasn't too sure about that.

Mrs Morgan appeared in the doorway with a tray on which she carried a pot of tea and her second-best cups and saucers.

'Goodness me, is that the time? I quite forgot I have a call to pay. Mrs Morgan, I'm afraid the tea has become surplus to requirements,' he said, glancing at his watch without any effort to look convincing. He levered himself out of his armchair. 'Miss Fellgate, would you see the commander out?'

Laura was astonished at Morgan's rudeness, to offer a guest a drink then suddenly eject him. But Alastair showed no reaction; he merely stood and held his hand out to Morgan, who gave him a swift, reluctant shake.

'I'm sure this won't be my last visit,' Alastair said. 'Perhaps next time we might even get as far as pouring the tea.'

'I'm sure,' Morgan replied, narrowing his eyes and darting a glance of annoyance towards Laura. 'Good day, Commander!'

Laura weaved past Mrs Morgan and led Alastair to the door. She whispered to him, 'I'm so sorry, that was very rude of him.'

Alastair shook his head and retrieved his hat. 'I've known enough admirals to deal with a blustering old vet,' he said as Laura opened the door for him.

'Miss Fellgate!' Mr Morgan bellowed. 'Five minutes, if you

would, madam!'

Laura's stomach twisted with anxiety. She wasn't looking forward to this.

'I'll collect my case and be on my way.' Alastair turned towards the open door. Just as he was about to go, he looked back at Laura and said, 'I don't suppose we could talk later, about what's been going on? Say, six thirty at the George and Dragon?'

Laura nodded. 'Of course.'

'I'll see you then,' Alastair said, then strode away down the path as Laura watched him go.

Standing by the gate was Smudge, the delivery man. He did a double-take at Alastair, then smiled a smile of affectionate recognition. Laura realised that Smudge knew him. But of course he did – Smudge was an ex-naval man, invalided out when he lost an eye at Dunkirk. He now sported an eyepatch, which gave him a piratical air.

Smudge suddenly snapped to attention and gave Alastair a naval salute, the back of his hand facing outwards.

'Commander, sir!' he said. For a moment Alastair simply looked at the man as though he had seen a phantom. Then, sharp as a whipcrack, he returned the salute.

Laura was amazed, Morgan's demand that she speak to him momentarily forgotten. The path outside the veterinary practice had turned into the deck of a warship. This didn't happen every day. And that salute of Alastair's, so precise, so keen... it seemed rather a shame that he no longer had a ship to command.

'Smudge!' Alastair said. 'Small world. How the devil are you?'

'Mustn't grumble, sir,' Smudge replied, beaming. 'And how are *you*? My goodness, the lads'll be pleased as punch when I tell them as I've seen you. They're always asking how you've got on.'

'Earning a crust on dry land, just like you,' Alastair replied. 'You're looking well. I'm glad you're getting on.'

'Miss Fellgate!' Mr Morgan bellowed. 'Now!'

'I'm coming, Mr Morgan,' Laura replied, and she reluctantly closed the door. Morgan's shout had brought her back to reality. The jovial men on deck retreated.

She took a deep breath and thought of the animals who were suffering for no reason thanks to the saboteur, and the terrible risk to the home front; from the Land Girls who would be blamed, to the empty plates on the nation's tables. That was why she was doing this. That was why she'd put herself on the line.

She went into the lounge, where Morgan was standing by the fireplace, his back to her and his hands planted solidly on his hips.

'Yes, Mr Morgan?' she said in a small voice.

'A naval commander? Poking around backwater farms and throwing his high-handed manner around in my own home? Why is he not at sea? Why is he not seeing off Jerry? Instead he has washed up here, with no experience of our ways of life nor the countryside and all its vagaries!' Morgan was ranting as he turned sharply to face her. His cheeks were ruddy with anger and he glared at her as he bellowed, 'Miss Fellgate, you have committed a grave wrong, young lady! An outsider from the city speaking to me as though he owns this establishment?'

Laura had seen Morgan cross before, but never as angry as this. He was furious, and she knew that there was nothing she could do or say to change that.

'I thought it was for the best that I reported what was happening,' she replied honestly, hoping he would understand that she had acted as a professional. Even if he did only think of her as his assistant. 'I didn't expect them to send someone so fast.'

'But I told you, there is nothing happening!' Morgan

snapped. 'Perhaps I should have spoken louder? What exactly did you misunderstand, Miss Fellgate?'

'I haven't misunderstood anything,' Laura said. What on earth would Morgan do? He wouldn't sack her, would he? She couldn't lose her job. She couldn't bear it. Who would protect the livestock and the village if she was gone, and who would clear the name of the Land Girls? 'I merely disagree, that's all. You're certain that the cyanide poisoning has come from the linseed cake, and I don't agree. It's from the dry feed, Mr Morgan. I tested the feed that I found on the ground, and I found cyanide.'

'Which could have come from the linseed cake,' Morgan declared impatiently. 'Do you know what a fool I will look? Do you? That man from the Ministry poking around on the farms, and the farmers will come after me with pitchforks demanding to know why I sent him! Only *I* didn't send him, did I, Miss Fellgate? *You* did!'

'Because I'm very concerned, Mr Morgan,' Laura replied, trying to keep her voice steady as she battled to stand up for herself in the face of his rage. 'Those animals are suffering, and then there's the fires... and, well, there's even the sheep too! I don't suppose you've heard about that!'

'What sheep?' Morgan asked dismissively, because apparently the only information worth knowing was what he already knew.

'The sheep on the line,' Laura explained. 'Constable Russell told me someone left a gate open, and—'

'Someone left a gate open!' Morgan mocked in a high-pitched voice. 'That happens in the countryside. It was probably one of the evacuees, down from the city and they haven't a clue how things are done here. And that reminds me – that little girl who came bursting in like all the devils in hell were after her. She follows you about like your shadow and behaves as if she's your assistant! I don't remember hiring a little cockney urchin of a schoolgirl, Miss Fellgate. She mustn't go with you on your calls. It's very unprofessional. I won't have it!'

Laura swallowed. Sarah loved coming out to the farms, and she couldn't bear the thought of telling the girl not to any more. 'She's not doing any harm, Mr Morgan. She's learning about the countryside, and she's very responsible. She'd never leave a gate open.'

'She's likely never seen a gate if the East End hovels I've heard about are any indication of her worth!' Morgan barked. 'No more brats on farm visits and no more letters to the Ministry! He should be on a bally boat, not in Bramble Heath! If you behave in this manner again, young lady, I shall have no option but to ask you to leave.'

Laura took a step back from him. Tears pricked the backs of her eyes, but she wouldn't let them fall, not in front of him.

Morgan pointed towards the door. 'Go and do your paper-work. And I don't want to hear any more female hysteria about poisonings! Out!'

Laura's shoulders sagged. It was like being dismissed by a headmaster. But she did as she was told and left the room.

But she wasn't going to do paperwork. Once again she went to the pharmacy, and ran a test on the dry food that Sarah had found at the Bryants' farm.

And once again there was a trace of cyanide.

The tears burning at the backs of Laura's eyes didn't fall. Morgan could chastise her and shout all he liked; it wouldn't change the fact that there was a traitor in Bramble Heath, someone who was trying to take the very heart of the village, and destroy the nation's morale just at a time when everyone needed to be strong, no matter how scared they were. And Laura was determined to hunt them down and bring their campaign of evil to an end.

TEN

That evening, Laura went home to change before her meeting at the pub with Alastair. On her way to the front door, she checked her hair in the oval hallway mirror, which reflected back the collection of coats and umbrellas on the rack, and Iris's impromptu gallery of countryside prints. Laura was terrible at remembering to set her hair before going to bed, but at least it had natural waves that she could tame into something almost resembling a style. She'd used some odds and ends of make-up to add some colour to her face, but it was something she'd never learned to do with great skill as she'd never had the sort of job where she needed to look polished. The sheep and cows she looked after didn't mind if she wore make-up or not.

Iris, with Sam on her hip, watched her with intrigue from the sitting room doorway.

'Just checking I haven't got any straw in there,' Laura explained to her audience.

Iris dimpled with amusement before asking, 'He's an airman, isn't he? I knew you'd be walking out with a fellow before long!'

Laura nearly dropped her comb in surprise. She turned to

Iris. 'Oh, no, I'm not walking out with anyone! And he's certainly not an airman.'

'So it *is* a he?' Iris's eyebrow quirked with interest.

'It's dreadfully boring,' Laura told her. 'Official agriculture business, you see. I just want to make sure I look smart.'

'You definitely do in that lovely suit,' Iris remarked. It was the one Laura had worn to her interview with Morgan, a sensible dark blue skirt suit with padded shoulders. It was the sort of thing she never got to wear doing her day job. 'You look like Joan Crawford!'

As if I look like a film star!

Laura chuckled. 'That's very kind, but I look more like a vet going to a meeting! I hope you don't mind me abandoning you for the evening?'

Iris shook her head. 'Not at all. You go and enj— you go and get to that meeting!'

Laura headed off, walking down the street lined with old cottages, their gardens coming to life in the light and warmth of spring. She was glad of the lengthening evenings; long, dark wintry nights gave the enemy planes too much time to attack.

The honey-coloured stone of the George and Dragon pub reflected the golden tones of the spring evening as Laura arrived. A queue of Land Girls from farms around Bramble Heath were at the door, some in their uniforms while others wore pretty dresses. Laura smoothed down her skirt, feeling rather out of place.

She spotted Frances and the two sisters, Martha and Lottie, from Goslings' farm, and waved hello. She really hoped the new girls weren't still blaming themselves.

Laura headed inside the pub, following Frances and the sisters. Martha had put up her long, dark blonde hair with ribbons in RAF blue, a lovely touch to show the boys from the airbase her support.

The pub was large and low-ceilinged with ancient, exposed

beams, and hadn't been divided into a saloon and a public bar. There was something very Bramble Heath about that, Laura decided – everyone was brought together. As she walked in, glancing around for Alastair while hoping she didn't look like too much of a pub novice, she spotted him.

He was sitting in a corner, not far from the fire, a pint glass on the table in front of him. He looked out of place in his smart city suit.

As soon as he spotted Laura, he rose to his feet, and came over to greet her. She detected a slight smile on his otherwise unreadable face, but she decided he was being friendly and polite. It didn't mean he was thrilled to see her; perhaps he felt quite the opposite.

'Miss Fellgate, thanks for giving up an evening to talk about cyanide,' Alastair said, with a definite smile this time. 'What can I get you?'

'What else is there to talk about of an evening?' Laura teased in reply, glad to see him smile. 'I'll have... half a pint of beer, please,' she decided. It was a sufficiently masculine drink for a woman who had taken on what Morgan called *a man's job*. She looked around and saw it was the preferred tipple of most of the Land Girls anyway.

Alastair gestured for her to sit down, and Laura took a seat at his table. The airmen and Land Girls were on the other side of the room, and some of the old farmers, in worn tweeds and corduroy, had taken up the opposite corner by the fire. They watched Alastair as he stood at the bar, the airmen parting like the Red Sea and letting him buy his drink before them.

Surrounded by the residents of Bramble Heath and the young airmen, Alastair still carried that air of respectable offi- cialdom with him. Laura couldn't decide whether it was diffi- cult to picture him commanding a destroyer or not, but from the way the RAF boys stood aside for him she decided that she *could*. There was something of the officer about

Commander Seaton, even to people who didn't know him from Adam.

The door banged open and, all at once, a crowd of airmen in their blue RAF uniforms burst in, cheering at the top of their lungs.

Everyone turned to look, the airmen who were already in the pub joining in with the cheering. Laura wondered what on earth they were so excited about; perhaps they'd restarted their cricket games beside the runway and were celebrating a win?

The farmers laughed, amused at the spectacle. They wouldn't begrudge the brave young men their fun, Laura knew. God knew they deserved some.

Laura spotted one of her patients, Wilbur the dog, who looked thrilled to be part of the rowdy gang as he was carried in the arms of Freddy, his owner. Sally, Freddy's fiancée, had somehow ended up in the gang of airmen and was cheering too.

'Round of applause for Flight Lieutenant Harvey!' Freddy announced to the patrons as his friends bundled one of their number to the front of the pack. 'Miss Martha, your man only went and made ace last night! You should've seen Jerry run and your George running right after them!'

An ace. So George had shot down five enemies during his last sortie.

'Oh, George!' Martha rushed forward and flung her arms round him. She held him tight, and George closed his eyes as he hugged her back. She and her sister hadn't been in Bramble Heath long, but she'd certainly made an impression on George. It was hardly surprising; she was a pretty girl, with rosy cheeks from all the time she spent outside working on the farm. And those RAF blue ribbons were clearly meant to show him how much she cared for him.

'It was nothing, really,' George said, as casually as if he had merely made a pot of tea. 'Just happened to be in the right place at the right time.'

'You should have seen him,' exclaimed Mateusz, one of the Polish pilots who flew from Heath Place. He'd made his home in the hamlet on the edge of the village, where the Polish refugees had found a welcome. Here, in Bramble Heath, they'd found an end to their agonising flight from their homeland... at least until they could return. 'Miss Martha, your man here was hiding in every cloud tonight.'

Martha blushed as she gazed at her boyfriend.

'And popped out to give Jerry a good kicking!' one of the other airmen hooted gleefully. 'Achtung, Fritz!'

Freddy and his pals gave a roar of approval and Wilbur barked along too as the entire bar gave the young pilot a round of applause. Even Alastair paused at the bar to join in, before he picked up the glass of freshly poured beer and made his way back to the table.

'What nice chaps those RAF boys are,' Laura said, nodding over to them. In their midst were Martha and George, the Land Girl gazing at her hero, although it was clear from George's affectionate smile that he idolised her too. Of course, Alastair would know that the pilots were good lads, as he'd been to the airbase. How many other airbases had he been to? The man was a mystery.

'I can't imagine the sort of nerve they must have.' Alastair resumed his seat. 'I won't keep you too long, Miss Fellgate, then you can be off and carousing with your friends.'

'Carousing? I haven't caroused since I was a student.' Laura giggled. 'Even then, I mainly kept my nose clean and had my head stuck in a book.'

'And now you find yourself in Bramble Heath...' Alastair sipped his beer. He was evidently fishing for Laura's back-ground. 'As unappreciated assistant to the erstwhile Mr Morgan.'

'I've been here a year,' Laura explained. 'Covering for the sainted Master Morgan, who's gone off to war. You'd never guess I was a fully qualified veterinary surgeon, would you? I'm just Mr Morgan's assistant. But I wanted to work on the farms, where I can do my bit. When I see a field full of cows, I think of all the milk they're producing, all the babies they feed, all the cheese that will be produced. Before I came here, I was in Coventry looking after people's cats and dogs, and, as much as I love looking after people's pets, when there's a war on... well, it changes your priorities, doesn't it?'

Did she see something change in his expression when she mentioned Coventry? But what had happened there had shocked the nation, and still did.

'It changes everything.' Alastair took a sip from his glass. Then he drew in a breath as though gathering himself, and said, 'Coventry, eh? That must've been... well, it was dreadful.'

It certainly was. But she sensed a note of caution in his voice; he didn't want to probe her about it, and she didn't want to talk about that awful night. She wanted to hear about *him* instead, this quietly fascinating man from the ministry.

'And where are you from?' Laura asked him. 'Is that a Yorkshire twang I can hear?'

And his expression changed again, a slight smile creeping over his face.

'It is,' Alastair confirmed. 'Up near Scarborough. Obviously the sea air got to me!'

'Gosh, you *are* a long way from home! I grew up in the Cotswolds, on a farm there,' Laura replied. 'Whenever the vet came to visit, I always followed him around. I was fascinated, and I knew it was the job for me. My brother's running the farm at the moment, with my father. Coventry's not too far from home, so that's where I headed. But when the vacancy came up here, I couldn't miss the chance to work with farm animals *and* help the war effort at the same time, so... here I am.'

'All of us doing our bit.' Alastair nodded.

Laura nodded. 'Even caring for cats and dogs, vets are still doing war work. I helped to train up animal guards in the ARP, so any cats or dogs hurt after a raid could be quickly cared for. I loved passing on what I know, and I've carried that on in a sense here, you know, showing the Land Girls the ropes.'

Laura took a mouthful of her beer while she watched Alastair, as he watched her in his turn. She wished he would give *something* away. Surely the way he had stood up to Mr Morgan suggested that he thought her concerns weren't just hysteria?

'The Land Girls...' he said eventually, tapping one fingertip thoughtfully against the tabletop.

She knew what he was implying, and she took a sharp breath.

Are we really back to that idea that all these poisoning cases are just accidents, with the Land Girls taking the blame?

'Before you ask, I make sure the girls all know how to prepare linseed cake properly,' Laura told him. 'And I also tell them how to spot the signs of cyanide poisoning – along with all sorts of illnesses and things.'

Alastair nodded carefully. Laura couldn't tell what he was thinking.

'You've no doubts about the feed prep?' he asked.

'As long as they follow the instructions, then there's no cause for concern at all,' Laura replied. She was completely confident in the girls. It was part of her wartime duty to teach them well, and she knew they took it as seriously as she did.

The Land Girls were laughing and joking with the airmen now, George and Martha glowing with affection as they gazed at each other. Laura thought how odd it was to be discussing them like this without the girls having a clue. She knew they would be devastated to think that anyone among them might be suspected of such dangerous carelessness, let alone a deliberate act of sabotage.

'So if it's not them, what other sources of cyanide are there?' Alastair asked. Laura frowned. Was he fishing for reasons to disbelieve her? He went on, 'In your professional opinion as a veterinary surgeon, that is?'

'Cyanide naturally occurs in apple pips, peach stones, cherry laurel...' Laura replied, counting them on her fingers. 'But pigs live happily in orchards, munching away. The quantity of apples you'd need to eat before it could have a serious effect is enormous, so I don't think it can be that. And farmers don't plant cherry laurel, it's too much of a risk. And that's why I think it must be...' She lowered her voice and leaned over the table toward Alastair.

But her words were lost in the sudden wail of the air-raid siren.

ELEVEN

Every conversation stopped. Ted Fenning, the landlord, rang the last-orders bell and announced, 'Everybody down to the cellars, come along now. You can take your drinks!'

He'd said the same thing so many times, and yet the edge of fear was still apparent in his voice.

The cellars. Laura shivered as her memories of that awful night in the basement of the veterinary practice began to resurface, the terrified mewls and whimpers of her animal charges as the bombs crashed down on Coventry. She had to put it out of her mind. She'd got through it; by some miracle she had survived, and so had the beloved pets she'd cared for through that nightmare. She could get through tonight as well.

George, Bramble Heath's latest ace, threw his arm round Martha and told his girl, 'Time to give Jerry another hiding!' He kissed her rosy cheek. 'I'll be back before you know it.'

Martha kissed him back. 'You better be, or I'll drink your beer!' she teased, even as her blush paled and her voice trembled. 'Take care, sweetie!'

'You look after your mum,' Freddy told the little dog he was carrying. He kissed Wilbur on his nose and bundled him into Sally's arms. 'See you in a bit, Mrs-Carr-to-be.'

Sally kissed him on the lips, then the airmen who had come cheering into the pub only a few minutes before had all put down their glasses and left. Laura tried to suppress a shiver as she thought of how suddenly their evenings had changed, from fun and flirting to facing their perilous duty to protect the village, not knowing if they would survive.

Laura got to her feet, but Alastair hadn't moved. Perhaps living in London he was more than used to air raids, more so than even the villagers of Bramble Heath, and took them in his stride. He took a deep breath and, in the moment before he rose to his feet, Laura was sure he almost squared his shoulders. Perhaps it wasn't a matter of being used to air raids after all? But surely a naval officer wouldn't feel any fear at the wail of the siren?

As they headed through the tables towards the door to the cellar, Laura felt his hand on her arm, guiding her. There was something stiff and awkward in his touch, and Laura wondered if, beneath his gentlemanly exterior, he actually felt uncomfortable.

'We'll be safe as houses down in the cellar,' she assured him, though she was sure a man who lived and worked in London, witnessing far more air raids than she had, wouldn't need to hear her say so. She was telling herself, really, reminding herself that a basement had saved her life on the worst night she'd ever lived through.

Ted and his wife had done their best to make the cellar inviting, with pictures tacked up on the wall and the cobwebs swept away. The Land Girls were already down in the cellar, making themselves at home on the trestle benches, crates and cushions among the barrels. The two inseparable sisters, Lottie and Martha, sat close together, their hands tightly joined, their knuckles white. The chairs were reserved for the oldest customers, and everyone still had their drinks. The conversation from upstairs carried on down here, but not as brightly. Even though the siren wasn't as piercing down here, there was fear in the shelter, so strong that Laura could almost touch it. And it wasn't just for themselves, waiting it out in the cellar. What about everyone else in the village? What if they didn't make it to their shelters in time? And would all the young lads who'd left their drinks on the bar to take to the skies make it home again?

Laura settled as best she could onto one of the benches. Alastair carefully sat down beside her, and stared straight ahead in silence. He laced his fingers together, slowly twisting his gold wedding band this way and that. He must be worried about his wife, especially if she was in London.

Laura knew he was a man of few words, but now he was a man of no words at all. Yet she knew they couldn't really continue their conversation, as they would be easily overheard down here.

'Is your wife still in London?' she asked him, hoping she could offer him some sympathy, some understanding of the terror he must feel knowing that his wife, too, might be facing the same terror from the skies at this very instant, and might not have made it to a shelter in time.

For what felt like a long time, Alastair said nothing. Then he turned to look at her, blinking in bewilderment.

'I'm sorry, did you say something?'

Laura was surprised that he hadn't heard her. He really must be worried about his wife. 'I was just asking, is your wife still in London? Or has she gone to live in the countryside?'

'No... no, she hasn't.' And he twisted his wedding band again. 'I lost my wife in the Blitz, Miss Fellgate. I'm a widower.'

Laura swallowed uneasily. She really shouldn't have asked him, and she felt dreadful for stumbling so carelessly onto his grief. After everything she'd seen in Coventry, how on earth could she have been so tactless? 'I'm... I'm so sorry,' she mumbled. 'I really shouldn't have asked you. It was very thoughtless of me. My word, I don't know what to say. I'm so sorry for your loss.'

But she knew that her words were inadequate after she had torn through such a painful, recent scar. No wonder the air raid impacted him so much. He must be thinking of what his poor wife went through in her final moments.

He shook his head, something suddenly awkward in the air between them.

'Thank you.' The response was almost prim, but there was such sadness in his eyes that Laura's heart blanched. So much loneliness was conveyed in that simple reply.

Wilbur's bark suddenly echoed in the cellar, and he hurried towards Laura with Sally in hot pursuit. He rested his paws on Laura's knee and looked up at her, his tail wagging with excitement. His simple joy was a world away from Alastair's grief.

She fussed Wilbur. It made her think of the basement in Coventry again, but reminded her that she'd given those animals comfort, and that in turn they had comforted her. While human beings tore each other apart, the simple innocence and affection of animals always warmed her. 'Hello, young man!' she said. 'Fancy seeing you here.'

'Hello!' Sally said cheerfully, even though Laura could sense that she was putting on a brave face, covering the dreadful worry that she must feel every time Freddy went up in the air. The small diamond on Sally's engagement ring caught the light, and Laura hoped like mad that Freddy would come back safely.

Please, God, you spared me – could you spare Freddy, to bring him home for Sally?

She thought that Sally was about to say something else when her expression abruptly changed to one of surprise.

Laura glanced around the cellar, wondering why, before realising that Sally's attention had been drawn to Alastair.

'Oh, meet Commander Seaton,' Laura said. She wasn't sure

what Alastair, a sensible man from the Ministry, would make of being introduced to a stunt pilot, but perhaps, she hoped, it might distract their thoughts for a few moments. 'Commander Seaton, this is Sally Toussaint. Do you remember Toussaint and Carr before the war – the young flyers?'

Alastair blinked. 'Yes, yes, I remember... before the war.'

Sally smiled. 'That's right, and didn't I chat to you at some of the airshows we flew at? It's funny how you remember faces, isn't it?'

'I think you did, yes.' Alastair nodded. 'I'm flattered you remember me. It's good to see you again, Miss Toussaint.'

Laura tried to conceal her amazement. Alastair didn't seem the type to enjoy standing in a field watching stunt pilots. Surely it was too frivolous?

'And it's good to see you again too,' Sally replied.

'Funny who you bump into, isn't it?' Laura said, quietly amused as she pictured Alastair watching the stunt pilots. But then, she thought, for a naval man he had a surprising affinity with flight, as she recalled what Alastair had said earlier. He'd been to Bramble Heath before, to the airbase, although what exactly the Ministry of Agriculture had to do with an airbase she still couldn't fathom.

But hadn't he made a point of saying simply that he was from *a* Ministry? Perhaps it wasn't Agriculture at all. With the poisonings and the fire so near to an airbase, perhaps someone important was taking this far more seriously than the likes of Mr Morgan were.

Alastair wasn't going to tell her, and she wasn't going to ask. As one of the government information posters on the wall declared: *CARELESS TALK COSTS LIVES.*

Sally went to sit down on another bench with one of her friends, who was wearing an Air Transport Auxiliary uniform. They watched Wilbur as he made a circuit of the cellar, sniffing and greeting everyone who was sheltering down there. Quite a few curious glances came Alastair's way, from the Land Girls and the farmers, clearly wondering who the man in the smart suit was. Martha and Lottie looked over at him too, before returning to their whispered conversation.

'I had a dog like Wilbur when I was a child,' Laura told Alastair. 'Friendliest little chap you could ever meet.'

'My parents' farm has a whole pack of dogs that rule the roost,' he said, and suddenly his ease with the ailing cow made sense. He'd grown up on a farm, before life had taken him away to sea and a career in the Royal Navy. A career that had, for some reason, ended. 'Soft as anything, though they're a fearsome sight.' Alastair flicked his gaze up to the ceiling, as though he might be able to see the aircraft passing far overhead. Then he took a deep breath and returned his attention to Laura. 'What were you about to say? Before the siren?'

'I was saying...' Laura spoke in a whisper, deciding that the air raid couldn't halt the investigation; they had no time to lose. The airmen of Bramble Heath were at this very moment risking their lives to save the village and the country. She too must play her part, and not allow the saboteur any further opportunity to snatch food away from the nation's plates. 'If it's not the linseed cake, and it's nothing that's just naturally occurring on the farms, then it's someone who wants to harm Bramble Heath, indeed our whole country. It's in the dry feed, you see. The farmers aren't feeding it to their animals at the moment, but it's turned up at two farms where the poisonings have happened. And I've run tests, both times, and...'

Alastair took a small notebook and pencil from his jacket. He opened the cover and scribbled something down in looping handwriting.

'Cyanide,' Laura finished.

'How about the other farms?' Alastair asked.

'I have no idea,' Laura replied. She thought back to the altercation with her boss earlier and clasped her hands.

'Mr Morgan attended the other cases. He's convinced I'm wrong, and that it's the linseed cake.'

'Yes...' Alastair said thoughtfully. 'He doesn't strike me as a fellow who welcomes debate. His way or no way?'

'That's exactly it!' Laura replied. 'He had a good old shout at me after you left. He's very angry that I wrote in about it. But what else could I do?'

And it felt good to be doing something about it, particularly right now while the sirens still moaned and the aeroplanes soared overhead. She couldn't bear to think of them, Freddy, George and Mateusz and their friends, risking their lives up in the clouds. But while there was nothing she could do to stop the terrifying air raids, she *could* do something to stop the saboteur.

'You did the only responsible thing,' Alastair assured her. He wrote something down and Laura saw the words DRY FEED with a determined line drawn underneath them. 'So... a saboteur. Any suspects?'

He held Laura's gaze, and she shifted on the bench. 'I don't know. It could be anyone.'

It could even be someone sheltering down here. What an awful thought.

'Someone on the farms?' Alastair thought aloud. 'Certainly someone with knowledge of cattle feed. Which leaves us with a county full of suspects if, indeed, it *is* a case of sabotage.'

'But what else can it be?' Laura wondered, fearing again that Alastair wasn't on her side. How could she ever stop an unknown poisoner on her own?

The other conversations in the cellar hummed in the background, and Laura strained to listen over them. Could she hear anything? The drone of enemy planes? She shivered and tried to put the thought out of her head. She hoped everyone had got to safety, and she wished she'd stayed at home so she could have helped Iris with the boys. Did they make it to their shelter in time?

But she'd needed to come out to speak to Alastair. She *had* to focus on the traitor. Who would want to harm Bramble Heath? Who would be acting against the nation just when it needed everyone to play their part?

An idea occurred to her. 'I've just had a thought. It might be significant, or it might not... the trough at Goslings' farm, the one the poisoned cows had eaten from – it's close to the road.'

Alastair gave a single nod. 'So you wouldn't need access to the farm at all to reach it.'

'Potentially,' Laura replied. 'Although that doesn't help at all. It doesn't narrow it down – it does the complete opposite!'

She leaned her head back against the cellar's cold wall and closed her eyes. She could feel a headache coming on. They were sheltering from an air raid in a cellar, while trying to identify a traitor within their midst. There seemed to be danger round every corner.

Laura sat up again and, trying to inject some levity, said to Alastair, 'I suppose there's worse places to shelter than a pub cellar. At least we won't be thirsty!'

His mouth twitched into a smile for a brief moment, then it disappeared.

'Or sober,' he replied, as he picked up his glass.

TWELVE

Once the all-clear siren sounded, a cheer went up from the Land Girls. Relief was evident on everyone's faces, and the old farmers laughed. Ted got up from his broken rocking chair with the missing runner to hesitantly open the cellar door.

He was being careful, Laura could see. No one knew what awaited them upstairs after a raid. Her heart hammered in her chest. Would there be a pub? Would there even be a village?

She fought back memories of Coventry, of the endless ruined buildings and the ashen-faced figures wandering the smoky streets in a daze.

But her nerves were getting to her. They wouldn't have been able to miss a direct hit, even in a shelter, and she hadn't noticed the *thud* of a bomb landing nearby. Hopefully, Bramble Heath was unscathed. This time. She couldn't bear to think about the consequences if there'd been a hit. What about Iris and the boys? What about Sarah? What about *everyone*?

Ted hurried up the stairs, then came back down again, beaming. 'The George and Dragon's still standing and at your service!' he announced. 'Not even a cracked windowpane! Our lads chased 'em off! Can't have Jerry take out their favourite boozer, eh?'

The pub had survived for another day and another cheer went up.

As Laura went up the stairs from the cellar, she asked Alastair, 'Can I get you a drink?'

He shook his head. 'I ought to get an early night, I'm afraid. But I'll walk you home.'

'You don't need to do that,' Laura told him.

'I insist,' Alastair said. 'I asked you to come out. It's the least I can do.'

He was doing the right thing, Laura knew, because gentlemen like Alastair always did. But perhaps, at the back of his mind, he was thinking of his wife, and the raid she hadn't survived. He could get Laura home safely, at least.

'All right, then,' Laura said. They put their empty glasses down on the bar, which was busy with customers putting in their orders. Laura waved goodbye to everyone, and they waved back. Alastair gave a polite nod.

The light was fading as Alastair escorted Laura home, and a flock of birds swooped noisily across the street before heading to their roosts. Soft pink clouds chased the sunset down to the horizon, and vapour trails from the warplanes hung in the sky as innocent as lambs' tails.

'I imagine this street looks very pretty when the lights come on in the houses at night,' Laura remarked. 'Not that I've ever seen it look that way...'

'One day,' Alastair assured her. He glanced up at the darkening sky. 'That was an early raid; perhaps someone in Berlin is panicking.'

'Now the Americans have joined in, I bet they're having more than a few sleepless nights over there.' Laura glanced at him. He'd lost his wife to this dreadful war and she didn't want him to think she was making light of it. 'I feel more hopeful now. I wonder if we'll see American pilots in Bramble Heath?'

'You never know,' Alastair replied. 'They do seem to turn up in the most unlikely places.'

She wondered if he knew more than he was saying, and was keeping deliberately taciturn on the subject, as he had to be. Or whether he just didn't like making conversation.

Or perhaps he just doesn't like me. I wouldn't be surprised – it really was thoughtless of me to ask after his wife.

Laura gestured ahead to Iris's cottage. 'I'm just up here.' She lowered her voice. 'So, you'll be off investigating tomorrow?'

'I will,' he replied. There was a pause, as if he realised that she wanted him to say more than that, but he didn't.

'If you need to come and find me, I'm either here or at the practice. Or on a farm somewhere,' Laura said. 'I never wander far.'

Alastair walked Laura as far as Iris's gate. He swallowed before holding out his hand and saying, 'Thank you, Miss Fellgate. For coming out this evening.'

Laura shook his hand firmly, noticing how cold it was. 'Don't mention it. Good luck, by the way. I hope this nasty business is cleared up very soon.'

'We'll get to the bottom of it,' Alastair replied. 'You have an ally, Miss Fellgate.' He gave her a nod.

So he is going to include me. My new ally.

'Thank goodness I do,' she replied with a gentle smile, relief spreading through her at the thought that she wasn't fighting alone any more. 'Goodnight, Commander. Sleep well.'

She saw something in Alastair's eyes then. Just a flicker, then it was gone. A look of sadness so profound that Laura had to look away.

She was nearly at the door when she heard Alastair whisper, 'And keep your eyes open. If there really is a traitor out there, someone hell-bent on harming the village and maybe even the entire home front, we don't want him to know you're on to it. Be careful.'

Laura half turned towards him. His words had taken her by surprise. 'I'll be careful, don't you worry.'

She shivered. The calm evening was full of threat. In the gathering darkness, there was someone lurking, who would do them harm; not just to everyone in Bramble Heath, but the whole nation.

I won't let this evil win. I can't.

THIRTEEN

The following day was suspiciously quiet, and the village felt peaceful as Laura arrived at the veterinary practice. Surely that meant that the pilots who set off last night had got home safely; and, as no desperate calls came in about cows struggling from the effects of cyanide, Laura hoped it meant that whoever had set out to harm the village had thought better of it.

Instead of hurrying off to a farm this morning, Laura was patching up Bramble Heath's smaller animal residents. But as she worked, bandaging a cat's paw, and peering into a dog's ear, the shadow of the traitor loomed over her. She tried to tell herself that the telephone's silence was a good thing. It might mean that the saboteur had stopped; maybe they'd realised that Laura was on to them. Perhaps they'd even heard about Alastair arriving in the village, or seen him as he went from farm to farm investigating. Anyone sensible would stop.

Or perhaps events had run their course and whatever unfathomable reason the saboteur had thought they'd had to poison the animals had been fulfilled.

Maybe.

Or maybe they were biding their time, planning something else. Maybe something even worse.

Before going back to her lodgings at the end of the day, Laura had a personal call to make. She'd promised to examine Winnie, the tortoiseshell kitten Alastair had found and Sarah had adopted. She walked through a sudden shower of spring rain, not bothering to put up her umbrella, and other figures in the street hurried by.

Annie drove by on her motorbike, carefully avoiding the puddle that was swelling in the gutter. Reverend Ellis, sheltering under his large black umbrella, was walking along the path from the church, lost in his thoughts.

Maybe the rain would put off the poisoner too, Laura hoped. If they were planning another attack, every moment mattered to find out who they were before it was too late.

She knocked on the door of the Hubbards' cottage and heard a rush of footsteps inside.

'I'll get it, I'll get it!' one child shouted.

'No, me, me! I want to open the door!' another replied.

'I bet that's Laura!' Sarah announced, and the door swung open. Winnie, tail pointing upwards like an aerial, was balancing on her shoulder while the four Hubbard children peered around her up at Laura. 'Sorry, everyone was excited to see you.'

Laura smiled. 'I always looked forward to seeing the vet when I was little too. I'm not sure the animals did quite as much.'

'Miss Fellgate!' called Mrs Hubbard, emerging from the kitchen carrying a mixing bowl. 'I'm sorry about these children. Come on, let the vet through...'

But there was nothing scolding in her tone, and the children giggled as they made a space for Laura in the hallway.

'That Winnie is full of beans,' Mrs Hubbard went on.

'While the kids were at school today, she chased me around the kitchen!'

Laura laughed. 'That's torties for you, I'm afraid. Let's check Winnie over.'

Mrs Hubbard led her to the large wooden kitchen table and laid a wax cloth over one end of it.

'There you go, Winnie!' Sarah said, and managed to peel the kitten from her shoulder, the claws on the cat's small, fluffy paws shining.

The five children and Mrs Hubbard gathered around Laura as she checked Winnie over. It went well, apart from a swipe from the kitten that left Laura with a scratch across the back of her hand.

Laura let each of the children listen through the stethoscope, and before long they were all using it on each other.

'Don't break it,' Mrs Hubbard said, but she couldn't resist having a go herself. Laura dreaded to think what Mr Morgan would've made of it. He'd be horrified, she was sure.

'Winnie is a healthy little girl,' Laura said finally, passing the kitten back to Sarah. The girl cradled her carefully, and Winnie purred loudly. Laura would have to tell Alastair; wouldn't he be pleased to know how well the crying, abandoned kitten he'd found was doing?

'Come and play with Winnie,' Edwin, the youngest of the Hubbard children insisted, dragging Laura by her hand to the sitting room. Laura didn't resist and soon she was kneeling on the floor among the children as they dangled a piece of paper on a length of string for the cat. Winnie swatted at it and everyone laughed.

Laura glanced at Sarah, a girl from the city, who could be so streetwise and appear older than her years. But seeing her play with the kitten, her face alight with innocent joy, Laura saw how she could still be a child; it was the same when Sarah turned up on the farms to lend a hand. There was a sense of curiosity about her that cut through her prematurely grown-up swagger.

Sarah turned to Laura and said, 'You know your friend with the hat?'

Laura wondered who she meant for a moment, before realising it must be Alastair. 'Oh, Commander Seaton?'

'Yes, the commander who don't command nothing,' Sarah replied. 'Well, he's really getting on everyone's wick.'

Laura was taken aback by that. Alastair had seemed a rather quiet sort of man, a gentleman. Maybe he was a little brisk in his manner, but he was a government official.

'How come?' she asked, as Winnie pounced on the piece of paper before it was twitched away.

'I went up to Goslings' farm after school finished,' Sarah replied. 'And Nicola said he'd been up there poking about. The Land Girls weren't very happy, and neither were Mr and Mrs Gosling.'

'He's investigating what's been happening to the cows,' Laura explained, although she knew his official air was probably grating. A man in a grey suit, arriving from London without any warning, asking questions and looking around the farms. That wasn't going to go down very well with the locals.

There was a knock at the door. The children made a rush for it again, leaving Sarah playing with the kitten. Moments later, two Land Girls were towed in by the excited children.

It was Nicola and Frances.

'Hello, you two,' Laura said, getting to her feet. 'Sorry, just... erm... playing with a kitten!'

Nicola chuckled. 'I'd play with kittens all the time if I had your job, pet! Sorry to burst in, but Iris said you'd be here – we just wanted to have a quick word.'

Concerned, Laura asked, 'It's not another cow, is it?' But the girls didn't seem to be in a great hurry.

'No, they're all fine,' Frances replied. She cast an uncertain glance at Nicola, before telling Laura, 'It's about that fellow from the Ministry, actually.'

The children were playing with the kitten again, but Laura was aware that Sarah was listening.

'He's been to see you up at the farm, hasn't he?' Laura asked. 'Sarah was just saying.'

Nicola nodded. She looked uncomfortable as she said, 'He turned up and asked loads of questions and demanded to see this and see that. Now, I'm not one as complains and I know them cows were ill as ill can be. Nobody wants to see any more of them getting sickly, but...'

'But he's not going to get anywhere walking onto the farms around here and poking his nose in here, there, and every-where,' Frances finished.

Laura shook her head in frustration. She'd hoped so much that Alastair's arrival would be the answer to her prayers, but now he was making himself unpopular with the very people he needed on his side.

'Look, I'll have a word with him,' Laura told them. 'Don't worry, this'll soon be ironed out.'

She left the Hubbards' cottage, Sarah tagging along and chattering about Winnie, her new best friend. From what Laura could glean, Winnie had received more visitors than the king himself since her arrival in Bramble Heath; and today was no different, as Sarah was off to summon her friend Peter, the next to be received by the kitten Alastair had brought into their lives.

'Peter's only fussed about dogs, but Winnie'll change that,' Sarah was telling Laura as they strolled along. 'It's because of Wilbur, so he's never even had a cat. But everybody needs a cat. Even people with dogs!'

'Winnie is quite a character, I'm sure she'll convert him,' Laura assured her with a smile. Sarah's love of animals was very endearing.

Just at that moment, she spotted a now-familiar figure in the street. The homburg and the smart overcoat made Alastair stand out.

'Ah, there's my friend in the hat,' Laura whispered to Sarah. She waved hello to him. 'Evening, Commander!'

'Who've you been upsetting now?' Sarah teased, but Alastair didn't look amused. In fact, he looked rather taken aback, and Laura could've winced at the girl's ill-chosen words.

'Now, now, Sarah,' Laura said quickly. 'I'm sure the commander hasn't upset anyone.'

'I hope I haven't,' Alastair told them as he crossed the road towards the pair. Sarah was silent for now, but somehow Laura could sense the mischief fizzing from her. She was going to say something, she just knew it.

'If you're not busy, maybe you'd like to pop round for a pot of tea?' Laura suggested, hoping Sarah wouldn't say anything more. Then she could speak to Alastair without the Land Girls' complaints about him being broadcast in the middle of the street.

Alastair glanced towards Sarah, perhaps waiting for her to offer her next insight, but instead the girl simply looked up at him, smiling a butter-wouldn't-melt smile. She waited until he opened his mouth to reply, then cut in and said, 'She's going to tell you off.' She dropped her voice to a whisper to assure him, 'But I think you're all right really.'

Laura stared awkwardly at Alastair. *I'm blushing, aren't I? Oh, heck!*

'Oh, Sarah, what can you mean? I don't want to tell anyone off, I just want to have a chat with Commander Seaton,' Laura said to the girl, but she wasn't sure she sounded very convincing. She was more relieved than she could say at the sight of three boys rounding the corner at the end of the road, one of whom she recognised as Sarah's friend Peter. It might be just the distraction the evacuee needed.

'Oh, I'm sure a pot of tea will make the telling-off more

bearable,' Alastair decided. 'Farmers don't like Ministry visitors, do they?'

Laura bit her lip. He knew, then. And maybe that would make the task of talking to him about it a little easier. 'You could say that, yes,' she said tactfully. 'They're a bit funny about anyone who's not wearing wellies and corduroys.'

'And East Enders,' Sarah assured him. 'But they've took to me by now, so they'll take to you if you forget the suits and all that city business. Right, I've got things to do. Evening, Laura, evening, Mr Commander!' She nodded her head, then trotted towards the boys with a bellow of, 'Oi, Peter! Winnie wants to see you before she goes to bed!'

Laura swallowed. She hoped Alastair's dry sense of humour would mean he'd take it in good part. 'Sorry about that, Commander. Sarah's rather... direct, isn't she? But she means well.'

'I'd certainly rather you tell me off than her,' Alastair admitted. 'You're a little bit less fearsome.'

Laura chuckled. 'Well, that's good to know!'

FOURTEEN

A few minutes later, Laura and Alastair were sitting in Iris's cosy front room.

'I'll just make you a pot of tea,' Iris said, but paused in the doorway, her attention fixed on Alastair.

'Thank you, Iris, that's very kind,' Laura said, and finally Iris closed the door behind them and left them in peace. 'Sorry, people in Bramble Heath don't see chaps like you every day. I suppose that doesn't help when you're going around the farms. How did it go today?'

Not very well, if what Nicola and Frances had to say was true.

'You don't have to be tactful. I come from a farming family; I know full well how little farmers like men from the Ministry turning up and asking questions.' Alastair smiled, which came as something of a relief. 'But I have to do it, Miss Fellgate. We're in rationing and we need our farms working as well as they possibly can. If this *is* sabotage, we need to get on top of it. But of course, I can't tell them it might be sabotage, because the last thing we want is panic.'

Laura sighed. 'I know – part of me wants to go around

warning them, but I can't do that when I don't have proof and when my own boss doesn't believe me. It's only when a case happens that they listen, and even then the first thing they all do is blame the Land Girls. But look, we need them on our side, don't we? You're not commanding a battleship now.'

'It was a destroyer.' His reply was rather brittle, a certain ice in the words.

Laura hadn't realised there was a difference, but she filed that piece of information away.

'I imagine that on a ship, when you say *jump*, everyone jumps,' Laura said as gently as she could. She wasn't sure he'd like to hear it, but it was the truth. 'And so you go onto a farm, and you do the same thing. But you said yourself, you know what farmers are like. It doesn't work.'

Iris knocked softly and opened the door, carrying the tea tray. She set it down on the table in front of Alastair, and had a good stare at him before bustling out again.

'Please have a think about what I've said, Commander,' Laura said as she poured the tea. She hoped he wouldn't think that Iris's curiosity was rude. 'When I first came to Bramble Heath, I was the first woman vet anybody had seen down here. They're a friendly bunch, and the Land Girls liked me, but the farmers weren't too sure. They thought I'd never cope because I don't have the manly brawn that's apparently needed to handle large animals. And of course, Mr Morgan thought the same thing.'

Alastair tutted. 'Mr Morgan. I've met a few of his type in my time.'

'And to start with, I acted the professional,' Laura went on, as she passed him his cup of tea. 'Reeling out long Latin names for this and that, so they'd know I knew what I was doing. But eventually, in desperation, I told them, *I grew up on a farm. I had a pet pig when I was four. I used to do the milking before school and when I got home.* And suddenly, things changed. I wasn't just an oddity any more – I was a farm girl, and they could relate to me.'

Alastair gave a tiny nod. He'd been listening to her, at any rate. Whether he was going to change his manner when he visited the farms remained to be seen.

'So please just think about that,' Laura said. 'I know you know animals – I saw how skilfully you helped me with the cows at the Bryants' farm. Let the farmers see *that* side of you, not Commander Seaton ordering about his men.' She put on what she thought was a sailor's voice, and said, '*Swab the deck, you landlubber!*'

'Miss Fellgate, I do appreciate your advice,' Alastair said, leaving the distinct impression of a man who was choosing his words very carefully. 'But it's been a long, *long* time since I grew up on a farm. I fought in the Battle of Jutland when I was four-teen years old; I've spent a quarter of a century in the Royal Navy. It leaves a man with an air of formality that isn't easy to shake off.'

Laura froze. Her father had a friend who'd fought in the Battle of Jutland, and she'd overheard him talking about it when he came to visit. What had stuck in her mind most of all was what her father had said about Jack Cornwell, who was only sixteen and had refused to move from his gun even as the shrapnel had flown around him. He was one of many who were killed.

'My goodness, I had no idea,' Laura said. 'You were so young. Fourteen, and seeing war. It's unimaginable.'

But he wasn't in the navy any more. All those years at sea and he was now tramping around country lanes. Why? Was it because his wife had died?

'Well...' Alastair nodded, then dropped his gaze down to the teacup he still held. The room was silent save for a ticking clock, until he glanced up again and settled his attention on Laura's scratched hand. 'Winnie?' he asked.

'Yes, that was Winnie!' Laura told him. He clearly wanted to change the subject, and she wasn't surprised. 'She's a sprightly little thing. You did the right thing, rescuing her.'

Alastair took a sip of tea. 'She just needed a helping hand.' He gave a nod, the sort of nod that seemed to say a decision has been made. 'Be less *commander*. Message received and understood, Miss Fellgate. Right, I'll let you get about your evening.'

And with that, he rose to his feet. 'But if I may issue *one* instruction, it's just a reminder to take care. We don't know exactly what we're dealing with here, what this traitor, if indeed there is one, might be capable of. Better to stay watchful.'

'Of course, Commander,' Laura replied. 'That's one order I *will* take from you.'

FIFTEEN

After Alastair had left, Laura helped Iris take the tea things to the kitchen.

'So *that's* him.' Iris chuckled. 'He's very smart, isn't he? Shame he's married, isn't it?'

Laura put the cups in the sink, glancing at Iris. She was very observant – clearly she'd noticed Alastair was wearing a wedding ring.

'Actually, the poor chap lost his wife in the Blitz,' she explained.

'Widower?' Iris's smile disappeared. She sighed. 'And still wearing his ring. Poor man. That's not a loss you get over easily, if you ever do.'

Laura thought back to what Alastair had told her; he'd joined the navy at fourteen and had experienced the horror of the Battle of Jutland. The years had passed, he'd married, then he'd lost his wife. He'd seen so much death, experienced so much pain. Was it any surprise that he came across as so officious, his emotions buried deep down inside him? But his dry sense of humour shone through, although Laura wondered if it was a weapon he used to stave off his sadness.

'Still, you grieve and you move on,' Iris observed, wielding her washing-up brush. Life continued; the dishes still needed to be done. 'I wouldn't be surprised if he's enjoying your company, you know. I bet he misses the companionship; I know I miss Bertie's. And you never know...' Iris's smile had reappeared, and she grinned cheekily at Laura. 'Maybe a bit more!'

Laura shook her head. 'If he's still wearing his ring, then I think he's still grieving. Besides, he's very busy. I don't think he's got time to go wife-hunting in Bramble Heath, even if he wanted to.'

And would he really be interested in me?

Iris seemed to realise that she wasn't going to get anything else from Laura about Alastair, and she changed the subject, telling her in great detail about her boys' new game. They had sat under the kitchen table, pretending they were soldiers in a pillbox looking out for Germans, and had demanded Iris say their special password every time she went between the sink and the hob.

The evening thankfully wasn't punctuated by an air raid, and Laura went to bed hoping the night would be peaceful too. As she started to drop off, she thought of Alastair, just a boy when he'd first fought in a war. There were children in the village who weren't much older than he'd been then; like Peter and Jamie, who rode bicycles and kicked a football about. Alastair's boyhood had been taken from him, and later his wife had been stolen away from him too.

No wonder he seemed so lonely.

But she liked him. It wasn't just because he believed her about the saboteur. She liked his sense of humour, and the fact that he clearly didn't see anything odd about a woman being a vet. Or least, if he did, he hadn't made it obvious.

Laura had fought over and over again to have the career she wanted; the career she was good at. From her teachers at school who'd tried to steer her towards *something more suitable for a girl* to her lecturers at veterinary college who had suggested she didn't perform surgery in case she fainted at the sight of blood, it had been a constant battle. Her biggest fight had been convincing her lecturers that she should be allowed to study farm animals, when they had insisted that she should focus solely on domestic pets because they were smaller.

She'd stuck to her guns, though. That was one of her best and worst traits. She was stubborn, with a willpower of steel. She'd never given up on her career, and she wasn't going to give up on the Bramble Heath poisoner. And now she had Alastair on her side as her ally, she felt even more confident that whoever was trying to sabotage the farms could be stopped. Facing it alone, with a boss who wouldn't look further than the end of his sexist nose, would've been terrible.

Laura rolled over and snuggled down into her bed. She was drifting off, picturing Alastair carrying Winnie the kitten in his arms, his city suit and hat looking so out of place in a country lane, when she heard a car drive past outside. The engine whined and the brakes squeaked, and then it was gone.

It wouldn't have been an unusual sound during the day, but night had fallen and few people drove around in the blackout. And there was something about the sound... it felt both familiar and out of place. It seemed...

But Laura's mind was fuzzy with sleep. Whatever it was, her thought was now unreachable. She was probably over-thinking things. It was only a car, after all. Perhaps it was something to do with the airbase? They never slept, so a car driving through Bramble Heath at night really shouldn't seem that odd at all.

Yes, something to do with the airbase. Maybe that's all it is...

SIXTEEN

Laura's day began early; Mrs Morgan banged on Iris's front door with news of an urgent call from Goslings' farm – but not so urgent that Mr Morgan would go himself. Petunia the pig had gone into labour in the early hours and everything had come to a halt. Laura knew how tricky these births could be, and she got into the Clyno as dawn was breaking and headed to the farm. It was a relief to be dealing with a case that had nothing to do with the saboteur.

As she drove out of the village, she spotted a figure in the shadows wearing slacks, a shirt and a cravat. They didn't look like someone from the airbase as they weren't in an RAF uniform. What were they doing out here?

But as she got closer to the figure, she realised that she recognised him. How had she not seen that it was Alastair? And what was he doing out and about so early in the morning?

She came to a stop beside him and opened her window.

'Commander Seaton!' she called. 'Fancy seeing you out here so early!'

'We don't have fresh mornings like this in London,' Alastair said, leaning down to address Laura through the open window. His brow furrowed and he asked, 'Has something happened?'

'I don't blame you for enjoying an early morning walk,' Laura replied. 'There's a pig in labour up at Goslings' farm.'

Alastair gave a little smile, one that Laura was sure contained a touch of nostalgia. 'A pig?' he mused. 'Do you fancy some company?'

'Why not? Hop in, Commander!' Laura leaned over to open the passenger door for him. It'd be good for the farmers to see him in his casuals, she decided, a chance for them to see beyond the civil servant in his suit and hat. And besides, she had to admit that she did rather enjoy his company.

Alastair strode round the car and climbed in, closing the door behind him. He looked to Laura with a warm smile and said, 'Bramble Heath's a beautiful place to live. It makes me so angry that someone could be trying to do such damage here.'

'It's terrible,' Laura said, with an involuntary shudder. 'I'm just so, so glad you believe me. If you hadn't come, I don't know what I would've done. The thought that someone's creeping about, poisoning the livestock, setting fires, intent on starving people and spreading division between the Land Girls, the evacuees and the villagers – I don't understand what can possibly be going through their minds.'

She started the car again, driving along the lane that cut between pastures and fields of crops, all geared towards feeding the nation.

'You're exactly right about division. Maintaining morale at home is vital...' Her companion shook his head. 'The last thing a close-knit community needs is to think that someone inside it is capable of poisoning cattle and heaven knows what else. We *will* get them, Miss Fellgate.'

'We have to,' she replied. She admired Alastair's determination, and it made her feel more confident that the traitor would be caught. But would they be in time to stop them from doing more harm... maybe something even worse? She nodded eagerly. 'We *will*. You're right about morale, and it's not just about the Land Girls and evacuees being blamed for the poisoning and the fires. Just imagine if the farmers all start to blame each other. They all get on so well and help each other out; the last thing we need is someone driving a wedge between them.'

Alastair suddenly sat forward in the car seat, squinting against the shadows.

'What's that?' he asked.

Laura followed his gaze. There was a glow on the horizon, in the direction they were headed. 'That'll be the sunrise,' she replied, turning her attention back to the road.

But then she froze, suddenly alight with panic. 'No, it can't be, that's not the east, that's over where Goslings' farm is. That's — oh, no, it can't be a fire!'

Laura slammed her foot down on the accelerator. The car grumbled, then lurched forward, taking the lane at speed. She tried to wrestle with the awful images filling her mind, the terrible destruction that could be caused by the fire rushing through the farm. Her terror was visceral; fiercely unwelcome memories bombarded her of the Coventry Blitz. The roar of falling bombs, the stench of burning, the smoke still rising from the ruins days later.

She coughed as the smell of smoke blew into the car, and as they got closer the glow grew larger, as if it was trying to fill the sky.

She took the turn for Goslings' farm too fast and skidded, but managed to get the car under control again, speeding down the lane. She tried to take everything in at once – the smoke rolling through the yard, the flames bursting out of one of the barns, the hurry of figures, the animals being ushered to safety, the glint of the flames on the metal buckets, the splash of water.

Laura skidded to a halt and leapt down from the car, Alastair following close behind. They ran towards the fire, despite the smoke that choked their throats and the terrifying waves of heat they could already feel on their skin. They had to help somehow.

Some of the Land Girls were shepherding the animals to safety, as smoke gushed from a barn and flames leapt above them. Mrs Gosling was filling buckets with water at a trough, and her husband was hurriedly uncoiling a hose.

'Lottie! Oh, Lottie! Someone get her out!' Mrs Gosling cried.

Laura's heart plummeted. The barn was ablaze, the flames licking holes through the tiled roof. The thought that Lottie, that sweet, earnest Land Girl, could be in there was horrifying.

'It's the crop store!' Nicola shouted to Laura and Alastair as she ran out of the barn, her arms wrapped round an enormous sack of produce. Behind her more Land Girls followed, their faces blacked with smoke, their arms full of the crops they'd managed to save. 'Someone set it bloody alight!'

Laura saw something in Alastair's gaze, and she knew he must see it in hers too. Not content with poisoning animals, the traitor in their midst was now torching the crops, endangering the whole farm and the people who lived in it.

Mr Gosling strode up, water gushing from the hose as he approached the door of the barn. He winced at the heat.

The air was rent by a crash, and sparks flew up from the barn. Everyone in the yard cringed a step away from it. The barn was about to collapse from the force of the flames.

'Where's Lottie?' Martha gasped, glancing from face to face. 'She was right behind me! Where is she? Oh, no, she can't still be inside the barn!'

Over the roar of the inferno, a cry rang out. 'Help! Help me, please! I can't get out!'

Terror tore through Laura; it was Lottie. She was trapped inside the barn.

Martha rushed forward, desperate to save her sister, but Mr Gosling caught her arm. She fought him desperately, screaming, 'Lottie! Oh, Lottie! Somebody help!'

Laura was aware of movement at her side and suddenly Alastair was running across the yard towards the burning barn. As he pushed open the door he shouted back to them, 'Get that hose in here now!' Then he lowered his head and dashed into the inferno.

She couldn't believe what she'd just seen – but then again, hadn't he been the commander of a battleship? He clearly had bravery in spades.

But so did she.

Without a second thought, Laura grabbed the hose from Mr Gosling and ran into the barn after him. She'd sheltered in a basement during that horrific night in Coventry. But now she could save someone.

The heat hit her at once, and the smoke stung her eyes. In moments they were streaming and she could barely see a thing.

'Commander Seaton!' she called, squinting through the smoke as she tried to find him.

'To the left of the door!' Alastair shouted, his voice strained as the tortured timbers of the barn snapped and creaked in the heat. Then she heard him say urgently to Lottie, 'Keep your head low and crawl underneath!'

Laura headed towards Alastair's voice, and aimed the water at the flames that were spreading in their direction. It was only now that she started to think of what must be going through Alastair's mind. This was a man whose wife had perished in the Blitz, in flames and in the crush of a fallen building. He hadn't been able to save her, but now here he was, in an inferno, fighting to save another life; risking his own.

Through the smoke, Laura saw Alastair bracing himself against a huge fallen beam, lifting it away so that Lottie could crawl to safety. She was coughing, her face mired with soot, as she emerged from beneath the beam. With the hose still in one hand, Laura bent down and grabbed Lottie's shoulder, and helped to pull her free.

'She's out!' Laura called to Alastair. The beam gave an ominous crack and Alastair winced as he slipped out from beneath it. No sooner was he clear of the timber than it crashed to the ground, then Alastair seized the hose from Laura's hand.

'Take Lottie and go!' he commanded.

Laura slipped her arm round Lottie's shoulder. The girl could barely stand, and Laura knew she might be seriously injured. As she dragged her to the door, she cried out desperately to Alastair, 'Get out, Commander! Now!'

As soon as Laura got out of the barn, Martha ran forward and clutched her sister as if she'd never let her go again. They staggered back from the stricken building and all Laura could think of was Alastair still inside it, among the merciless flames and toppling beams. Tears began to course down her face.

She couldn't lose him.

Bells clanged, and Laura looked through her tears at a fire engine that was speeding along the lane towards the farm. But would they be in time to save Alastair?

Then her heart leapt as a figure appeared in the doorway of the barn. Alastair was alive. He was shrouded in smoke but straight-backed and determined, training the hose on the fire that still threatened the barn. As he directed the water, he glanced over his shoulder and shouted, 'Is everyone out?'

'Aye!' Nicola replied over the clanging bell of the fire engine, which had now pulled into the yard. 'Everybody accounted for!'

A cheer went up from everyone in the yard, but their jubilation only lasted a moment. The Land Girls formed themselves into a conveyor belt, passing buckets of water along from the trough to be thrown into the barn by Mr Gosling, and back again. The fire engine came to a stop and the firemen jumped down, some joining in with the buckets while others uncoiled hoses.

Laura approached Alastair. 'Are you all right?' she whispered urgently, wiping a large speck of soot from his cheek.

He blinked at her through eyes that were red with smoke, then said, 'I'm fine. They're all safe, Laura.' His next breath was deep and shuddering, then he closed his eyes for a long moment.

'You take the load off.' Mr Gosling took the hosepipe from Alastair and patted him on the shoulder. Then the farmer looked towards Laura and nodded towards the edge of the yard. 'Go on, we'll manage it now.'

Laura guided Alastair away from the flames. 'I don't suppose you'd like to help with Petunia?' she asked him, hoping that aiding her might take his mind off what had happened. And hers too; the memories of Coventry were receding again. 'She still needs us, even with all this going on.'

'Petunia...' Alastair murmured, looking down at his soot-blackened hands. 'Yes... I'll wash my hands.'

Laura led him over to the pigsties. Although she could still hear shouts and the crackle of the flames, they couldn't drown out the contented grunts and snuffles of the pigs. There was no sound of a sow in distress, and when Laura looked over the wall of Petunia's pen she found the pig lying on her side, a row of tiny piglets suckling her.

'It looks like Petunia sorted herself out. Nature got along perfectly well without us after all,' she told Alastair with relief. At least *something* had gone right this morning. Alastair said nothing, but replied with a gentle nod as he watched the new mother and her young.

Only after a minute or more had passed did he murmur, 'I'm going to find out who's terrorising this village, Miss Fellgate.' Then he looked to Laura, his gaze filled with a pain that could only have come from memories of the wife he had lost. 'They're not going to win. But I need your help. I can't do this without you.'

SEVENTEEN

Bone-tired and shaken, when Laura arrived back at Iris's she trudged up to the bathroom to wash away the soot. It was only as she dabbed it off that she realised there were little burns across her skin, which she'd been too shocked to notice before. But as she cooled them with water she saw that, thankfully, they were all minor.

Completely wrung out, she went into her bedroom and fell asleep in her clothes, which still carried with them the smell of the fire.

When she woke up it was nearly the middle of the day, and her first thoughts were of Alastair. He had seemed so distant when she'd dropped him off on the way back from the farm. He'd been so brave, running into the fire, but she knew he'd had to confront the distressing memories of his wife's death to save the life of another. No wonder he'd looked so pale under the patina of soot on his face.

Laura could hear the comforting sounds of home, as Iris worked in the kitchen and her boys played with their toy cars in the hallway. She pulled on her dressing gown and went downstairs, stepping carefully past the twins' precious toys.

'Ah, there you are!' Iris said jovially as she laid the teapot on the kitchen table. 'I thought you might appreciate a nice big breakfast after the morning you've had!'

Laura smiled at the sight of toast in the rack and the brimming bowl of porridge. She sighed as she sat down at the table, remembering that she should've been at work. 'I don't suppose you heard from Mr Morgan while I was asleep?'

'I did,' Iris said, putting a jar of home-made strawberry jam on the table. 'And I told him you were having a well-deserved rest! A fire up at the farm, I ask you. And all this business I've heard about, with those awful poisonings, too – everyone's talking about it. You've had your work cut out for you!'

So, news about the poisonings had spread. But it was hardly a surprise; gossip spread through Bramble Heath just as quickly as the deliberate fires that now threatened everyone's safety.

Laura poured the tea, wondering about the effect the news was having on the village. 'It's frightening stuff,' she admitted. 'But that's why Commander Seaton's here. I wrote to London, and he's come down to put everything to rights. He's such a brave man, Iris, he'll find out who it is and stop them, and I'm going to do everything I can too.'

Iris toed the kitchen door half-closed and lowered her voice, no doubt to avoid the boys overhearing and getting upset. 'Everyone thought it was the Land Girls and the evacuees to start with, that's what Mrs Farthing said at the post office,' she whispered. 'But it's a dreadful thing to think that someone in the village is going about poisoning the animals and burning down barns full of food!'

She dropped down into the chair beside her lodger, and Laura gently put her hand over hers.

'I know,' Laura replied. 'One bad apple...'

'One *very* bad apple,' Iris went on, her expression twisting with fear. 'But I just can't think who it could be. Bramble Heath's such a lovely place, everyone gets along just dandy, whether they've lived here years, or they've just arrived, like the Land Girls, or the Poles or the airmen. And now some-one... someone's taking food out of my boys' mouths, Laura. Someone's trying to scare us all with these fires, and worse... It isn't right!'

'You've already got enough to worry about with Bertie being away, please don't let this affect you so,' Laura said, trying to console her. But how could she? It wasn't just the farms that were impacted but the whole community, all of whom seemed to be the target of these vicious attacks. 'I want you to know that Commander Seaton and I are doing everything we can to get to the bottom of this.'

Iris nodded, but she was clearly still unnerved; her hands trembled. 'What about my boys, Laura? What about the fires? What if this monster hurts them? If they go out to play and...'

It was horrible to see Iris so frightened. She was a good person, doing her best to keep her chin up in very trying circum-stances, and she didn't need another burden. No one in Bramble Heath did.

'As long as they don't go gallivanting off, they should be all right,' Laura assured her. 'Just... keep an eye on them, won't you? I know you already do, but it doesn't hurt to be even more vigilant at the moment.'

Iris sighed. 'You're right. I mustn't let whoever this is scare me, must I? That's exactly what they want. But I will keep an eye out. We all can do our bit, can't we?'

'That's it,' Laura said, smiling gently at her. 'We all can do our bit.'

EIGHTEEN

Later that day, Laura was working in the pharmacy when she heard a knock at the front door. She hoped it was Alastair, with news about the fire.

Horrible though it might be, it simply wasn't believable that the fire could have been an accident. Someone targeted that barn on purpose, because it was a food store. Someone wanted to make the nation go hungry; they were prepared to let innocent people and animals die horrible deaths in order to do as much harm as they could to the home front.

And beside her desperate desire for any news he might have, Laura was worried about Alastair. Rescuing Lottie from the flames must've brought back so many distressing memories for him, and she didn't like to think of him being alone at such a painful time.

Laura went along the hallway past the paintings of racehorses and gundogs, and opened the door. But it wasn't Alastair. Smudge, the former sailor who'd known last night's hero as the commander of a Royal Navy destroyer, was waiting there with a parcel.

'Morning, Smudge,' Laura said. She wished she could ask

him to tell her more about Alastair, but she wasn't sure she could.

'G'morning, miss.' Smudge beamed and passed the brown-paper parcel over to her. 'It's not much of a weight. Are you all right to manage?'

'That's very kind of you, Smudge, but I'm sure I can,' Laura said as she took it. She was sure it was the charcoal she'd ordered in case the Bramble Heath poisoner struck again. It wasn't too heavy, but she appreciated Smudge's gentlemanly offer of help nonetheless. 'I hope you don't mind me asking, but you were in the navy, weren't you?'

He nodded, his smile proud. 'And I was honoured to serve under Commander Seaton from my first day to my last.' So perhaps he *might* be willing to share a few stories, then. 'It's on account of him that I'm standing here talking to you now, even with my pirate's patch.'

'Really?' So Alastair was a hero to Smudge, the reason he was alive today. Lottie was now added to the list of lives that he had saved. How many others were there? 'He was in the navy right from when he was fourteen, he told me. That's a long time at sea.'

'The commander was at sea man and boy,' Smudge confirmed. 'He was my first commander and I was lucky enough to stay with him all the way through. He fought two world wars and they made a hero out of him in both, so don't let him tell you,' and here he affected a gentle mimicry of Alastair's precise Yorkshire tones, '*It was nothing. Just a job.*'

Made a hero out of him? But now he's away from the navy, far away from the sea in rural Bramble Heath, fighting battles on the home front. Why?

'He didn't say a word to me about being a hero, but then he doesn't seem the type to brag,' Laura said. And yet, it didn't come as a surprise. He'd shown such selfless bravery while tackling the blaze. He was a hero to everyone in Bramble

Heath now too. 'I was impressed that he commanded a destroyer.'

'HMS *Nemesis*.' As Smudge said the words with undisguised relish, a smile spread over his ruddy face. 'Oh, Miss, there was a ship. A real beauty of a thing. And the commander could handle her as delicate as a racehorse.'

Laura swallowed. How hard it must've been for Alastair to leave the navy when he had earned such a position – and was clearly so respected by his men.

'Gosh, Commander Seaton must miss the sea.' She sighed. 'We don't have a lot of it around here.'

'Happen as he just needed a bit of a break from it all,' Smudge said, but something in his reply struck Laura as very careful. He had chosen those words deliberately, she was certain. 'The man earned that DSC and two bars. *Two*. Now, that takes some getting. I'll tell you this for nothing, every man on *Nemesis* who lived to see his missus and kids again would've given the commander the bloody Victoria Cross if he'd had his say!'

Laura blinked at Smudge in amazement. She'd had no idea that the quiet man from the Ministry, in his homburg hat and neat grey suit, had done something so extraordinary while he was in the navy. No wonder Smudge had looked at Alastair with such admiration when he'd met him the other day. And no wonder Alastair hadn't given it a second thought when he'd heard Lottie's cries for help. Those memories of his lost wife had combined with his well-practised bravery to drive him on and risk his own life to save another's, once again.

But what did Smudge mean about Alastair needing a break? Surely the navy didn't allow their officers to go off on sabbatical, especially not during a war. A man of Alastair's talents would be badly needed at sea.

'I really had no idea,' Laura replied. 'How extraordinary! What's a DSC? It sounds very impressive.'

'Distinguished Service Cross.' Smudge said the name of the medal with awe, almost in a whisper. 'They gave him that when he was still a lad in the Great War. Dunkirk got him the first bar and saving our necks in the middle of the Atlantic got him the second. I don't mind telling you, miss, I thought we'd be shaking hands with the *Titanic* that day.'

Laura regretted her silly impression of a pirate giving the order to swab the decks. Alastair's career in the navy was one of extraordinary bravery – but then, he'd never hinted at it, beyond the fact that he'd told her he'd fought in the Battle of Jutland when he'd been only a boy.

'I still run for cover when I hear a car backfiring.' Smudge chuckled. 'But I'm here and I'm breathing and that's all down to our commander, God bless him. It was a surprise to see him down this way, but a happy one.'

'I'm sure it was a surprise,' Laura replied. How often did two sailors bump into each other on land? Smudge must've gone through a dreadful time. And... what had happened to Alastair? She knew life had dealt him many a cruel card, but what had driven him away from his work, away from the sea?

Oh, Alastair, what happened to you?

'You must know how grateful we all are for what you did,' she said. 'For the risks you took.'

Smudge gave a polite nod of acknowledgement, but, just like the men from the airbase, he didn't seem overly concerned with receiving thanks. To them, it really was their duty to risk their lives for their country and their fellow men, like everyone should.

'I'd better crack along, miss.' He smiled. 'You have a good day now, won't you? And give Commander Seaton my best if you see him again.'

'I definitely will. Goodbye now,' Laura said, her mind spinning. She watched her visitor amble along the path back to his waiting van, wondering once again at what had brought the man in the smart grey suit to Bramble Heath.

'Curiouser and curiouser, said the veterinary to the one-eyed old salt,' Mr Morgan announced as he stepped into the hallway from his sitting room, appearing to read her mind. 'Ah, there's a story there, what, about our gentleman from the Ministry? Diddling the admiral's wife? Caught quaffing the rum ration?' He pulled on his overcoat and took his hat from the peg. 'What brings a fellow from the deck of his ship to our humble village? I think I shall make some enquiries into our commander-who-no-longer-commands.'

Laura bit back a retort. Why did her boss have to assume such horrible things about Alastair? And after news of his bravery during the fire had spread through the village. Even Morgan must've heard about it by now. How could he be so rude about a man who was clearly a hero?

More and more, Laura was coming to realise that Alastair's ability to face the war at sea had somehow worn itself out. He'd reached a point where he simply couldn't go back on a ship; but he was still determined to do everything in his power to protect their country. How dare someone like Morgan, who had never worn a uniform, be so judgemental about someone who had spent most of his life in one?

'Commander Seaton is a very brave man,' Laura told him. *Braver than you.* 'There must be a reason why he left the navy, but I can't imagine it's for anything scandalous.'

'We shall see. Now, I am away to East Grinstead to see our good friend Mr Pullen and his racehorses,' said Mr Morgan.

Laura knew Mr Pullen by reputation if not in person, and she knew he had made his fortune by supplying feed to the farms of the south-east. The very same feed that even now might be being poisoned. 'Work, not pleasure, of course. But I shall, alas, be busy for the duration.'

Work, not pleasure, my foot. And I'm left to hold the fort. Thank you very much.

As annoyed as she was to be left the only vet in the practice while her boss went off on a jolly, there was nothing she could do to stop him.

'Hopefully we'll have a quiet day here,' she said. She dreaded to think what would happen if the traitor had been busy overnight harming even more livestock or taking their vendetta to the next stage, with only her to manage things. 'Goodbye, Mr Morgan.'

'Farewell, young Miss Fellgate of the Overactive Imagination, farewell!' Mr Morgan called as he left the house. A car was just drawing to a halt at the bottom of the path and Morgan paused, narrowing his eyes at the driver. He called over his shoulder, 'Your suitor is keen, Miss Fellgate!', then strode away without waiting to greet the new arrival.

Thank goodness Alastair couldn't have heard that from inside his car. And she was embarrassed that Morgan had blanked a visitor so rudely, especially one who had risked his life for a fellow Bramble Heath villager only the day before.

'Hello, Commander,' Laura called as Alastair got out of the car. Had he come with news about the fire?

Once again he wasn't in his city clothes but casually dressed in slacks, wearing a shirt with a cravat. His sleeves were rolled to the elbow, showing his toned arms. She tried to read his expression, wondering how he was coping after yesterday, and was dismayed to see a look of fear, anger and urgency spreading across his face.

'You're needed up at Hillside Farm,' Alastair called urgently. 'The herd's been poisoned!'

NINETEEN

It wasn't much when compared to a destroyer, but the car Alastair had borrowed from the George and Dragon's landlord was at least faster than the Clyno Laura normally drove. And speed was of the essence.

'How many have been poisoned?' Laura asked Alastair as he drove through the lanes. She held tight to her bag, hoping against hope that they'd arrive in time. The saboteur was stepping up their campaign; a fire and a whole herd poisoned in one day. Was this person acting alone? Heaven forbid, but could there be more than one traitor in their midst, to have achieved so much at once? How on earth could they be stopped before people started to go hungry, or lost their lives in a terrifying attack like the one that had nearly killed Lottie?

'They've lost a dozen this morning. The Land Girls turned them out before breakfast and somehow the poisoner got to them.' It was the news Laura had dreaded hearing, and her heart sank. 'There's no question this is linseed cake or any of that rubbish. And it isn't only happening here.'

Despite the green hedgerows and white puffs of hawthorn

blossom rushing by the windows in the spring sunlight, Laura shivered. Everything suddenly dimmed.

'A dozen deaths... this is exactly what I was scared of! Why wouldn't Mr Morgan listen to me?' She sighed heavily. 'This didn't have to happen. Those poor creatures must've suffered so. And as for the Parker sisters... what a blow to their farm. Twelve cows? It's so awful.'

And then there was the hit the local milk production would take. Twelve cows gone all at once from a herd that helped to keep the country fed.

But Alastair's last sentence rang in her ears too.

It isn't only happening here.

'We've had a farm on the Welsh borders lost half its herd this last week. There's been crop damage and fires set. It's not just a local issue any more,' Alastair went on as they sped onwards. 'The truth is, it's been building over the last couple of months, and I've been trying to convince my bosses that there was more to it than coincidence and the needless fretting of a man with cracked nerves. I wish I'd been wrong, but...'

A man with cracked nerves.

With those words, Laura knew that Alastair had let her into his confidence. And not only that, but now she knew that what had seemed like a one-person vendetta against the farms around Bramble Heath was something more. It was part of a wide-spread attack against their nation. An attempt to destroy them from the inside, while the Germans attacked by sea and air.

'Half its herd?' Laura shook her head, unable to conceal her shock. 'And fires too... we've only had the one barn torched here, alongside those fires people thought the evacuees had caused... but are there going to be more? We can't let any more animals suffer and die; we can't afford to lose any more food. Farmers, Land Girls, even the little evacuees – any of them could be killed if a farm is set alight. We can't let this monster destroy Bramble Heath. We can't!'

And yet, Laura felt helpless. She'd been battling her boss and Alastair had been battling his. They had been proved right, but what a bitter victory it was, and they seemed no closer to knowing who the enemy among them was.

'I was walking in the blackout last night, before the fire, and I heard a car engine,' Alastair told her, and Laura wondered if they'd both heard the same vehicle. But something else struck her too: Alastair was out walking as she was falling asleep and this morning, as she drove though the village just before dawn, he was out again. He needed rest, but the burdens he carried never gave him the chance. 'It seemed odd in such a quiet village, but I didn't see who it was. If I had—'

Alastair broke off and shook his head, but it wasn't his fault. It was bad enough that something had left him tormented and walking the streets after the world had fallen silent, but to have him blame himself... no, he had nothing to feel guilty about.

'I heard it too,' Laura told him, and gently touched his arm. It was only for a second, and yet perhaps it was enough for him to know that she didn't think he was at fault. No one would. 'It seemed so out of place, but I told myself it was something to do with the airbase. And yet... there was something about it... I can't quite put my finger on it, but it seemed familiar. But I suppose if the wretch who's doing this is local, that shouldn't come as a huge surprise.'

'I've spoken to my bosses in Whitehall,' Alastair said. 'We can't risk sabotage on the home front. The war effort has never been more critical than it is now. There's too much at stake.'

'And they know our poisoner is an arsonist too,' Laura said grimly. 'Hopefully they will take it seriously now. But how are you, Alastair? You were so brave, rescuing Lottie, but it must have been so frightening. You're such a quiet sort of hero.'

'I'm not a hero,' he replied. 'Are *you* all right? Did you manage to rest?'

'I did, thank you,' Laura replied. She knew he wouldn't

have, though, and that saddened her. 'But more importantly, did you? Only, you must've been exhausted. I know I was.'

'I don't sleep well these days. Too much to think about,' Alastair admitted. As he glanced towards Laura, he swung the car onto the long lane up to the farm. He looked almost stricken, and now she understood why. His suspicions had been proven true, but it was something he hadn't *wanted* to be right about.

'The traitor in Bramble Heath must be connected to a network operating across the nation, threatening to bring us all down from the inside just as our brave lads are out there dying to keep us safe. But if we can catch one of them,' he said, 'we could stop them all. We just need one thread to unpick the whole tapestry.'

TWENTY

When they arrived at Hillside Farm, a group of Land Girls were clustered around a cow lying on her side, not far from the hedge. The rest of the herd had been guided to the other side of the field.

The cow had to be dead, just like the twelve poor, gentle beasts who had already died. Laura's heart sank. 'It looks like another one's been poisoned.'

'We've got half a dozen more ailing in the barn!' Shona, one of the Land Girls, shouted urgently as she broke from the group and ran towards the approaching car. Her eyes were bloodshot with emotion, her voice thick with sorrow. 'But they're all still standing, for now. Daisy here just went down as we were helping her!'

'Don't worry, Shona, I'll do what I can,' Laura assured her as she climbed out of the car. *Curse my boss, gallivanting off and leaving me to deal with all of this on my own!*

Laura and Alastair were silent as they hurried across the field. The ground was soft, sucking against Laura's shoes, but she ignored it, her mind reeling.

What if I can't save her? What if all the cows at Bramble Heath die? What on earth will we do?

The Land Girls stood aside as Laura and Alastair reached them. Bridget, who Laura had met before, was sitting down beside the cow, stroking her head as she struggled to breathe. It was awful to see an animal in such a condition, and all the Land Girls were pale with concern.

The Land Girls were so occupied with Daisy that they'd barely registered Alastair's presence, but Laura told them, 'I hope you don't mind Commander Seaton being here with me. I think you met him yesterday? He told me about the cows and drove me here.'

'I saw Miss Parker while I was walking this morning,' Alastair explained. 'She told me what'd happened.'

Shona nodded. 'This is why we need a bloody telephone, all the way out here!' She exclaimed despairingly. 'Miss Parker's in the barn with the other girls now; she said the vet was on the way. Thanks for fetching her for us, Commander.'

'Can you do anything for Daisy?' Bridget asked, looking up at Laura as she blinked away tears.

'I'll do what I can,' Laura replied, hoping Bridget wouldn't notice her uncertainty.

'Come on, sweetheart,' Shona whispered, her gaze fixed on the ailing creature. 'You're a big strong lass...'

Laura began to examine Daisy, and Alastair knelt down in the grass beside her. She opened the cow's mouth, releasing a slight scent of bitter almonds, and saw the dark red colouration inside. She knew he could see it too and, when she glanced at him, a knowing look passed between them.

It was a terrible case, worse than the others, and she wasn't sure there was much hope.

'I'm just going to give her an injection,' Laura told the girls as she primed her syringe. There was a tremble in her voice that she couldn't hide. 'Can you steady her for me?'

Bridget and Shona held on to Daisy, trying to keep the struggling, frightened cow as still as they could.

'Come on, Daisy,' Laura whispered, resting the cow's head on her lap. Alastair reached out and settled his hand on the animal's shoulder.

Laura gave the injection.

No one spoke, or even moved. And in the silence, Laura realised that Daisy was no longer moving and her struggling breaths had ceased.

She lowered her head and closed her eyes. She couldn't cry. Not in front of everyone. She couldn't.

I was too late. I've lost her. At least her suffering's over, but... I was too late.

'She's not...?' Bridget sobbed. 'She's not dead, is she?'

Laura could only keep fighting her tears, her words trapped in her throat. What more could she have done?

She heard the cows on the other side of the field shifting and mooing. They knew something was wrong. Did they know when one of their herd died?

Laura's eyes were still closed when she felt something warm and wet rasp against her hand. She opened her eyes and saw Daisy's tongue, poking out from between her teeth. The rasp came again, and Laura realised that Daisy was licking her hand.

'She's still alive!' Laura gasped, amazed, and the Land Girls around her cheered.

Alastair ran his hand back over his hair, even though not a strand of it had come loose. 'Thank God,' he whispered.

'She's not quite well yet,' Laura warned them, but moment by moment Daisy was rallying, licking Laura's hand with more enthusiasm.

'Daisy'll lick your hand right off!' Shona joked.

'Once she's back on her feet, I'll give her some charcoal to soak up the rest of the poison,' Laura told them.

'It's from the linseed cake again, isn't it?' Bridget sighed.

'That's what Mr Morgan said when he came up the other week.' She turned towards two of the Land Girls. 'Mary, Harriet, we went through this.'

'But it can't be,' Mary replied. 'We *definitely* boil the mash. We made sure, especially after last time.'

'Yeah, we check and double-check!' Harriet added defensively. 'I don't see how it can have happened *again*.'

Alastair stayed where he was for another couple of seconds, his hand still steady on Daisy's shoulder. Then he seemed to gather himself, and rose to his feet as he said, 'Right. We need to take some action.'

'Oh, we do, we *do*,' Laura said with determination. 'Because whoever has done this has come for us, for Bramble Heath, and they're not going to get away with it. We won't let them!'

TWENTY-ONE

While Laura stayed with her patient, making sure she didn't suddenly relapse, the Land Girls listened attentively, their faces a picture of horror and dismay, to Alastair as he told them about the cases across the country that mirrored theirs.

'I know I put a few noses out of joint when I started asking questions, but there was no other way,' Alastair told them. 'There have been cases all over this part of the countryside and a few further afield too. I've been asked to find out if there was something to it.'

'So, it's not us after all?' Mary sighed with relief. 'Mr Morgan certainly thought it was.'

What an arrogant fool Laura had for a boss. He'd been so busy blaming the girls that he hadn't seen the truth that was right there in front of him, and it had wasted precious time. If he'd taken her seriously, she wouldn't be the only vet on the scene. Once Laura was sure that Daisy was out of the woods, she'd have to go and treat even more of the herd alone – perfectly healthy animals who were suffering and might die because her boss had laid the blame in completely the wrong place.

'I grew up on a farm and I know how much pride and effort you put into your work,' Alastair continued. 'I had an instinct from the off this wasn't accidental and none of you were to blame; now I'm sure of it. I'll speak to the Ministry and to the police. What we have here is a clear attack on the home front, a concerted effort to disrupt the food supply and do as much damage as possible to our nation's farms.'

A gasp of astonishment ran through the Land Girls.

'How dreadful!' Bridget exclaimed. 'Hillside's lost twelve cows already. What'll we do if they come back? We can't lose any more of the herd!'

'I'll speak to Miss Parker, but from now on we need someone on watch around the clock if the cows are out,' Alastair told them. Laura could well believe he was a military man now; he seemed much more at ease here than he had acting as the besuited Ministry pen-pusher. 'Every morning, every afternoon, every time the cows are to be put out, check the troughs, check the meadow and check the grass along the roadside of the fields. If you see any dry food out that shouldn't be there, or anything that strikes you as odd, keep the cows in, or take them to another field. And let me know right away. You'll find me at the George and Dragon.'

'Dry food that shouldn't be there?' Bridget asked, her voice shaking in anger and dismay. 'That's how they're doing it, isn't it?'

All the girls talked at once, and Laura, still nursing Daisy, shushed them.

'Daisy's still recovering, let's try to keep calm,' she said. 'But yes, that's how they're doing it. Did anyone see Daisy eating?'

Harriet nodded over to a trough by the hedge. 'Yes, I did. She goes over to that trough every morning. First thing. She was straight over there this morning too.'

Alastair was already on his way to the trough Harriet had

indicated before she'd finished speaking. He looked down into the trough, then stooped to retrieve something from inside it.

'I'll gather some of this,' he said, looking back at them. 'Then this trough needs emptying and sluicing down. The grass around here too.'

The Land Girls glanced at one another, their fear obvious. Nobody was saying it, but everyone knew the attacker could just as easily target them in their attempt to harm the home front. They would've heard about the fire at Goslings' farm by now, and would've known that Lottie, one of their number, had barely escaped with her life. But Laura sensed a steely resolve in their faces too. The poisoner hadn't reckoned with the courage of the Land Girls.

'Don't worry, we'll give it a good scrub. We won't let any more of the girls get ill,' Shona promised, with iron determination in her voice. 'They're not going to hurt our cows again.'

Once Daisy was out of danger, Laura left her to the care of Bridget and Harriet, then she hurried over to the barn to treat the other patients while Alastair went to speak to Miss Parker. It was hard work, but with the help of the Land Girls she examined and treated all six of the ailing creatures.

Laura would have to give an official opinion on the dead cows too, seeing as Morgan wasn't around to do it. It was never a job she relished, but it would have to be done.

She came out of the barn, tired and with mud and bits of straw stuck to her, to find Alastair in the yard, talking to Miss Parker. The wind fluttered the farmer's faded silk headscarf, and she pulled a large handkerchief from the pocket of her over-sized cardigan to dab at her red-rimmed eyes. Miss Parker had the look of someone who had lived most of her life outdoors, her skin lined from sunshine, wind and rain. Farming was a hard job, a calling, really; it was backbreaking and heartbreaking in equal amounts. There were always triumphs and tragedies, but never usually on this scale. And when it was something that nature had no hand in, but something perpetrated by a traitor twisted enough to cause pain and suffering, and threaten the whole country at the same time, it was almost impossible to bear.

Losing so many of her herd was catastrophic, and what made it worse was that Miss Parker and her sister, like Laura, had to fight against outdated views that said women couldn't handle large animals on their own. Of all the rotten luck, it was Miss Parker who'd lost twelve of her cows to the poisoner, and Laura worried how she'd cope.

'Miss Parker, Mr Ministry Man, good morning to you now!' Farmer Bryant called as he rolled into the yard atop his pony and trap.

'Morning,' Miss Parker replied. Despite the tears that Laura had watched her wipe away, there was something about the determined tilt of her head that told Laura that Miss Parker wasn't going to cry any more. 'We've lost twelve cows, Nobby. Twelve... I still can't believe it.'

The farmer climbed down from his trap and took off the flat cap he wore. He wrung it between his hands as he approached.

'It's all over the village,' he admitted. 'I've been on the blower to old Risby and Cotter down the way; Gosling too. They're on the blower to a few others while I'm here.' Bryant shuffled on the spot, awkward. 'It's bloody criminal, is what it is. And after that fire over at Goslings'...'

'What on earth can be going on?' Miss Parker said, anger detectable behind her despair. 'Who would do such terrible things?'

'I'll be coming to your farm later to brief you and the Land Girls,' Alastair told him. 'I'm afraid we've got a traitor in our midst, someone trying to harm the farms, the whole of Bramble Heath, indeed the home front itself.'

Bryant nodded. 'Miss Parker, I know you and your sister haven't always seen eye to eye with some of the menfolk when it comes to women running a farm,' he said, wringing his cap again. 'But a farmer's a farmer and you're one of us.'

'I'm glad you think so,' Miss Parker replied. 'We work very hard at Hillside, no matter what some people might think. To have this happen to us... and through no fault of our own. The commander here has been telling me it's been going on all over, but we're the only farm to have lost any cattle around Bramble Heath.'

Laura stepped forward. 'If you don't mind me saying so, I think it's because the traitor knows there's now a man from the Ministry in the area, and we're on their trail. I wouldn't be surprised if that's why they've increased the doses they've been using – to cause more damage before they're stopped. I'm so sorry, Miss Parker. It's devastating. But I promise you, we're doing everything we can.'

Miss Parker sighed bitterly, her hand tightening round her handkerchief. 'It is devastating. It really is.'

'The other lads and me... well, we want to make it right,' the farmer said. 'We'll make up the loss to the herd, Miss. It's a family we've got in Bramble Heath.'

Laura was amazed at Nobby Bryant's words. Even when there were so many shortages, he and the other farmers were going to give Miss Parker some of their own animals to make up for her dreadful loss. Bramble Heath really was a wonderful place.

'My word, I don't know what to say,' Miss Parker murmured, her voice thick with emotion. 'I thought Hillside might be finished, but... Thank you. Thank you so much. I won't ever forget your kindness. And you're right, we *are* a family in Bramble Heath. They've forgotten that, whoever this wretched traitor is. They've forgotten that we stick together.'

TWENTY-TWO

After finishing up at Hillside Farm, Laura arrived back at the practice to find that a pregnant ewe at Bishops' farm had gone lame. It wasn't a serious case, and Laura was relieved that it wasn't another poisoning, but it had to be dealt with right away. Mrs Morgan, who knew the busy vet had missed lunchtime, appeared as if by magic with a cheese sandwich for her, which Laura ate as she drove to her next patient. She knew the cheese was from local farmers, because Mrs Morgan refused to buy anything else; the very animals Laura cared for kept her going. And the rest of the nation too.

As she went about her day, Laura thought of Alastair. She'd seen a little bit more of the commander today behind the civil servant; the man who faced peril with bravery. The man who ran into fires without a second thought for his safety. The man who would do everything possible to protect the home front. And she admired him for that.

When she finally arrived home, bone-tired and longing for a warm meal and her bed, Iris was all a-flutter and held out a note for her.

'It's from him – from Commander Seaton!' she exclaimed as

she passed it to Laura. 'I suppose I should ask him if his intentions towards you are honourable, but I held my tongue.'

After the tragedy at Hillside Farm, Iris's excitement made Laura smile. If only life was really that simple.

'He said he wanted to speak to you, but he couldn't wait,' Iris said. She stared with interest at the note, clearly hoping Laura would open it right there.

Not wanting to disappoint her, Laura read the note.

'Commander Seaton's had to go back to London for a couple of days,' she told Iris. Something twisted inside her – what was it? Disappointment?

But she wasn't surprised that he'd had to go. Alastair now had proof there was a conspiracy to disrupt the country's food supply and destroy its farms, and he had to act fast. Goodness knows how many telephones would ring on ministerial desks, and how much hurrying up and down ministerial corridors would go on. And yet, Laura wished she'd been at home to say goodbye to him before he'd had to leave.

That night as she lay in bed, stretching out her aching limbs, she realised she already missed him. But not in the way Iris would assume, not romantically. Laura saw him as a friend, someone who respected her and recognised her as a professional. And she thought a lot of him too, such a brave man, trying to do his best on dry land after a lifetime at sea.

As she drifted off to sleep, she tried to keep an ear out for the car that she'd heard the night before. But the village was peaceful tonight, at least.

The next morning, with no urgent cases to deal with on the farms, Laura went to church. She didn't go very often, but there was something important she had to do today. She joined in with the hymns, listened to the sermon, and followed everyone to the altar rails for communion. As she did, the thought struck her that the traitor could be in the church with her at that exact moment. She glanced surreptitiously at the local men in their Sunday suits, and the women in their best hats, the pilots in their RAF blue and the Land Girls in their brown and green uniforms.

No one stood out. She truly couldn't imagine a single soul in Bramble Heath being capable of something so terrible. And yet whoever it was had knowledge of the local farms, was close enough by to keep committing such terrible acts. It was entirely possible, probable even, that it was someone right within their midst.

As Reverend Ellis held a communion wafer out to Laura, a jolt of panic ran through her. She suddenly thought of the dry feed that was poisoned and left for the cows to eat. What if the traitor switched to humans? Just how easy would it be to poison the wafers and everyone at the church?

Reverend Ellis patiently waited for Laura to take the wafer.

'Sorry,' she whispered to him as she finally took it.

I can't panic like that. That's the worst thing I can do. I need to face this calmly and bravely. Like Commander Seaton would do.

Once the service was over, Reverend Ellis asked anyone with parish notices to come forward. Taking a deep breath to steady herself, Laura stood up and went to the front of the church.

Curious faces turned to look at her, but the farmers and the Land Girls were solemn. They knew exactly what Laura was about to say.

She didn't beat around the bush either. Without introducing herself – although she didn't need to, as she had become a familiar face in the village over the past year – she said, 'Quite a few of you will already know that there's been some cyanide poisoning cases on our farms lately, and a suspicious fire too.'

Shocked gasps ran through the congregation, and Laura

waited until the alarm had subsided. It was horrible to think that she could be standing in front of the traitor at that very moment.

'I want you to know that it's being taken very seriously and is being investigated right now. Some of you will already have seen Commander Seaton in the village. He's from the government, and he's handling things. He's already given information to everyone on the farms on how to deal with this threat to the farmers' livelihoods and our food supply, but you can do your bit to help as well. I'm asking you to keep vigilant. I know you already are because we have an airbase in Bramble Heath and we must be careful, we are a target for the enemy.'

The pilots nodded in agreement. They of all people knew how important it was that anything untoward was reported.

'So now I'm asking you to think not only about the airbase, but about the farms as well,' Laura went on. 'If you see anyone behaving strangely around the farms, or anything suspicious in the village at all – even something that just doesn't feel quite right – then please let Commander Seaton know right away. You'll find him at the George and Dragon in the next few days. He's away right now, but I'm working with him. So, in the meantime, let me and Constable Russell know.'

The alarmed congregation whispered to one another, their shocked voices rising into the high vault of the church's ceiling and echoing like the murmurs of phantoms. No one was untouched by the news; every face before her was a study in dread. Laura suspected that the poisonings would become the main topic of conversation in the village for the next week or two, and that was no bad thing. The more people who were aware of it, the better.

Unless it spurred the traitor to even greater acts of violence, in an attempt to do as much damage as they could before they were caught.

Because they would catch them, wouldn't they, she and

Alastair? They couldn't let the enemy win. They couldn't let Bramble Heath and the villages and farms like it, the very heart of England, be defeated.

'Everyone on the farms is keeping watch,' Laura told them. 'And if we all stay alert too, then someone will see something. God willing, we'll stop whoever is doing this to us, before they cause even more harm.'

TWENTY-THREE

Laura did her best not to be late to work the next morning, but every few steps she encountered someone who wanted to ask her about the poisonings and the fire. All she could do was repeat what she'd announced in church the day before.

'Just stay vigilant,' she told everyone. 'Be on the lookout for anything that doesn't seem quite right.'

She arrived at work, knowing that Morgan would by now have heard about her announcement to the village yesterday. News travelled fast in Bramble Heath, even to a vet who had gone to another village to quaff port with another of his race-horse-owner friends.

But she wasn't afraid. She'd done the right thing by reporting it. She couldn't face the thought of any other farms losing their cattle.

Laura hung up her coat, and called, 'Good morning, Mr Morgan.'

'Good morning?' Morgan shouted as he emerged from his consulting room, red-faced already. 'How dare you make announcements on behalf of this practice, girl? How dare you?'

Girl? I'm nearly thirty, you patronising toad.

Laura stood her ground. 'I did no such thing,' she replied. 'Commander Seaton needed the information to get around the village as fast as possible, and the quickest way I could see to do that was to tell everyone at church.'

'Commander Seaton!' He scoffed. 'Mr Pullen has had visitors from the Ministry of Agriculture. On a *Sunday*!' He jabbed his finger towards her. 'I was perfectly capable of establishing poisoning cases and would have done so had you kept your paperwork in order. My failure – if I can be accused of such a thing – is entirely down to you!'

Laura blinked at Morgan in utter astonishment. How on earth could he stand there and blame her for his failures? It had nothing at all to do with paperwork.

She clenched her hands, trying to control her anger. She could easily have stamped her feet and ranted and raved at him, but she was better than that. She wouldn't stoop to his level, no matter how much he goaded her.

'I'm sure when Commander Seaton returns from London, he'll explain to you what's been going on,' she told him, doing her best to keep her voice calm and even. 'All I have done, right from the beginning, is to look at the facts, and it was very obvious to me that this had nothing to do with the Land Girls and the way they prepare the food. I had to tell the Ministry; it would've been negligent of me not to.'

There was implicit criticism in Laura's words, but what else could she say? Morgan had held back the investigation by being a pompous windbag.

'You are on the thinnest of ice,' he warned, livid as ever, his eyes popping. 'I've had a parade of farmers at my door and on the telephone wanting to know why I took no action – why I missed cyanide poisoning! You deliberately neglected to inform me of the weight of evidence so you might seize the glory!'

Laura couldn't believe he was blaming her. The only person

at fault was Morgan, because he couldn't trust women to do their work properly.

'I *did* tell you,' she replied carefully, trying not to let her fury show. 'I came back from Goslings' farm, after the first cyanide case I saw, and I told you. And you suddenly said that you'd seen other cases – but you had not mentioned them to me before. You were so sure it was all down to the Land Girls that you wouldn't listen to what I had to say.'

'Land Girls!' Mr Morgan spluttered. But Laura could well understand his anger: her tenacity had shown up his own complacency, his belief that he simply *couldn't* be wrong. 'I shall be making farm calls today, Miss Fellgate, while you are to remain here in the surgery. Now get out of my sight!'

She wasn't surprised at all at his blustering rage, but it still stung. *He* had made the mistakes, and was now desperately trying to cover himself by blaming her. She'd never done anything for acclaim; she'd only ever tried to do the right thing.

Laura's shoulders sagged as she headed for the pharmacy. Twelve cows would still be alive today if it hadn't been for Charles Morgan and his startling arrogance. Twelve cows would still be alive today if a merciless traitor wasn't stalking the farms around Bramble Heath. They had taken lives and threatened livelihoods, and were hell-bent on destruction.

Laura lifted her head. She was resolved. Whoever this was, somehow, they would be stopped. And they would dearly wish they'd never picked a fight with Bramble Heath.

TWENTY-FOUR

Laura didn't want to be cooped up in the practice all day. So at lunchtime, when the sign on the door was turned to *CLOSED,* she decided to go for a walk. Maybe stretching her legs might rid her of the anger and frustration she still nursed towards her boss.

As she headed down the path to the street, she pictured Morgan smiling and nodding at the farmers. She was sure he'd be letting them all know that he'd realised there was a traitor all along, and that it was *his assistant's* fault that nothing had been done straight away.

Whether the farmers would believe him or not remained to be seen.

Everything she had worked for was hanging by a thread. Because Morgan's opinion carried weight. He could tell everyone she was incompetent and the farmers' hard-earned trust in her would evaporate, just when she needed them to work with her to catch the person who threatened to harm them all.

Once she arrived in the high street, she saw Joan, the farm

delivery girl, up ahead in her van. Maybe she might've seen something? Laura raised her arm, trying to flag her down.

With a friendly wave, Joan pulled her van in to the side of the road and climbed out. She wasn't a tall woman, but she was strong from all the supplies she lugged about, and always wore a brown warehouse coat and stout, sensible shoes. But like a lot of young women who'd taken on practical wartime jobs, she still wanted to look fashionable; her long blonde hair was kept back from her face with a brightly coloured scarf.

'Something up?' she asked Laura. 'Isn't all this business rotten? Every delivery I've made today, the farmers are talking about nothing else. Who would've thought we've got our very own quisling?' Joan shook her head. 'It makes me sick.'

'It's terrible.' Laura shivered at the mention of the name of Quisling, the infamous politician who had sold his own people to the Nazis. 'I suppose you've heard that twelve cows died at Hillside? I was just wondering, actually... Bearing in mind you're often driving around here, have you seen anything unusual?'

But Joan shook her head. 'I wish I had,' she admitted. 'I don't like to think about some sort of Mosley skulking about after dark.'

'It's horrible, isn't it?' Laura agreed. 'Be careful when you're out and about, Joan. We don't know what this wretch is capable of.'

'All of the drivers are keeping an eye open,' Joan promised. 'And there are more of us than there are Lord Haw-Haws trying to run us into the ground.'

Anger swirled in Laura's stomach at the mention of that name. Lord Haw-Haw broadcasted from somewhere inside Nazi Germany in an affected upper-class British voice. He told the listeners who tuned in of Allied losses, and extolled the virtues of Hitler and his cronies, clearly revelling in it. What a monstrous traitor he was.

'You're right, Joan,' Laura replied, 'there are more of us than there are traitors like them, and it's something we should all be grateful for. Who wants to have that man with the silly moustache take over our country? No one who's got any sense!'

At that moment, Laura heard a familiar bark, and she turned to see Wilbur, Freddy and George strolling down the street.

'We're keeping our eyes peeled,' George told her, flicking back a loose strand of his blond hair. 'No one comes to Bramble Heath and poisons our cows!'

Freddy nodded as Joan stooped to fuss Wilbur. 'And whoever it is had better remember that some of us have a bird's-eye view.' He made a telescope of his clenched fist and peered through it, as though looking down at the ground. 'And some pretty hefty firepower on board.'

Joan took a little biscuit from her pocket and held it out to Wilbur, who had already turned his attention to Laura instead.

'It's no more than they deserve,' Joan said as she scrubbed behind Wilbur's ears despite his lack of interest.

'Dropping bombs on traitors on our own land?' George teased. 'It's exactly what I signed up for!'

Laura couldn't help but smile. The poisoner had definitely chosen the wrong village to try to destroy. They wouldn't succeed.

She wouldn't let them.

TWENTY-FIVE

Later that afternoon, Sarah and Mrs Hubbard arrived at the practice with Winnie. She was meowing from inside a wicker basket, which rocked from side to side; she was clearly desperate to escape.

'Winnie's full of beans,' Laura observed as she helped Sarah to lift the basket onto the examination table. 'What seems to be the matter?'

'Nothing really,' said Mrs Hubbard apologetically. 'But I've never had cats before and I thought it might be worth you giving her the once-over. Just so we know we're on the right track!'

Sarah nodded, keen as ever. 'We want to make sure Winnie's doing just right!' she told Laura. 'She likes to come up to the clubhouse in the woods with us kids. She's an evacuee herself!'

'I wish more pet-owners were as sensible as you,' Laura told them as she carefully opened the basket.

A paw, tipped with little razor-like claws, lashed out. But Laura knew what to do. She reached inside the basket and took Winnie by the scruff of her neck. Winnie stopped moving and Laura was able to bring her out.

'Let's take a good look at you, then,' Laura said, and stood Winnie on the examining table. She started to check – Winnie's eyes were bright, and her ears were clean. Her heartbeat was fine. Her skin and fur all looked to be in perfect condition. She peered inside Winnie's mouth, and saw an excellent display of sharp, white teeth. 'I think you've done very well, looking after your first kitten. Winnie's in the pink!'

Sarah beamed proudly and stroked Winnie's sleek back. The little kitten closed her eyes and enjoyed the fuss, which Laura was sure she'd get plenty of in Mrs Hubbard's house.

'I drew a picture of Winnie and sent it home to Mum,' said the evacuee. 'And she said Winnie can come home with me after the war ends if we like. And if Ma Hubbard says it's all right.'

'That's wonderful news,' Laura replied. 'There's vets like me in London who can help, you know. If your mum wants to go and speak to one of them, I'm sure they'll tell her everything she needs to know about looking after a cat. They train people to help any cats and dogs who get caught up in the air raids, you know.'

Sarah nodded, intent on her words. Laura had no doubt that Winnie would be in good hands with the girl, no matter where she was living.

'I'm going to be a vet like you when I grow up,' she told Laura. 'And I'm going to help save animal lives just like you do. Even when there's people out there trying to hurt them. At school today, we had a special assembly and Miss Lewis told us all about the poisoned animals and the fires. Constable Russell said we all have to keep an eye out!'

Laura smiled, both at Sarah's spirited determination and at the fact that the children had been included in what was going on. It might be frightening for them, but the situation was desperate. And the more eyes and ears they had, the better.

'Yes, if you see anything unusual, or anyone behaving

strangely, you must make sure you report it,' Laura said. 'We don't want any more of the animals on the farms falling ill.'

Sarah looked up at Mrs Hubbard and said, 'What about the bang?'

Mrs Hubbard shook her head indulgently. 'That was just a car, love.' She smiled. 'Folks shouldn't be driving during the blackout, but sometimes people don't follow the rules. We do, though, and that's what matters.'

Laura glanced at Sarah. She was a bright girl, and she wouldn't have mentioned something like that if she hadn't thought it was important. And besides, Laura and Alastair had both heard the sound of an engine during the blackout that night. Couldn't it be the same one?

She picked up Winnie and stroked her. The cat purred happily in response. 'What night did you hear that noise, Sarah?' she asked.

'Friday night,' Sarah replied. 'I should've been asleep, but I was up playing with Winnie. And I heard a car out in the street and the engine made a really big old bang, like the coal wagon that backfires back home.'

'That's useful to know, thank you,' Laura replied. Someone was driving through the village at night during the blackout, while everyone else stayed inside ready for the next air raid. Could this give them a clue as to the direction the poisoner came from? 'I'll pass that on – and well done, Sarah. That's just the sort of thing you need to tell us. It might be perfectly innocent of course, but then again… it might not.'

Alastair would be back in Bramble Heath soon, and Laura would tell him. But that wasn't the only reason she was looking forward to his return; she missed her friend. They'd have a drink at the George and Dragon together again soon.

TWENTY-SIX

When Laura arrived for work the next day, she was surprised to see a Rolls-Royce pulled up outside. She hadn't seen it before, but she wouldn't have been surprised to learn that it belonged to one of Mr Morgan's many wealthy friends.

Please don't tell me he's friends with the king. That's all I need.

The brass plaques by the front door were gleaming as Laura headed past them into the practice. As she hung up her coat, she could hear voices coming from the sitting room.

Laura hoped Mr Morgan would be too busy discussing stallions and racing to hear her arrive, and she headed for the peace and quiet of the pharmacy.

But she had only just begun to settle into her work when a rat-a-tat-tat sounded on the door, and she looked up from the pestle and mortar to see Mrs Morgan peering in.

'Miss Fellgate, my husband would like to see you in the sitting room,' the other woman told her.

Would like to see you was Mrs Morgan's polite way of saying, *demands to see you at once.*

Laura put down the pestle and wiped her hands before

making her way to the sitting room. This didn't bode well. Whoever this visitor was, she was being dragged out to see him. Would Mr Morgan parade her as a curiosity, or was he going to blame her for his own shortcomings again?

'Mr Morgan?' Laura said, knocking on the half-open door.

Mr Morgan and his guest were sitting in armchairs by the fireside, looking like an advert for life in the country. His barrel-chested visitor could barely be contained by the armchair. His red face was just visible behind his ginger whiskers.

'Ah, Miss Fellgate.' Mr Morgan rose to his feet, his face lit with a scheming smile and his eyes gleaming like a cat that had cornered a mouse. He took the cigar from his mouth. 'I would *love* you to meet my very good friend, Mr Pullen, of Pullen's Fodder and Feed. Mr Pullen, this is our young troublemaker, the erstwhile Miss Fellgate!'

And as Mr Pullen levered himself from his seat, extracting his own cigar from between his lips, Laura gritted her teeth.

Young troublemaker? That's what he calls me in front of his friend?

'Pleased to meet you, Mr Pullen,' Laura said guardedly. She would try to be polite, at least. 'You're a popular man on the farms around Bramble Heath – with the animals, anyway.'

She'd meant it as a little joke to try to lighten the mood, but as soon as the words were out of her mouth she realised Pullen could all too well find something insulting in what she'd just said.

'Am I now?' he asked in a thick Lancastrian burr. 'Is that why my office and factories have been bombarded by farmers wanting to know why I'm poisoning their beasts? And Mr Morgan here tells me as you're the one put it about!'

'Indeed she was,' said Mr Morgan. 'She and that yellow-bellied sailor!'

'Sailor!' Pullen scoffed. 'Well, we know a thing or two about that one now, don't we? A nutty fantasist, running around the countryside putting a man's livelihood at risk!'

Yellow-bellied? Nutty fantasist? How dare they!

Laura glared at the pair of them in disgust. 'Is that Commander Seaton you're talking about? You do know he was awarded the Distinguished Service Cross no fewer than *three times*? And just the other day, he ran into a fire and risked his own life to save one of our Land Girls? How da— how can you possibly accuse him of cowardice?'

'Mr Pullen has friends in well-connected places,' said Morgan with relish. 'We know a thing or two about your commander.'

Pullen nodded and took a puff on his cigar. He blew out a plume of yellow, foul-smelling smoke.

'You and him have as good as accused me of killing off whole herds,' he said. It wasn't true, of course, not that he was likely to listen to Laura's explanations. 'I've had the Ministry of Agriculture knocking at my factory doors and, where they knock, the taxman follows. You'll cost me money and I don't take kindly to folk who cost me money.' Pullen took another draw on the cigar. 'I'm in the business of making cash, not losing it to idiot girls who're fluttering their lashes at lunatic sailors because they've got a couple of medals attached to their chest!'

Laura wasn't about to stand for this. Insulting her, insulting Alastair, and after everything they were doing to try to protect Bramble Heath. No, she wasn't going to take this. She'd had enough. Just because he was wealthy, it didn't mean he could talk about people as if they were dirt.

'How *dare* you speak to me like that?' she snapped, her voice boiling over with anger. 'Idiot girl? Really? I went to veterinary college. I've got "MRCVS" after my name. Do you really think they let any old fool become a member of the Royal College of Veterinary Surgeons? And no one has been blaming you for killing whole herds – but it's an unfortunate fact that the saboteur is using *your* feed to poison cows. This is being taken very seriously by the Ministry of Agriculture, as it should be – there's a war on, if you hadn't noticed.'

'Let me tell you a thing or two about your commander,' Pullen sneered with sadistic glee. 'They kicked him out of the navy because he went off his rocker. He's not right in the head... he probably poisoned them cows himself and doesn't even know it!'

Mr Morgan nodded sharply. 'You've shown poor judgement, Miss Fellgate,' he said. But Laura knew what was really at play here: Pullen had taken the perfectly understandable investigation as a personal insult, because it might dent the profits that paid for his precious cigars and Rolls-Royces, while Mr Morgan simply couldn't bear the fact that she had proved him wrong. Not only wrong, but inept too.

'No, I haven't,' Laura retorted. She felt sick to the stomach at the thought of Pullen poking his nose into Alastair's past. 'And you know it too. You could've stopped this, Mr Morgan. You. If you'd listened to me, we might have caught the poisoner by now and we wouldn't have lost so much livestock. But you didn't listen, because you have such a poor opinion of women. You blamed the Land Girls, and you refused to listen to me. And now...'

She thought of Daisy the cow, lying so still that Laura had thought she'd died. She thought of the Parker sisters' murdered cows. Laura shook her head. It was too horrible; something to consign to the depths of her mind and never revisit. Along with the memory of the fire in the barn, walking into the inferno that had nearly claimed Alastair and Lottie. She had seen too much; too many burnt-out ruins, too much death.

'And now your friend is standing here making baseless accusations about a good man.' Laura gestured in frustration at Pullen. She swallowed, trying to steady her voice. 'There's an ex-navy man who comes here sometimes with deliveries. He's lost an eye. And he has nothing but good things to say about Commander Seaton. You're talking about a man who was in the Battle of Jutland when he was only fourteen. Do you remember the story about Boy Cornwell? The commander was younger than him, and Boy Cornwell was held up as a hero. But the commander survived and fought through goodness knows what else as the war went on, miles from home, salt dried onto his face, bullets and bombs flying, enemy submarines on the prowl. Where were you? Then there was Dunkirk and protecting our ships in the North Atlantic. Is it any wonder his nerves were shredded? Where were you, Mr Pullen? Where were *you*?'

Laura knew the answer, though. Tucked up safely in his big house, telling himself that he was doing his bit by selling fodder for farm animals and making the highest profit he could while his fellow countrymen struggled.

And probably tucked up at home with his wife, just like Mr and Mrs Morgan had been, while Alastair's wife had been lost to the Blitz.

'You're lucky I haven't had you up on a charge of slander,' Pullen told Laura, jabbing his cigar towards her like an accusing finger. Laura couldn't believe he'd dare say such a thing, after the insults the two men had just spat about Alastair. 'If you worked for me... well, you wouldn't work for me a day longer. I'm a wealthy man, Miss Fellgate, and my stables brings in a lot of the money that pays your wages.' He turned to Mr Morgan. 'I wouldn't presume to tell another gent how to run his business, Charlie, but this one's trouble. She's got it written through her like Blackpool rock.'

The ground lurched beneath Laura's feet. Mr Morgan couldn't sack her. As furious as he was, he couldn't easily replace her. And especially with the poisoner still at large – he couldn't risk it, surely. If another farm suffered like Hillside, he'd be on his own.

'All I've ever done is my job,' Laura told him. 'And I never come to your stables – I'm out on the farms. It's the *farmers* who pay my wages.'

'Nevertheless, I cannot have you upsetting my clients,' Mr Morgan told her. 'You may work out the week, Miss Fellgate, but no longer. As of Monday, you shall find yourself unemployed.'

Mr Pullen gave a firm nod. 'Now run along,' he told her. 'Find something to dust, eh?' And he and Mr Morgan chuckled together.

Laura's mouth was suddenly dry. She'd been sacked. Just like that. And all because she'd told the truth and done her duty. As she backed away, out of the room, out of the presence of such odiously arrogant men, she told them, 'You'll regret this. You've made a very big mistake, Mr Morgan.'

'Aye, I'm sure.' Pullen laughed. 'Fear the wrath of the WI, eh? Look out Charlie, Miss Fellgate and her nutty sailor have marked your card!'

'On your way now, girl.' Morgan waved the cigar dismissively. 'Mr Pullen and I have business to discuss.'

Laura turned away and headed back to the pharmacy. The little room that had been part of her life ever since she'd accepted the job in Mr Morgan's practice already seemed to be receding, sliding out of her grasp. A week, that was all she had left. What on earth would she do?

She didn't care so much about herself, as sad as she would be to leave Bramble Heath. But far more importantly, somewhere out there in the village was the traitor. They knew full well the suffering they were inflicting, and the lethal potential of what they were doing, but that hadn't stopped them. They had crept through the darkness, through gaps in the hedgerows, trespassing as they tipped out their poisoned feed.

Had they smiled as they'd done it? Were they proud of their work? What were they planning to do next, and how could Laura stop them if she were no longer here? How could she protect the animals and the villagers she'd come to love so dearly?

Laura tried to picture the traitor, but nothing solid came into her mind; just a faceless figure made from nothing but shadows.

TWENTY-SEVEN

When Laura arrived home that evening, she felt too dismal to settle. She couldn't bear to tell Iris that she'd lost her job, because it would mean Iris losing her lodger. And she couldn't stop worrying about what would happen to Bramble Heath now that she was being forced to leave. Alastair had reported back to Whitehall; even Churchill must know about it by now. But she loved the village so much, she couldn't bear to leave them while they were under attack. She needed time to think, so, instead of going in, she'd turned away from the door and headed out for a walk.

The countryside around Bramble Heath was gorgeous all year round. In summer it was a sea of green, with yellow crops, and pink and white flowers. In autumn, the trees were a riot of orange and gold. In the winter, it looked like a Christmas card. And now, in spring, everything was coming back to life again with the promise of the warm months to come.

Over the year she had lived here, Bramble Heath had become like home to her, and the thought of leaving it behind brought tears to her eyes.

Laura climbed over a rickety stile with ease and made her way through a field, the grass swishing against her tweed trousers. She'd enjoy the countryside while she could, because who knew if she'd find work in another country practice? A year she'd worked for Morgan – a wasted year, because there was no way he'd give her a reference now. She'd be back working in a town or a city, but it wasn't where her heart was.

Swifts circled and tumbled through the air above her, singing as they flew. They seemed to be following her as she headed up the field towards the hill with its view of the village below.

The sun was beginning to sink in the sky, and as she neared the top of the hill she saw a figure. At first she thought it was a farmer or a Land Girl, but suddenly she realised who it was.

Alastair! Oh, thank goodness he's back!

'Commander Seaton!' Laura called, waving to him, as she picked up her pace to a run. He was in his casuals again, no doubt pleased to step out of his suit and take off his homburg as soon as he'd arrived back in Bramble Heath. 'I didn't expect to see you here!'

'Three days in the city is three days too many!' Alastair replied as he greeted her with the brightest smile she had so far seen him give. 'It's lovely to see you, Miss Fellgate.'

'And you too.' Laura beamed at him, her miserable thoughts banished for a moment. 'It's lovely up here, isn't it? You can see the whole village—' Her voice was choked by a sudden sob that caught in her throat.

The village I'll have to leave.

'I'm sorry...' she murmured. 'I've had some rather bad news since you've been away...'

'What's happened?' he asked, his brow furrowing with concern. 'Not another attack?'

Laura shook her head. 'No, thank goodness, it's not that. It's just... I had a very unpleasant conversation earlier with my boss, and a horrible friend of his, Pullen, the animal feed man.' She didn't want to tell Alastair what they'd said about him. It was too hurtful. But as she said that name, she saw something change in Alastair's expression. Had Pullen thrown his weight around at the Ministry? 'The upshot is... in a week, I won't have a job. Morgan sacked me.'

Laura tried to wipe away a tear, hoping Alastair wouldn't notice.

'*Sacked you?*' he asked, disbelieving. 'How on earth can he sack you? He should be upping your wage if anything! Pullen's been complaining about me to my Ministry too; a nasty piece of work.'

'I still can't quite believe it, you know,' Laura admitted bitterly. 'He's blamed me, would you believe? He said I didn't keep my paperwork in order, and that he would've known if... He's lying, of course. He's just trying to cover the fact that I showed him up. Pullen said some horrible things, and I stood up to him, so he told Morgan to sack me. And Morgan, well, he doesn't want to lose a friend who drives a Rolls-Royce and owns racehorses...'

'I'm so sorry, Laura.' Alastair laid his hand gently on her shoulder. 'I promise we'll get this resolved somehow. I never could stand a bully.'

He called me Laura...

She did her best to smile at him, and took a chance when she replied, 'Thank you, Alastair. I'm afraid I don't know what to do. I haven't told Iris yet. I've got some savings, so I can stay in the village for a little while, but not for long. I can't leave yet, not when we still haven't caught the traitor. But I don't have much time.'

'I'll speak to Morgan,' Alastair suggested. 'He must see reason.'

After Pullen and Morgan's cruelty, Alastair's gentle kindness threatened to undo her. But how could he resolve it, especially after what the two men had said about him? They would clearly never listen to him.

Laura really hadn't wanted to tell Alastair what they'd said, but she couldn't bear the thought of him going to speak to a man who would attack him with such vile words.

'Pullen has been asking around, trying to find out about you,' she began, hating the fact that what she was about to say would hurt him. 'Alastair, I think you're a very brave man. Smudge told me about your Distinguished Service Cross. And it's very easy for a man like Pullen who's never seen a bullet fly apart from on a pheasant shoot to judge. He... he found out why you left the navy. And he wasn't very kind about it.' She looked away from Alastair, unable to bear the hurt that she was sure she'd see in his eyes.

'I'm sure he couldn't judge me more harshly than I judge myself every single day,' Alastair said quietly. 'I take it he told you?'

Laura nodded slowly and looked back up at him. She chose her words carefully. 'He said it was because of your nerves. Because of that, he doesn't trust your judgement and he doesn't believe there's a traitor trying to sabotage our farms. And he called me an *idiot girl*. But we're right, we *are*. He's just in denial, he can't bear the thought that he might not be able to buy another Rolls-Royce, that's all, if people panic and think it's the feed he's selling that's poisoned. He's got no right to carry on like he did. None at all.'

'The truth is, the Ministry parcelled me off down here because they thought it was all nonsense when I saw the pattern between reports that were coming in,' Alastair told her. 'I imagine it seemed like a harmless way to occupy my time while I tried to stop shaking at every backfiring car.' And Laura remembered Sarah's words, and the car *she'd* heard. She thought of Smudge too, who had said something very similar about the terror even that simple sound could usher in. 'But you were right. *We're* right. Someone's out to cause havoc, Laura, they're intent on doing serious harm to Bramble Heath, to the whole country, and we're going to put a stop to it.'

Laura gently took Alastair's hands in hers. How sad that people didn't trust his judgement because all they focused on was his shattered nerves. 'We definitely will. We can't let—' A sudden patter of rain against the leaves on the trees in a nearby grove interrupted her. 'Oh, it's raining, and I didn't bring my umbrella! Quick, we can go to that old shepherd's hut over there.'

It wasn't much, a tumbledown stone building with half a roof, but it was better than nothing. Laura led the way, pushing open the door that was half off its rusted hinges. It was a small room, with straw and hay that had been left for the sheep that wandered up this way.

'We'll be dry in here,' she promised him, as they sat down in the corner under what remained of the roof. 'I'm so sorry for what happened to you, Alastair. And I'm glad you came to Bramble Heath.'

Alastair glanced towards her as he asked, 'Not much of a *commander*, eh?'

'Smudge begs to differ, and so do I,' Laura said. 'You went through so much. How could anyone be surprised that you... everyone has their limits, don't they? Smudge told me that there's a lot of men who only lived to see their families again because of you. And after what I saw in Coventry... there's things you try to bury deep, but it's hard.'

'Smudge is a good lad,' Alastair replied, with that gentle smile of his. 'I've never known much beyond the sea... but these past two years—' He glanced down at his wedding band, then clenched his fist for a second, as though catching the words. 'Tell me about yourself instead, Laura. Did you always want to be a vet?'

The rain pattered down against the hut, dripping from the edge of the roof. It felt safe here; a world apart.

Laura knew he wanted to be distracted, to think of something else. 'Always,' she told him. 'Even when people told me I couldn't, because I'm a girl. *I'll show them*, I thought. And I did. Well... I thought I had.' In her mind, she saw Morgan and Pullen again, their faces red with fury. 'I'll show them again. I love what I do, you know. Someone once called it my *hobby*, but it's my reason to get up in the morning. It has to be more than a hobby, especially when you're shivering in a barn in the middle of the night with an icy, wintry gale blowing in. And in wartime, it's definitely more than a hobby. After Coventry, I knew I had to do more, and that means standing shoulder-to-shoulder with the farmers, caring for their livestock and keeping the nation fed.'

'Is it a family business, or are you the only vet in the Fellgate household?' he asked. 'My father and brother are pig farmers up near Scarborough. It's a glamorous old business, I can tell you.'

'Pigs?' Laura grinned at him. 'I love pigs. But no, it's only me who's a vet in my family. They're all farmers in my family.'

'Vicky and I always talked about a farm...' Alastair's voice trailed away and he absent-mindedly linked his hands, twisting the gold wedding band again. 'Tell me about the Fellgate farmers?'

Vicky. Laura hadn't heard him mention his wife's name before, and she paused for a moment. How sad that they'd talked about starting a farm together, but their dream, Alastair's hope of a happy future, had been killed by the bomb that took Vicky's life.

'Well, we've got lots of Cotswold sheep,' Laura told him, warming to her subject as it meant she could talk about home and not think about what was happening in her adopted village. 'They're wonderful – tough as old nails but they look like clouds on legs. We've got some cows too, some Herefords. And pigs, chickens, ducks on the pond... it's a lovely farm. They've got Land Girls working there now, of course. They're lucky girls, it's a very nice place to be!'

Alastair smiled. 'We have Tamworths – the finest of pigs,' he replied, his voice warm with nostalgia. 'Your farm sounds a lot more picturesque than the Seaton hog homestead!'

'Tamworths are wonderful!' Laura grinned, even as the rain fell more heavily. It looked like they would be stuck here for a while. She wondered why Alastair had left the farm at fourteen. Had he wanted to see the world? It wouldn't have surprised her. 'I suppose you decided that pig farming wasn't for you, and took to the high seas instead?'

'My friends and I thought it sounded very exciting,' Alastair admitted, and Laura understood, because he wouldn't have been alone. Plenty of young men had gone off to face the German guns expecting to be home by Christmas, with a wealth of stories to share with their pals. 'And I'd grown up on the coast, so the navy was the only choice for me. I thought maybe I'd get to travel the world and, if I had to do a little bit of fighting on the way, well, so be it.' He shook his head at his own innocence. 'It didn't turn out quite that way. But when you're fourteen, you think you're immortal.'

'Oh, yes!' Laura nodded. 'When my big brother said he wanted to join up, Dad hid his shoes so he couldn't go to the recruitment office!' She chuckled at the memory, then said, 'But in some ways, it's a good thing that you did. What a career you've had at sea, and how many lives you've saved.'

Laura didn't know much about Royal Navy medals, but she knew full well that they didn't hand out awards for distinguished service like sweets. And though she knew Alastair likely wouldn't want to share how he had won them, he *had*. Whatever Pullen and Morgan said, he'd done his bit.

The rain was still coming down, and night was falling. Laura stretched out her legs to get more comfortable.

Then suddenly, splitting the night air, came the mournful wail of the air-raid siren.

TWENTY-EIGHT

'Alastair, what are we going to do?' Laura whispered, her voice taut with fear. Coventry had taught her that she was safe protected beneath the earth. That basement under the veterinary surgery was the only reason she was still alive today. They were so exposed out here. Surely they weren't safe at all, here in the middle of a field. 'We're too far from the village, or any of the farms, to get to a shelter.'

He swallowed and cast his eyes heavenwards, looking up at the patchy roof above them.

'It's not nightfall yet,' Alastair whispered. 'Perhaps it's a false alarm?'

Laura hoped so too, but they'd know soon enough. If it wasn't a false alarm, the last place they wanted to be was out in the open. No, this shelter might not be much, but they would have to stay there. It might not be safely underground, but it was better than nothing at all.

'We'd better wait it out...' This time his voice was quieter still, his eyes still fixed on the ceiling as though he might be able to will the Luftwaffe away.

The pilots who'd been having a drink over at the George

and Dragon would be running back to their planes right now, and, even so soon after the siren had sounded, Laura could hear the sound of engines starting up over at the airbase.

'Good luck, boys,' she said, a lump in her throat. If she felt exposed in a hut in a field, then just how did they feel, going up into the air? 'Can't be fun flying in weather like this, can it?'

Although she was talking to a former sailor; she couldn't imagine that Alastair had any fear of getting wet. Alastair gave no indication of having heard her at all and she followed his gaze to the heavens, from where they heard the distinctive sound of incoming planes. Alastair had paled to a deathly white and his hands, which had been loosely linked, were now tight together, one gripping the other. Laura could see the bleached knuckles, so fast was he holding one hand to the other.

And that was when the whole world seemed to shake, a shuddering crash not so far away splitting the evening wide open.

Instinctively, Laura grabbed hold of Alastair and pressed her face against his shoulder. He was rigid with terror, and Laura didn't know what to do. How could she soothe him and tell him it would be all right when a bomb had just fallen, and when she was terrified too? She couldn't bear it, the thought of the village being hit, but that sound couldn't have been clearer. Having lived through the hell of the Coventry Blitz, she couldn't fail to know what it meant. Had anyone died? Who, right now, would be taking their last breath?

'Th-they've hit Bramble Heath...' Laura stammered fearfully. What about Iris and her boys? What about Sarah and all the other children who'd left London to come here for safety? What about the farms – surely a bomb hadn't hit there? Not the poor animals, not the Land Girls. 'Alastair...?'

There was an almost mechanical quality to Alastair as he pulled one hand from the other with an effort that made it look as though they were weighted with lead. Then he put his arm round Laura's shoulders and she felt a tremble running right through him, just as he must feel it in her. There was nothing to be ashamed of in being afraid, though, not when the sky was raining bombs.

'They won't bother dr-dropping a bomb on a field,' Laura told him, trying to think of something to say that might help him. Not that it helped much; bombs could land off-target, and planes could crash. An image shoved its way into her mind, of Iris sheltering with her sons. They'd be so afraid. What if it had landed on—? No, she couldn't try to guess where it had fallen. Instead, her words nervously ran away from her. 'Iris will be with the boys. They're so used to air raids now. They've never known any different. We try to make it a game for them, so they won't be scared.'

But Alastair was. And Laura wasn't sure she could blame him; he'd lost his wife to the bombings and had been through who knew what he had been through out at sea? Enough to cost Smudge his eye and win him a DSC; whatever it was, it had shattered the nerves of the man who was holding her so tight.

Laura heard planes flying overhead, but she was so afraid that she gave up trying to work out if they were RAF or enemy. She clung on to Alastair, and, just as she did when she was sheltering with Iris's boys or comforting a poorly animal, she whispered to him, 'It's all right, it's all right...'

But it wasn't. She knew it wasn't. Only she wished so much that she could take his terror away.

'She shouldn't even have been in London,' Alastair whispered, his voice thick with emotion. 'She always wanted to help—'

He was struggling, and Laura fought past her own fear, past the visceral memories of fire, and smoke, and terror, to try to reach him, comfort him. She gently took his free hand. 'Vicky sounds lovely,' she told him, her voice trembling. 'She sounds brave. Just like you are.'

Even if he might not feel very brave at that moment.

Alastair didn't reply. Instead he clung to Laura's hand, his arm still tight around her as they listened to the drone of planes and the crack of guns far overhead.

'You've been through so much,' Laura said, thinking of Alastair finding the courage to battle the flames to save Lottie. He was so brave, and yet so frightened too. 'I can't imagine what it's been like for you. All that time you were at sea, and then losing...' *Vicky.* 'You are so strong. But I think, even though I haven't known you long, I think you're a gentle soul at heart. And that's a wonderful thing to be.'

Because he *was*. He might've commanded a destroyer, but he was the same man who'd stepped off the train in Bramble Heath and rescued a kitten. He'd knelt beside Laura as she treated a cow, and he had dreamed of living on a farm with Vicky.

'They chased us morning, noon and night.' His voice was faltering, barely even a whisper now. 'We were crippled, Laura... I still don't know how we got home.' He drew in a shuddering breath. 'All those souls on board, all looking to me to keep them safe.'

And you did.

Just as Smudge had said, Alastair's crew had lived to see their families again, but fate had played such a cruel trick. They went home to their loved ones, while Alastair's wife was lost.

'It must've been terrifying,' Laura said. A relentless pursuit at sea, with nowhere to hide. It was no wonder Alastair still bore the scars of that terror. 'I would've been so scared... but you got home. And all those men who trusted you, they were right to, because you saved them. I'm just so sorry that... it's not fair, is it? That Vicky...'

Laura couldn't say anything more. She was too choked up to speak.

'I'm sorry.' That struck Laura as saddest of all, that he felt as though he should apologise for grieving, for fear. Nobody should feel sorry for that.

'What for?' she asked him gently. 'You don't have a thing to apologise for. Not one thing.'

Alastair buried his face against Laura's hair as sobs racked through him. She couldn't begin to imagine what he'd suffered, but it couldn't do any harm to weep. Half the world was weeping with him.

As she held him tight, she tried to keep her mind away from what could be happening in the village at that moment, as her memories of Coventry tried to superimpose themselves over the cottages and ancient houses of Bramble Heath. Shattered glass glittering on the pavements; heaps of brick where homes had once stood; silent, grieving figures, too stunned to cry, as stretchers carried away the dead. Laura felt helpless and afraid. Tears rolled down her cheeks.

TWENTY-NINE

The rain finally stopped just as the all-clear sounded.

Laura whispered to Alastair, 'Are you all right for us to head back to the village now? I know the way in the dark.'

She would much rather have stayed up on the hill and not known where the bomb had landed, but she couldn't stay away, not when she might be able to help. She might be qualified to treat animals, but she could use her skills to help injured humans too. She just hoped against hope that the bomb hadn't taken any lives. It could've landed in an empty field, couldn't it?

'Yes, of course. Let's go. I'm sorry I—' Alastair mumbled. 'You certainly didn't need to listen to my ravings while Lord knows what's happening in the village. I'm sure the bomb didn't hit them, it probably just landed on a field nearby. The blackout will have done its job. Are *you* all right?'

'I'm alive,' Laura told him. 'It's you I'm worried about. You've carried so much on your shoulders, and you're so—' *lonely*. That was it, wasn't it? He no longer had any crew, and he no longer had a wife. His family were all in Yorkshire, and who did he know in London? All of that sadness and fear, all that grief that he'd carried around with him; who was there to hear him? 'You needed a friend to listen. And I don't mind at all.'

Alastair gave Laura's hand a gentle squeeze of acknowledgement.

'I'll speak to Mr Morgan tomorrow,' he said, a little more firmly now. 'And if he won't budge... well perhaps *I'll* need a local colleague while we run our traitor to ground. You won't need to worry, Laura.'

A colleague. Not an assistant. Not an *idiot girl*.

'I'd love to work with you, officially,' Laura admitted. But the thought of sending Alastair into Morgan's firing line made her uncomfortable. 'Thank you, Alastair. But... Mr Morgan's probably still fuming. He's got a horrible temper, you know.'

'It's the bombs that terrify me,' he said. 'Not a blustering old curmudgeon.'

Laura smiled at him. 'That's the sensible way to be. Now, let's get down to the village.'

Once they'd got to their feet and made it to the door, Laura could see the sky, studded with stars, and the darkness of the hills and trees below.

'Your landlady must be worried about you,' her companion observed as they stepped out into the cool spring evening. His gaze settled on the glow on the horizon. 'Oh... oh, no.'

Over to the edge of the village, the sky wasn't dark at all. It was lit up in an angry red.

'That's where Goslings' farm is,' Laura said, her voice tight with fear. 'It must be where the bomb landed.'

She clutched Alastair's arm. The thought of the farm being hit, when it was still recovering from the fire, filled her with horror. What about the girls, sitting through the raid in the shelter, desperate to come out and tend to the animals who were entrusted to their care? And now Nicola and Lottie and Martha would be hurrying with buckets and hoses again, leading animals to safety, calling hoarsely to one another through the smoke-heavy air.

They barely spoke as they picked their way down the hill, the grass wet against their legs, the ground soft beneath their feet. Laura's heart raced as they got closer and closer to the village, the flames from the bomb still bright against the night sky.

Perhaps it wasn't as bad as it looked?

They reached the old stile, and Alastair, ever the gentleman, helped Laura over. But when it was his turn, Laura helped him too. Despite the darkness, she saw something in his expression as she held his hand and he climbed over. Something that spoke of friendship and the closeness that now existed between them.

They soon reached the high street. The blackout curtains were still drawn, and Laura knew that the inhabitants of Bramble Heath would have hesitantly left their shelters by now and, after seeing that their own homes were still standing, tucked up their children in bed. Yet, knowing that a bomb had hit the village, they wouldn't be able to rest.

And over at the farm, certainly no one would be sleeping.

They were nearly at Iris's cottage when Laura saw a figure approaching through the near-darkness. She tensed. Who would be out there in the dark, just after a bomb had hit the village?

But a moment later she heard a familiar voice. 'Why aren't you indoors?' Constable Russell called. He came a little nearer with his shaded blackout torch and said, 'Goodness me, sorry, Commander Seaton, Laura. I didn't realise it was you two.'

'We were caught on the hill in the rain,' Laura explained. 'Then the sirens went off...'

'It seemed safer to find shelter where we were,' Alastair added. 'Luckily, Laura here knows her way around the country-side by night. I'd have been stuck otherwise.'

Henry nodded. 'You did the sensible thing. You must've

heard the bomb drop?' He didn't wait for their reply; of course they had. 'I've just got back from Goslings' farm, where it hit. Oh, what a mess... the field was on fire!'

Laura could make out Henry's expression in the darkness. Someone had been killed, she knew it. She could sense it. But what were they doing in a field in the blackout?

'Did anyone...?' Laura began, but she couldn't finish her question.

'It could have been much worse. But...' Henry replied solemnly. 'Poor young girl didn't stand a chance. One of the cows took fright when the sirens went off and she ran after it. She must've got lost in the dark. The cow came home, but... but not Martha.'

Laura went cold. Martha, one of the new Land Girls, who had turned up in Bramble Heath to work on a farm with her sister, Lottie. George Harvey's girlfriend. She was dead. The girl with rosy cheeks and RAF blue ribbons in her hair. Another young life lost in this terrible war.

'That poor girl,' Alastair murmured. 'God help her family.'

'Best be getting along now,' Henry said. His voice was full of sadness, even though it wasn't the first time he'd reported a death. 'Goodnight, both.'

Laura took Alastair's arm as they continued on their way. She felt hollowed out, and desperately sad for Lottie and George. Had he daydreamed about marrying his Land Girl? Had he thought about a life together after the war? And Lottie – she was so close to her sister, who had nearly dashed straight into the fire to rescue her just days ago. They had a life of love and happiness ahead of them. But all of that had been taken from them tonight.

'So many people are losing so much,' Alastair murmured. And he knew that better than any of them; he knew what Lottie and George would be feeling.

'I know they are, and there's nothing we can—' Laura

stopped herself. 'Well, there is, there *is* something we can do. Look at what the farmers face losing. Martha died trying to save one of the cows, she cared about them, and she knew exactly how important they are for the war effort. We're going to stop the traitor. We're doing our bit too. I know it won't bring poor Martha back – but we *are* doing something.'

Alastair nodded. 'We are,' he assured her as they reached the gate of Iris's home. 'And all over the country, we've got people working just as hard as us to capture their own saboteurs in this network of traitors.'

'We'll get them,' she promised him. She glanced over her shoulder at the cottage and back at Alastair, then said, 'Better say goodnight. Before I do, though, I just wanted to say thank you... for keeping me safe earlier.'

'I should be saying that.' He smiled softly. 'Thank you, Laura, for being such a kind friend. It can be a lonely job sometimes.'

'I imagine it must be,' Laura said. 'Don't worry, we're chums now. You don't need to be lonely any more, Alastair. Sleep well, won't you? Goodnight.'

'Goodnight, Laura.' There was that gentle smile again, the smile he had seemed so unwilling or unable to show. 'I'll wait until you're safely inside.'

She liked that smile. It made him look younger, and rather dashing. He was quite a handsome man, really.

Laura paused, for a moment thinking that she ought to give him a kiss. Because she wanted to. But she wasn't sure what he would make of it.

So she gave him a quick hug, then she pecked a kiss to his cheek. 'Goodnight, Alastair,' she whispered, and made her way along the short path to the door. She opened it and stepped inside, then turned to wave goodbye. 'Goodnight!'

He gave her a wave in reply. 'Goodnight, Laura!' he called. 'I'll see you tomorrow!'

'See you!' Laura waved back to him, and finally closed the door. He didn't seem to have minded her kiss. She stood for a few moments, leaning back against the door, thinking of Alastair making his way back to the George and Dragon, to the bed he would sleep in alone.

But she hoped that now at least he wasn't lonely.

And yet, up at Goslings' farm, a young woman had been killed, and her sister was left on her own.

THIRTY

A smell of burning still lingered in the air as Laura walked to work the next morning. She kept thinking about Lottie and George, and dear, brave Martha who had given her life for her country. The weight of their loss settled, grey and heavy, in her mind and wouldn't move, and it made her feel even sadder when she thought of Alastair and how he had lost Vicky. Poor man, the things he had lived through. It was no wonder he'd been so petrified during the air raid.

As she walked along, she saw Ewa and Zofia, with Zofia's little girl in her pram. Ewa's husband flew from the airbase, and Laura couldn't imagine how hard it was for her, day after day, knowing that he could leave for work and never come back.

They had come to England from Poland as refugees, and had found safety in Bramble Heath. Relative safety at least, for nowhere in England was truly safe any more, especially not a village so close to an airbase. Indeed, now a bomb had fallen right here and claimed a life. Laura had heard that Ewa had lost her sister in their escape from the Nazi advance; Martha's death, the young girl ripped away from her own devoted sister, would surely bring back sad memories for her.

'Morning,' Laura said gently. 'It's awful what's happened, isn't it?'

Ewa shrugged her characteristic one-sided shrug, but Laura had been in the village long enough to know that the gesture wasn't a casual one: it was simply how Ewa answered many questions, from the serious to the frivolous.

'It is a terrible thing,' she said. 'And to lose a sister... the pain doesn't leave you.'

'She was a sweet girl,' Zofia said. 'So very sad. And she had a boyfriend too.'

The heaviness inside Laura grew. 'Yes, poor George, they looked so happy together. I can't imagine how Lottie feels. It's a terrible loss.'

'George has the men on the base. Mateusz and the others will take care of him.' Ewa nodded. 'And we in the hamlet will send a note to Lottie,' she went on. 'Her loss is all of our loss. We all grieve for Martha.'

'I'm sure she'll appreciate it,' Laura replied, touched by Ewa's heartfelt thoughtfulness and care. 'Take care of yourselves, won't you?'

'And you too,' Ewa said. 'It was good to see you.'

'Goodbye, both,' Laura said, then she continued on her way. Martha's death and Alastair's terror made her own worries look very small. She'd lost a job – one she cared about enormously, but she could find another. Even if she had to leave dear Bramble Heath, she shouldn't mourn for herself.

Just outside the vet's, swinging her legs as she sat on the wall, was Sarah. The usually lively girl looked glum and, as she swiped her hand across her face, Laura realised she was trying to hide her tears. Sarah had known Martha, of course, and would be mourning her along with everyone else.

'Hello, Sarah,' Laura said, sitting down beside her. She loosely slipped her arm round Sarah's shoulders. 'I know you were friends with Martha. It's very sad that we've lost her.'

'It's not fair,' Sarah replied in a small voice. She snuggled against Laura. 'She wasn't fighting or flying a plane or nothing. She was just trying to keep the animals safe.'

'I know,' Laura replied gently. 'There's nothing fair about it at all. But you know, she died doing such an important job. If it wasn't for all those girls like Martha, who are willing to work so hard on the farms, we'd all be hungry.'

And Sarah gave a little, brave smile. 'That's why I wanted to see you,' she explained. 'Because they're going to need all the help they can get up on the farm now Martha isn't there any more. She did her bit and I'm going to do mine; I'm going up there now to help them clean up after the fire. We'll show them Jerries what's what!'

Laura smiled at Sarah, impressed by her determination to help. Imagine what would happen if everyone had the same attitude as this brave, enthusiastic girl?

But Laura did too. She felt it there, like a fire inside her. 'That's the spirit, Sarah! That's exactly what you should do. They'll need a hand, and I'm certain they'll be pleased to see you, despite everything that's happened.'

And I'm going to do my bit too. I'm going to stop the traitor.

Up ahead, she saw a familiar figure approaching the vet's. *Alastair.*

'I'm off to help the Land Girls,' Sarah said as she waved at him, and he lifted his hat politely. 'You two behave!'

And she hopped down from the wall, exchanging a greeting with Alastair as they passed one another.

Despite her sadness, Laura smiled as he approached. She was surprised to see him calling on Morgan so early. He was back once more in his unofficial uniform of the man from the Ministry, in a neatly cut grey suit, his homburg placed with exactness on his head.

'Well, this is a treat,' Laura told him as they met. 'I wasn't expecting to see y—' *Oh, no, not again! Even after all those warn-*

ings we gave! 'Goodness me, there wasn't another poisoning last night, was there? Did he take advantage of the chaos when the bomb struck?'

'No, no. I'm here to speak to Mr Morgan,' he told her, lifting his hat. 'As promised.'

Laura sighed. At least the poisoner hadn't struck again. But she didn't envy Alastair, facing Mr Morgan. 'I apologise in advance if he's rude to you,' she said. In the distance she heard an engine, and it reminded her of something. 'By the way, I completely forgot to tell you, there was so much going on yesterday. Remember we both heard someone driving about in the blackout? Well, it turns out my little friend Sarah did too. She heard an engine backfiring!'

'Did she now?' he asked as they approached the door. 'How's little Winnie getting on with her?'

'Oh, she's very we—'

The door banged open before Laura could finish her sentence, and Morgan strode out. He flared his nostrils like a furious bull and glared at both of them.

'So *you're* back in the village, intent on spreading more of your nonsense?' he snapped at Alastair. Then he turned his attention to Laura and she cringed inwardly. 'And as for you, girl – paperwork!'

'I'm back in the village to stop someone poisoning half the cattle in the district,' Alastair replied coolly. 'Mr Morgan, do you have ten minutes to speak to me?'

'No, I most certainly do not! I'm a very busy man,' Morgan declared. He poked a sausage-like finger at Alastair. 'And I'll have you know, myself and my very good friend Mr Pullen, who is in line for a knighthood, have both complained to your superiors at the Ministry!'

Then he shoved past them and headed for his shiny Austin 12, which was parked up outside the house ready for him to leave. He climbed in and, just as he drove off, he aimed

one last narrow-eyed glare through the window at Laura and
Alastair.

The sound of the other engine grew louder, but Morgan
was so busy making his wrath known that he wasn't looking at
the road ahead. A dark blue car shot into view, but Morgan
plainly didn't see it. He carried on driving, heading straight into
the path of the other car, and Laura waved both arms at him
frantically, hoping he'd look away.

Something must've clicked in Morgan's head, finally, as he
turned his attention back to the street and jammed on his brakes
with a squeal. The dark blue roadster jackknifed across the road
trying to avoid colliding with Morgan's car, and threw up dust
from its wheels.

Morgan raised his gloved fist at the other driver and flung
open his door. He leapt out, bellowing, 'What the devil do you
think you're doing, driving like a maniac in *my* village?'

The door of the roadster opened, and the driver stepped
out. As he did, Alastair murmured, 'Oh dear,' and tutted. But
there was a distinct air of amusement in his tone.

Laura had never seen the driver before. He was handsome
in a steely sort of way, with a square jaw and a prominent nose,
his dark eyes glaring from beneath arched brows. His hat was
tilted at a precise angle, and he wore what looked like an expensive, broad-shouldered overcoat over an immaculate and well-
cut suit. He didn't look like the sort of person one usually found
in Bramble Heath.

'You bloody spivs, coming down from London to sell black-
market nylons to the Land Girls!' Morgan ranted on. 'Driving at
a hundred miles an hour with your bloody eyes shut!'

The stranger said nothing. Instead, he watched Morgan as
he ranted, unmoving and seemingly impassive. Only when her
employer was done with his outburst did the new arrival ask,
'Finished?'

Morgan didn't reply at once. He was staring at the driver, a growl in his throat like a bull that was about to charge but was suddenly unsure. Laura hadn't seen Morgan stopped in his tracks like this before.

'Yes, I have!' Morgan finally shouted in reply.

'Get in your car and leave, Mr Morgan,' said the man. 'Trust me, it's the best thing to do in this situation.'

'Is that a threat?' Morgan asked, but he was already climbing back into the car, as if he was genuinely worried about what the man might do. The man who somehow knew his name.

I doubt that other chap has taken kindly to being called a spiv by a man who can't drive.

Morgan slammed the door, stalled in the middle of reversing, then finally got the car started again and sped off.

'I'm terribly sorry,' Laura called to the man. 'That was very rude of him. We're not all like that in this village, you know.'

'You can only be Miss Fellgate,' was his surprising reply. Then he said, 'Commander Seaton, if you can tear yourself away?'

But Alastair, it seemed, wasn't about to be deterred by this curt new arrival.

'Miss Fellgate is the person who raised the alarm,' he said. 'She's the first vet in the district who did. Miss Fellgate, this is Mr Wyngate. He's with the Ministry.'

Another man from the Ministry.

'Pleased to meet you, Mr Wyngate,' Laura said, and held out her hand to shake. 'Yes, I wrote in, and Al— Commander Seaton arrived to investigate.'

'Good work, Miss Fellgate.' Mr Wyngate looked down at Laura's hand as though he was unsure of the protocol. Alastair gave a gentle clear of his throat, and that seemed to be the prompt his colleague needed. He took Laura's hand and shook. 'Sorry about the cows.'

Then he released Laura's hand and addressed Alastair: 'We've got a lot of ground to cover.'

'Thanks for coming.' Surely another Ministry man in the village could only be a good thing, if it meant there was even more hope that the traitor would be stopped. Even if this Wyngate fellow was rather brisk. 'I'll be here all day if you need me, unless I'm called out. Good luck, Commander; Mr Wyngate.'

'And I *will* speak to Morgan,' Alastair told her as Wyngate strode over to the roadster, apparently too busy to wait. He touched Laura's arm and lowered his voice to say, 'Thank you for being so kind last night, Laura.'

'Not at all.' Laura smiled as she replied in a whisper. 'We're friends now, Alastair. Good luck with Mr Wyngate. You'll make sure he doesn't upset the farmers, won't you?'

He nodded. 'I'll try.' Then he turned and strode away towards his waiting colleague.

Laura had never met a man like Wyngate before, a man whose strength seemed to be wound up tight and was ready to strike. He wouldn't have come down from London for nothing; the traitor had stirred a hornets' nest. Did they realise that the net was closing in?

THIRTY-ONE

Without Morgan around Laura was busy all day at the practice, which left her with no time to go up to Goslings' farm and offer her condolences. She felt guilty about that, but wondered if they needed a little time. Although was she protecting herself? She'd seen so much fresh grief in Coventry, so unstaunchable and raw, that now she found herself flinching away from it, hiding behind a thin excuse.

It was only just as she was about to leave that she got a call from one of the farms. Her heart was in her throat when she heard Nicola's voice, a sensation of guilt spreading through her. She should've gone up to see them. She shouldn't have hidden away.

And what if it's another poisoning?

'Oh, Nicola, I'm so sorry about what's happened,' Laura said, feeling even more guilty now at how inadequate the words seemed.

'Aye,' Nicola replied sadly. 'We didn't think we'd lose one of our own. It's a rotten business.'

'You girls are like family up there on the farms,' Laura

sympathised. 'It must have been such a painful shock for you all.'

'Keeping busy helps, but... it's like losing a sister.' Nicola gave a sigh, her usual exuberance gone. 'Can you come up and have a look at Petunia? Her bairns aren't fastening on.' Then, as though she'd read Laura's mind, she added, 'I know folks don't know what to say to us, but it'll be nice to see you.'

Those piglets had been born on the night of the fire, when Lottie had nearly died. For them to struggle now seemed a cruel irony.

'Don't worry, I'll come up now,' Laura said. 'And it'll be good to see you too.'

A couple of minutes later, Laura was in the Clyno and driving up to Goslings' farm, her heart heavy as she thought of Lottie and her appalling, sudden loss. She couldn't imagine the devastation of losing a sister, especially when Lottie and Martha had been so close. As she drove, she gripped the steering wheel as she pictured the washed-out faces she'd seen in the streets after the Coventry Blitz, standing in lines for the soup kitchens, or just wandering through the ruins, smoke still rising from the rubble. She heard again the tired voices calling out the names of the missing; despite all the devastation, there had still been tiny shreds of hope, but was that how they would be feeling at the farm? Was there any hope left?

As she drove down the lane to the farm, she saw the field where the bomb had dropped. It was charred and blackened, a crater torn into the earth. Laura had to look away as memories of Coventry tried to push their way into her mind again.

When she arrived, Frances and Nicola were waiting for her. They looked exhausted, their eyes red from tears and lack of sleep, Laura was sure. She wished there was something she could say to make it better, to take away their pain, but what could she do?

They took Laura past the burnt out barn to the pigsties

where her patients were waiting for her, with Sarah leaning over the wall, gazing with concern at the piglets. She was glad to see Sarah there. She was such a good little friend to them at the farm.

'I'm sorry we called you out,' Frances told her. 'Only Petunia's piglets aren't suckling, and we're worried.'

'It's not a problem at all. I'm here to help,' Laura replied gently. She lowered her voice as she asked, 'By the way, how's Lottie?'

Nicola shook her head. 'She's broken into pieces, poor lass. She's up in bed, but I don't reckon she'll get much rest,' she said. 'We're looking after her as best we can, but what can you do? I'll tell you one thing, I ever get my hands on the bugger who killed our hinny Martha, I'll baste the bastard good and proper! But Martha would want us to keep going with our work, focus on the animals and make sure they're okay. We'll never forget her.'

Laura wished that she could give Lottie a hug and console her somehow, but she didn't want to disturb her. But right now, the best thing Laura could do was to do her job; to care for Petunia and her litter, and reassure the girls that there were good things in the world.

Frances patted Nicola's shoulder. There was so much anger, so much sadness. Laura hoped that she'd be able to treat the piglets and give the Land Girls a much-needed ray of sunshine, even just a tiny shaft to break in on the gloom.

Laura examined Petunia and her piglets, and discovered that the sow had milk-fever. No wonder the piglets hadn't been suckling. Within half an hour, Laura had had Frances and Nicola round up the girls and they were each bottle-feeding a piglet, even Sarah. But not Lottie, who stayed indoors; Laura didn't expect her to join in.

She took a bottle of calcium from her bag and hooked it up on the wall above Petunia, connecting it intravenously to the pig.

'I'll need to stay for a while, if that's all right, we can't rush the calcium drip,' she explained, and settled in the straw beside the girls, a piglet in her lap. She thought of Alastair's family farm. She couldn't wait to tell him about Petunia and her piglets. It'd give him a welcome reminder of home.

Laura let the girls decide what to chat about as they sat there, waiting for Petunia's treatment to work. They didn't skirt around the subject of what had happened to poor Martha, and it seemed that the warmth and comfort of the sty made it easier for them to talk about it. Any of them could've run into the darkness after the frightened cow. Any of them could've been killed when the bomb hit. If the bomber's aim had been even slightly altered, he could have taken out all of them, the entire farm.

Mrs Gosling came into the sty with a plate of sandwiches, looking careworn and sad. But Laura sensed that it mattered to her to bring them some food, that she could look after them, even though she couldn't look after Martha any more.

When it was time for Laura to leave, the piglets looking fed and happy, and Petunia perking up, it was already dark.

'I'll come by tomorrow and check on everyone,' Laura told Nicola as she headed out of the sty. She didn't just mean the pigs either, but the human occupants of the farm as well.

Nicola dropped her voice to confide, 'Your commander friend was here first thing this morning. Asking after our Lottie. Not to see her, but wanting to know how she was.'

Laura paused and glanced at Nicola. 'Gosh, that's ever so kind of him. He's a sweet man, the commander, really.'

And he knew only too well what it was like to lose someone you loved to the sudden, merciless violence of war.

'He left a note for her, so I passed it on,' Nicola said. 'I thought it was right kind of him. He's not even from these parts, but he proper cared.'

'He understands, I think, how she's feeling at the moment,' said Laura gently. 'He's lost someone too.'

Nicola nodded. 'Aye, I thought that might be it,' she said. 'You can tell the folk who have. They wear it on their faces.' And she glanced back towards the quarters where the Land Girls made their home, where Lottie must be even now. 'But she's got all of us to take care of her.'

'I'm so glad that she has,' Laura said. 'Pass on my condolences, won't you? And let her know, if there's anything I can do...' She had no idea what, exactly, but she wanted to help somehow. 'I'll see you again tomorrow, Nicola. Goodnight.'

'You drive careful,' Nicola said with a smile. 'Thanks for sorting out Petunia and her bairns.'

'Don't worry, I will,' Laura said. 'Night!'

She set off, driving back to the village. At least the pigs would be all right now, she hoped. The lanes were dark between the high hedges, and the white hawthorn blossom stood out like ghosts.

Somewhere, she knew, the traitor was lurking. Perhaps they were laying low, now that everyone was on the lookout for them. These dark night-time lanes belonged to the traitor, and Laura shivered at the thought.

As she passed a gate into a field, she gasped.

There was someone there, just beyond the gate, heading into the field. It wouldn't be anyone from the farms; they kept early hours, not late ones. But it was so dark that she couldn't make anything out beyond the fact that it was a person – it was someone who Laura was sure shouldn't be there.

Prickles of fear ran back and forth across Laura's skin. She'd have to tell Alastair.

Not far ahead, at the crossroads, there was a telephone booth. She wouldn't waste time driving to the village. It was better to let him know right away. She drove on, wondering if the sound of her car would spook whoever it was lurking in the field and send them home. But she wasn't going to take any chances.

She parked up near the telephone booth and got out. The night was dark and silent, a complete contrast to the evening before when hell had fallen from the sky. She glanced this way and that, but she seemed to be the only person about.

She was put through to the George and Dragon and waited tensely for someone to answer. Ted came on the line in two rings.

'Evenin', the George and Dragon, Ted speaking,' he said.

'Ted, it's me, Laura, is Commander Seaton there?' Laura asked quickly. 'It's urgent. I must speak to him.'

'He's just come in from calling on you.' Ted chuckled, and Laura wondered what Iris would have to say about that when she got home. Ted muffled the receiver and called, 'Commander, sir, Miss Fellgate for you.'

Laura peered out through the glass panes of the booth, trying to see if there was anyone around. She felt like a sitting target, even though the booth was unlit.

Is it you, the traitor? Are you out here tonight, with death on your mind? Your days are numbered. We're going to stop you.

'Laura?' Alastair said. 'Are you all right?'

'I just saw someone in a field, not far from here,' Laura told him, looking over her shoulder. 'I'm in the phone box at the crossroads on the road down from Goslings' farm. It's not that far from the old shepherd's hut. Can you come out?'

'Come back to the village,' Alastair said urgently just as, in the little hut where they had sheltered the previous evening, Laura saw the faint flicker of a candle on the horizon. 'I'll go out and look around.'

'I think they're in the hut,' Laura said, her breath catching. 'I can just about see it through a gap in the hedge from here.'

'Come to the pub,' Alastair instructed as the pips sounded. 'I'll—'

The call cut off, her money spent.

Laura didn't have any more coins. And she knew she should go back to the village, but what if the traitor had run off by the time Alastair arrived? Perhaps she could get a little nearer to them, without them seeing her, and try to see more of them than she had. Something, some clue that might lead to finding out who the wretched traitor was. Because she had to do her bit, even if it was dangerous. She had to play her part to protect her country, just like Martha had, and here was her chance. All she had seen was an anonymous figure in the darkness and nothing more. She needed to get closer.

She put down the receiver and slowly opened the door. It didn't squeak on its hinges, and Laura took that as a sign of good fortune as she crept along, close to the hedge.

The gap was just large enough for her to squeeze through. Having grown up in the countryside, Laura didn't stop to worry that her clothes might get caught on branches and thorns; she forged her way through and found herself in the same field as the hut.

Who are you, lighting a candle in the dark?

She tried to keep low as she stalked through the grass. Candlelight was still glowing from the hut. Who was there?

She stopped, and rolled her eyes at how silly she was. Couldn't it be a courting couple, slipping away to somewhere private to spend some time alone?

If that's all it is, then good.

She carried on, still not seeing or hearing anyone around. Once she reached the hut, she pressed her back against the wall and took a deep, steadying breath.

I'll just have a little look inside.

She inched towards the open door, closer and closer, and when she reached it she peered inside with one eye.

And saw no one. Except—

'What on earth?' Laura whispered to herself.

In the corner, opposite the one where she and Alastair had sheltered only the night before, the straw and hay had been dragged aside to reveal a box with a dial on the front of it.

A radio? Why is there a radio in the old hut?

She went inside, keeping close to the door.

Then she heard a footstep close by; a starburst of sudden pain struck her head, and everything went black.

THIRTY-TWO

The world was spinning, lurching; a sickness was in Laura's stomach as she rose up from the dark reaches of the depths she'd been sent to.

My head... oh, gosh, it hurts so much...

She had the impression that there was someone near her, and she recoiled.

Don't hurt me again. Don't!

'It's all right, I'm here,' said a gentle voice. 'Don't try to sit up.'

Laura tried to open her eyes, but they hurt. Everything hurt.

But she knew that voice. She knew, without looking, that it was Alastair.

'Alastair...? Where am I?' she whispered. Bits of memories were falling into place like jigsaw puzzle pieces. She was inside the shepherd's hut. She was lying on something soft... on the hay. And someone had— 'No... wait... the hut. There's a radio in the hut...'

'Someone hit you,' Alastair said, and she felt the gossamer touch of his fingertips brushing her hair back from her face. 'Can you open your eyes?'

With an effort Laura managed to open them, and found herself looking up at Alastair's concerned face. 'Hit me? Oh, I'm such a fool, Alastair. A silly, silly fool... I just wanted to do my bit...'

'You're not a fool,' he assured her kindly. 'It was very brave.'

'I saw someone, I definitely saw someone,' Laura told him. The world wasn't spinning quite so fast now. 'And I heard their footstep too, just before they... But it was so stupid. I have no idea who it was.'

'Whoever it was,' Alastair said, 'they've got a backfiring engine. I heard it as I was halfway up the field to the hut.'

Laura reached for Alastair's hand and held it. Through her foggy thoughts, she worried about him hearing a backfiring engine. Wouldn't that make him scared? 'Just like Sarah said...'

Then she heard something, footsteps swishing through the grass. She tightened her grip on Alastair's hand and whispered fearfully, 'Alastair, someone's coming!'

'Hey, Commander Seaton, is that you there?' a familiar voice called. *It's Henry. Thank goodness.*

'Constable Russell!' Alastair called in reply. 'Miss Fellgate's been attacked. She tracked down our traitor!'

The footsteps hurried, and suddenly Henry appeared in the doorway, with Bob Knapp the greengrocer in his tin ARP helmet.

'Attacked?' Henry gasped. 'You best get her off to see my Annie. Me and Bob'll take over h— And what's that in the corner? Blow me down, unless I'm very much mistaken that's a radio!'

'Whoever did it took off as I arrived,' Alastair told the policeman, the efficient commander once more. 'I need to look after Laura. Would you be able to telephone the Black Bull in East Grinstead and ask for Mr Wyngate? Let him know what we've found.'

'Will do, sir,' Henry replied. 'I'll get some more bodies up here, too, to look for the fellow. Don't worry, sir, everything's in hand.'

Laura tried to sit up, but only succeeded in making her head feel even worse. She groaned in pain. 'I'm so sorry,' she moaned.

Alastair hushed her gently. 'I'll carry you down to the car. I want you properly checked over,' he said. 'Ready?'

'Ready,' Laura said. He was going to carry her. Laura hadn't been carried by anyone since she was a little girl. 'Some vet I am... *I'm* supposed to be the one looking after poorly patients.'

'As bad as a commander who's lost his ship.' There was humour in Alastair's voice, despite the gentle concern in his dark gaze, and Laura was suddenly ridiculously glad all over again that he had found her. Then, with great care, he slipped his arms beneath her and scooped her neatly up from the straw.

She felt rather wobbly for a moment, but the sensation passed, replaced with one of contentment. Alastair's hold was reassuring, his firm arms strong as he carried her. She gazed up at him, dimly aware of Henry and Bob busying themselves as she was taken away.

A dark field in the middle of the night, on her own... what had she been thinking? But she'd only wanted to do her bit. She could've caught the traitor tonight, and they'd all be celebrating. Instead, she'd been caught off-guard. She'd failed. But she was alive at least, and Alastair was here.

'Thank goodness you found me,' Laura whispered up at Alastair. 'You're a hero, Commander Seaton.'

'You're the hero. You did a very brave thing tonight,' Alastair replied, glancing down at her as he picked his way over the uneven ground. 'I just wish I could've been here sooner. When I saw you on the floor, I thought—' But he left the thought unfinished, swallowing his words down.

You thought I was dead.

'I'm still here, though,' Laura assured him, snaking her arm round his waist. 'Just about. Unluckily for our traitor!'

'And now we know where they were hiding out... and if we're lucky, they left the radio tuned.' Laura could see her own car in the lay-by, with Alastair's borrowed vehicle parked snug behind it and, behind that, the van she had seen doing the greengrocer's rounds. Soon they'd be in the village again, and she'd be with Annie, the district nurse. And they'd both be safe. 'I'll pop you on the back seat for now. I don't want any more heroics until Nurse Russell's looked you over.'

The traitor was long gone by now, though. But Laura still tried to be alert, even while her head was pulsing. What if she saw something again? What if...?

But she forced herself to relax. She needed to recover. 'I've got to go back and see Petunia tomorrow, I promised,' she told Alastair.

'The new mum.' Of course Alastair would know all about that. He was from pig-farming stock and had been visiting the farms, after all, and not only on professional business. Laura didn't think there would be many Ministry officials who would spare the time to leave kind words for a bereaved Land Girl. 'A touch of milk-fever, I think?'

He stooped a little, somehow keeping Laura close as he opened the car door.

Laura beamed at him. 'I'll make a vet of you yet,' she said, before adding, 'It was very sweet of you to leave a note for Lottie, by the way.'

As Alastair settled her against the back seat of the car with all the care of a parent tucking their child in for the night, he told her, 'I hope I didn't make her feel worse. I just wanted her to know that she's not alone; there are people out there who know exactly what she's feeling, and that we care.'

'I'm sure it meant a lot to her,' Laura replied, her voice gentle. 'A little light shining in the darkness.'

'And they can be the brightest of all in the end.' Alastair

took off his overcoat and leaned into the car to cover her, using the coat as a makeshift blanket.

He was very close to her at that moment, and Laura held her breath. He was her friend, she shouldn't think anything of it, and yet she liked it, that feeling of closeness. She liked the soft touch of his overcoat's lining against her skin, and she liked the scent of his spicy cologne that lingered on the woollen cloth. Had he bought it on his travels in the navy?

She smiled at him. Her friend, the sailor. The commander without a ship to command.

'Thank you, Alastair,' Laura said. 'I feel cosy now. Thank you for looking after me.'

'That's what friends do.' He stood back. 'Let's get you to the nurse.'

THIRTY-THREE

Laura still felt woozy a couple of hours later as Annie and Alastair helped her along the path from the Russells' home.

'It's a nasty bump, but nothing's broken,' Annie assured her. 'But that dizziness you're feeling is concussion, and you mustn't be left on your own.'

'Thanks for sorting me out,' Laura said. Annie's job, like Laura's own, didn't guarantee any time off the clock. At whatever time a cow fell ill, or someone got hit over the head, they had to be there to help.

'Can Iris help you? I know she's got the boys to keep an eye on, though,' Annie said.

She couldn't ask Iris to sit up all night and watch her, concussion or not. Her landlady had enough on her plate; she couldn't be a nursemaid too.

'She has...' Laura murmured. 'I really don't want to trouble her.'

'If you'd like, I'd be happy to stay with you.' Alastair opened the car door as he spoke. 'You can't take concussion too lightly.'

Laura blinked at him, surprised. But she was pleased too.

'That's so kind of you, Commander. But are you sure you wouldn't rather get some kip?'

'I'm sure,' he said kindly as he helped her into the passenger seat of the car. Laura felt very looked after, warmed by the thought that someone would be staying with her after the frightening turn the night had taken. And not just anyone, but Alastair – the very person who made her feel safer and more connected than she'd ever felt before. 'Nurse Russell, thank you. These so-called quiet villages, eh?'

'Never a dull moment,' Annie replied. 'Just be careful, won't you? Dad's told me all about what's been going on, and no one in the village could talk about anything else. Well, at least, not until what happened at Goslings' farm last night. That poor girl, I can't stop thinking about her and her sister. But don't take any more risks, Laura.'

Laura nodded, then regretted it. Her head still hurt. 'I'll be good, Nurse Russell. Don't you worry. Commander Seaton will make sure of it!'

With a final goodbye, Alastair climbed into the front seat and they set off into the still night. The village was so peaceful that it was hard to imagine that only last night a bomb had threatened them all and taken the life of an innocent young woman. And while the brave men at the airbase were doing all they could to protect the village from further attacks from the sky, someone right here in their midst was a danger to them all. It wasn't the sort of place that kind of thing was supposed to happen, was it?

But perhaps that was the point. Anyone would expect a traitor to attack the airbase, but it was well protected. The farms, on the other hand, with unlocked gates designed to keep animals in rather than people out, were open season.

'I know Annie means well, but I'd do it again in a heartbeat if I thought it meant catching the traitor,' Laura admitted.

'Oh, I know you would.' There was a note of resigned

humour in Alastair's voice. Laura found she quite liked it; it was another glimpse of the man who had seemed so unreadable. 'If I were him, I'd be looking over my shoulder.'

'I do hope that radio yields something,' Laura said as they neared Iris's cottage. 'If only we'd found it yesterday! There could be fingerprints on it, couldn't there?'

'If there are and they're on file, then we could be on the verge of having a name.' The car slowed to a halt outside Laura's home. 'But even if not, us finding the radio has cut off our poisoner's communication line with whoever they're talking to. And that's not a small thing.'

'They're on their own now...' Laura said. And that was good, wasn't it?

Unless it made them more desperate. Who knew what they might try to do next? Laura looked up at Iris's cottage and shivered. 'They wouldn't come here after me, would they? What about Iris and the boys? They're only little.'

But Alastair shook his head. 'Whoever attacked you just wanted to get away,' he assured her. 'And I'm bloody glad of it.'

He'd given up chasing the traitor to be with her. But of course he had; they were friends and he was a gentleman, in every sense. 'I hope so,' she replied. 'I couldn't bear it if I brought that monster to Iris's home.'

Iris must've heard the car arrive as the front door cracked open. Alastair had been back to see her while Laura was being patched up with a plaster, so that she knew not to worry. And yet, as Iris came outside, she *did* look worried. She came down the steps and out to the car, her arms folded across her chest against the chill of the night.

'Laura?' she said. 'My goodness me...'

'Nothing a good rest won't cure,' Alastair assured Iris as he opened the door. There was something very calm about the man who had commanded HMS *Nemesis*. Laura could well imagine him keeping the cool head under fire that had brought his ship home. 'A nasty concussion, Mrs Pearson.'

'Let me help her out, Commander,' Iris said. 'Thank you for bringing her home. We all love Laura in Bramble Heath.'

Iris's words struck home, and Laura sniffed back a tear. She was so cared for, and that thought made the attack, and the fact that she'd lost her job, far easier to bear.

They helped Laura out of the car, and over to Iris's front door.

'Iris, the commander's going to sit up with me,' Laura told her. 'Annie said I can't be left alone, and you've got the boys – they need you.'

Iris glanced at Alastair, then smiled. 'That's very kind of you, Commander.'

'If you've no objections, of course?' Alastair said politely. Then he deadpanned, 'I'm a civil servant rather than a sailor these days. Entirely trustworthy.'

'I don't object at all,' Iris replied with a chuckle. 'You're a proper gent, Commander. Would you like me to bring you up anything? A cup of tea? A little snack?'

Iris's attempts at matchmaking saw no bounds, it appeared. Even when Laura had been hit over the head, Iris was making Alastair as welcome as if he had come to call on his sweetheart. Even though he and Laura were just friends.

'I don't want to put you to any trouble,' Alastair replied politely. 'Do you need anything, Lau— Miss Fellgate?'

'A glass of water, if you wouldn't mind, Iris?' Laura replied.

Iris's cheeks dimpled as her smile widened. She'd clearly heard Alastair's slip with her name. 'Of course. You two go on up, and I'll bring a tray in a jiffy.'

She closed the front door behind them and went through to the kitchen.

'On the left at the top of the stairs,' Laura told Alastair. 'My room's not too untidy, I promise.'

She hoped she'd tidied everything away, at least. How embarrassing if he'd gone in and found yesterday's socks in the middle of the floor.

'You should see some of the ships I've served on.' He smiled. 'Can you manage the stairs?'

'I'm not sure I can get up them on my own,' Laura admitted. 'I feel so pathetic, Alastair. I'm sorry.'

'You were brave,' Alastair said simply, though Laura didn't feel terribly brave at that moment. Instead, she felt helpless and frightened. But above all that, she felt cared for.

Then, without another word, Alastair scooped her into his arms.

THIRTY-FOUR

Alastair carried Laura up the stairs, past Iris's prints of country scenes and family photos. She had looped her arms round his neck, and she gazed at him.

'I don't get carried about like this often enough,' she teased gently. 'I rather like it!'

'Then your own gentleman must be a gentleman indeed,' Alastair observed with a deliberate air of wisdom. He quirked an eyebrow and asked, 'If there *is* a gentleman?'

Laura hoped that she was too woozy for her surprise to register.

'There isn't one,' she replied. 'There was one, once, but there isn't one now. There hasn't been for quite some time. On the left,' she added as they reached the top of the stairs. He glanced down at her and gave a tender smile, then pushed open the bedroom door.

Laura flicked the light switch, illuminating her cottage bedroom. It wasn't much different from her bedroom back home on the farm. The room was dominated by a cosy double bed with a wooden bedstead, and the dressing table bore one tub of cold cream and a stack of veterinary textbooks. More books stood on the chest of drawers. The windows were concealed by pretty floral curtains, the dour blackout blind hidden behind. A Constable print of a rural scene hung on the chimney breast and Laura's odds and ends stood in a row across the mantelpiece. Her dressing gown was draped over the back of a wooden chair beside the bed, and her spare trousers hung on the wardrobe door.

On the bedside table was an alarm clock, almost hidden behind a frame of snapshots from home. A worn, one-eyed stuffed rabbit sat on her pillow, and she chuckled with embarrassment.

'Sorry, that's Mrs Ruggles...' she told him.

'Very pleased to meet you, Mrs Ruggles,' Alastair deadpanned. He stooped to settle Laura against the pillows, then cleared his throat and looked around the room. 'Well... I'll just pop out onto the landing while you get yourself comfortable.'

'Thank you,' Laura said. What a gentleman he was. She took her pyjamas out from under her bedclothes and dragged her dressing gown from the chair. A worn cushion lay on the seat, and she felt bad that Alastair wouldn't be more comfortable. 'The chair isn't very comfy, but there's a spare blanket on the top shelf of the wardrobe, if you want to keep warm overnight?'

He nodded and, with a polite 'Thank you,' stepped out onto the landing to wait for her.

Laura changed into her pyjamas, each movement slow and careful. She put her clothes away in the chest of drawers, then draped her dressing gown over her shoulders before sliding under the covers.

'I'm ready now,' she called softly.

'A child was looking at me,' Alastair whispered as he opened the door and slipped back into the room. He took off his coat and hung it over his arm. 'I don't think I was supposed to have spotted him, so I pretended I hadn't. But I did.'

'Tom or Sam,' Laura explained with a smile. 'I couldn't tell them apart when I first came here, they're peas in a pod. But after a while you notice little things, things you can't quite put your finger on, and you know which one is which.'

Alastair hung his coat on a spare hook on the back of the bedroom door. As he did, he glanced over his shoulder and said, 'There'll be talk by morning.'

'As long as they remember to mention the plaster on my head, I'm sure no one'll gossip,' Laura said, but she knew that plaster or no plaster, and no matter how innocent Alastair's reason for being in her bedroom, rumour would get around. 'Gosh, you're not going to get in trouble with the Ministry, are you? Do they have rules about men on government business going into women's bedrooms?'

She was only half teasing; she really didn't want him to get into trouble.

'I'll tell them I slept in my emergency hammock, like a good naval man.' Alastair settled onto the wooden chair beside the bed and gave a long sigh. 'Which reminds me, Mr Wyngate would like you to sign some papers; I spoke to him while you were with Nurse Russell. The radio, you understand?'

'Oh, of course, I'll sign them,' Laura said. 'I've left my pen on top of the chest of drawers.'

'Tomorrow is soon enough,' was his gentle assurance.

There was a soft knock at the door and Iris called, 'Can I come in?' Without waiting for Laura's reply, the door slowly swung open and Iris peered round the edge, eyes wide with interest.

For heaven's sake. Was she expecting to walk in on some sort of soft-focus Hollywood clinch?

'Yes, Iris, of course you can come in,' Laura said. As soon as she did, Alastair was on his feet again. He looked exhausted, but protocol clearly wasn't forgotten.

Iris was carrying a tray, with her best tea service and some biscuits. She winked at Alastair. 'It's not every day I have a commander in my house.'

'I'm afraid one of your boys might wonder who the odd man is in the house,' Alastair said apologetically as he took the tray from her. 'And I can't even claim to be Father Christmas.'

'Or the Tooth Fairy,' Laura added. 'You'd need to be wearing something more sparkly for that.'

'I'll let them know you're Auntie Laura's special friend,' Iris replied. 'They've got past the stage where they call every man they see "Daddy" – got quite embarrassing when they did that around the village, I can assure you!'

Iris was in her element, Laura knew. She had the patient to fuss, plus the polite and concerned widower to entertain, and, to top it all off, she had the chance to matchmake. Not that there would be any point in *that*, obviously.

'The boys called Mr Morgan "Daddy" once,' Laura went on, picking up Iris's story for Alastair's amusement. 'And Mrs Morgan gave my boss such a glare, as if she thought he'd been having a dalliance with Iris. And Mr Morgan looked horrified!'

'As if I'd go behind my husband's back, and with the likes of Mr Morgan, for goodness' sake!' Iris pulled a comical grimace, then backed away to the door, slowly, as if she didn't want to miss a second. 'I'll leave you to it, but just give me a shout if you need anything. And if that dratted siren goes off, it's straight through the kitchen door at the back and into the garden to the shelter. Oh, and she takes her tea with a little splash of milk, and no sugar.'

'Thanks, Iris,' Laura said, with a smile. Although she could've told Alastair that herself, Iris was enjoying looking after her.

With that, Iris left the room and softly closed the door behind her – but Laura suspected she might lurk on the landing for a little while. Just in case.

'The siren better not go off; I've been on my feet all day.' Alastair poured the tea with one hand as he stifled a yawn, and Laura wondered where he had gone with the mysterious Mr Wyngate. 'A little splash of milk and no sugar, as instructed.'

He brought the cups of tea and plate of biscuits back to the bed and put them down on the bedside table. Then he resumed his seat and told Laura, 'We'll sign papers in the morning. I don't think you're about to rush off and start telling everyone you found a radio tonight.'

'That was *exactly* what I planned to do,' Laura said drily. Signing papers because she'd found the radio was actually quite exciting, but she wasn't sure that she should let on. 'Fling back the bedclothes, jump out of bed, and run down the street waving my arms about and yelling, *I found a radio!* No, I'm going to stay here with you and hope the siren doesn't go off, because I really don't fancy those stairs at all at the moment.'

She reached for her cup and took a sip, before saying, 'This Wyngate fellow...he made short work of Mr Morgan, didn't he? Very impressive.'

'He'd make short work of Hitler.' Alastair took a sip of tea. 'I'm still going to speak to your employer, but I haven't had a moment today. A whistle-stop tour of county farms, Ministry business and back too late for supper.'

'And did Mr Wyngate...?' Laura wrinkled her nose. She didn't want to sound rude, but she had to know. 'How did he get on with everyone on the farms?'

Alastair pursed his lips comically. 'It got the job done. Eventually.'

'Oh, dear,' she replied. She wondered how the two of them got on. They were two quite different men. But she got the impression that Alastair couldn't tell her anything more about Mr Wyngate; he'd no doubt had to sign a lot of papers himself. She looked at him, not looking particularly comfortable in the chair beside her bed. But he wasn't the sort to complain, she knew, so she said, 'You know, I do really appreciate it, you being willing to sit on that hard chair when you've been going non-stop all day. Do you want to come and sit on the bed? It's softer. And I'm under the covers, so if you're sitting on top of them Iris won't be shocked.'

Alastair, who had leaned forward to untie his shoelaces, paused at her suggestion, and Laura wondered if she'd shocked him. But when he looked towards her, she knew she hadn't.

'I'm a widower.' He smiled. 'We no longer shock landladies.'

Then he kicked off his shoes and left the chair to settle on the bed, sitting at Laura's side.

It felt rather strange for a moment, rather personal, but the sensation lifted, and it soon seemed just *right* for Alastair to be sitting beside her on the bed.

'More comfortable?' Laura asked him. She felt as if, letting him sit on the bed beside her, the room looked different, as if she was seeing it from a different angle. Something had changed; she had shown Alastair that she trusted him, liked him.

'Very.' He looked down at her. 'How's the headache?'

'I've felt better,' she admitted. 'But it's not as bad as it was. And you're here, and...'

When was the last time he had sat on a bed like this, next to a woman? Perhaps the last night he'd been on shore, before he went off to sea, and Vicky had been taken from him.

'No more frights like this, all right?' Alastair offered the plate of biscuits to Laura. He was being light-hearted, but there was real concern behind it.

Laura looked down at the plate as she took a biscuit. She smiled her thanks to him, before saying, 'I'm sorry. It must've been horrible when you found me out cold like that.'

'I'd never make a Mr Wyngate, put it that way,' he admitted. And Laura suspected that the stony-faced man from the Ministry would have chased the backfiring vehicle and come back for her later. 'I'm allowed to tell you that the radio was still tuned, and we found tyre tracks. You led us to a couple of good clues... so far, the only ones we've found.'

Laura gasped. 'Well, that's something! Who's on the other end of the radio? Can you call them on it? I must admit, I have no idea how it works. And as for the tyre tracks – is Mr Wyngate going to check everybody's wheels? Although I'm not sure I can really see him doing that, somehow.'

Not in those expensive-looking clothes. He must've found an excellent tailor on the black market.

'Oh, he's full of surprises.' Alastair dipped his biscuit into his tea. 'One of the tyres is bald. So, we have a backfiring engine and a bald tyre... every other car in London, but not every other car in Bramble Heath.' He shook his head. 'I don't know how people in this country could be stupid enough to do this: to harm their own nation's war effort, to side with the enemy. And all for a lunatic in Berlin.'

'I suppose they didn't manage to round up all the Blackshirts,' Laura said with a shiver, as she recalled the fascists who had proudly marched in England in the 1930s. 'I know a lot of them suddenly changed allegiance when the war broke out, but there must be some around who still have those views, privately at least, and who would see sabotage against the home front as a *good* thing.'

With a sigh, Alastair nodded. 'Mosley's lot,' he agreed. 'Vicky's grandmother had one of his supporters living next door to her in Greenwich until— Well, even fascists aren't immune to Hitler's bombs.'

'Oh, no,' Laura sighed. 'I hope Vicky's grandmother was all right, though, even if her neighbour wasn't?' And yet, as she said the words, her woozy brain regretted her clumsy question. Was that how Vicky had died?

'No...' Alastair murmured. 'The whole row of houses, you see— just one lone bomber, after the all-clear.' He shook his head. 'Sorry.'

'*After* the all-clear?' Laura had heard of things like that happening but had always pushed them to the back of her mind, trusting that the all-clear meant it was safe to come out from the shelter. 'Oh, no, and if she was elderly, and couldn't get about very quickly... The poor woman. I'm so sorry, Alastair, that's a terrible thing to happen. And what brutes – bomb a factory or a railway station if you must, they're fair game in a war, but not houses. Not where ordinary people live.'

Alastair closed his eyes for a long moment and drew in a breath.

'Vicky had gone down to London from Yorkshire to help her out of the city,' he explained. 'One day later and they would've been safe on Dad's farm, away from it all. One more day, Laura.' She saw his fist clench, the knuckles white for a second. 'And all they can tell you is that they wouldn't have known a thing about it, as if that makes it hurt less. But nothing does.'

Laura didn't reply at first. The room was silent, except for the steady tick-tick of the alarm clock by the bed. Her mind was somewhere else, hearing the whine of a bomber's engine overhead, then the blast and the ground shaking as if it would split in two. Choking dust filled the air, and bricks and masonry flew as if they weighed nothing at all. And as the dust began to clear, figures – people – lying twisted on the ground. Still. Unmoving.

Dead.

She swallowed, and gently laid her hand over Alastair's. 'I'm so very sorry, Alastair. It's everyone's worst nightmare, that either we won't get to see the morning or someone we love won't instead. I can't imagine how awful it's been for you. If only that bomber hadn't hit all those homes, if only it'd been a day later. If only.'

But as Smudge had told her, every man aboard HMS *Nemesis* had got home because of the commander. Even as his heart was shattered and his nerve gone, he had saved hundreds of families from the same sorrow he'd had to face.

'And that's why I'm going to catch this traitor. They passed me all the notes from crackpots and curtain-twitching do-gooders so I could send a nice, harmless reply,' Alastair murmured with a fresh purpose in his words. 'And I might've lost my nerve, but when I read your letter... I *knew*, Laura. I knew it was true.'

'I was worried I'd sound half-barmy,' Laura admitted. 'So, I decided, *I'll just write the facts*. Because they're the same facts that made me realise what was going on. I'm so glad my letter reached you. I rather think that had it landed on anyone else's desk I'd be facing this on my own. But I'm not alone any more, Alastair – because you're here.'

He handed her another biscuit. 'And with a very fetching plaster too.'

Laura took a bite from the biscuit, before saying, 'It's what all the fashionable vets are wearing this season. Especially in Bramble Heath. And we also have dashing commanders sitting on our beds to give us biscuits too, you know.'

She smiled gently at him. It was fun, oddly, sitting in her room with Alastair, just talking, just *being*. It shouldn't have been – she should've been afraid; after all, she'd been attacked by the traitor. And yet she felt safe here with Alastair.

'Dashing?' Alastair blinked. 'That must've been quite the bump on the head!'

Laura took another bite, then told him, 'But you are! You commanded a whole ship, and saved all those men, and you rescued me. Now if that's not dashing, I don't know what is.'

And you're rather handsome too, but I really won't say that out loud.

'All that and I hand out biscuits too.'

'Exactly, you're very dashing indeed,' Laura said. Without thinking, she rested her head against Alastair's shoulder. He tipped his head towards her too, so his cheek was resting against her hair. And for a while they sat in contented silence just like that, holding their cups of tea that Iris had so kindly brewed.

She wished Alastair could see how dashing he was, how heroic. But he'd seemed surprised, and Laura thought of all he'd been through, of all the terror he'd faced, and how somehow he'd kept going. It was all buttoned up in his civil servant's uniform, even though tonight he was casually dressed. He still had that bearing. More and more, she felt as if she was getting to know him and was allowed to peek behind his armour. She wished she could free him of it, but she knew it wasn't something to rush. He needed to know that she was there for him; that he wasn't alone. To coax him out, like a tortoise emerging from hibernation in its bed of warm hay. And sitting like this, in their companionable silence, was just one way to show him.

'Tomorrow,' Alastair said eventually, his voice utterly content, 'I'm going to employ a little Wyngate on your boss.'

Laura smiled at him. 'You are? Oh, I have to see that. It's high time he was put in his place. Gosh, when you think of all those poison cases he knew about, and he just did nothing at all... Will he get in trouble for that, do you think?'

He could do, she knew; it might be seen as dereliction of his professional duties, especially during wartime.

'That's a decision for someone further up the chain than me,' he said. 'But I expect he'll have some questions to answer. And from people who won't take well to being bellowed at.'

Laura chuckled. 'He does like a good bellow, doesn't he? Gosh, do you know what would *really* get on his wick? If whoever gives him a dressing-down is a *woman*. He's got such old-fashioned views – he only employed me because he couldn't find a man!'

'I'll see what I can do,' Alastair murmured contentedly. 'We need a few more inquisitive Miss Fellgates and fewer disinterested Mr Morgans. And from what Mr Churchill was saying this afternoon, I think he'd tend to agree.'

Clearly Churchill had been giving a speech that chimed somehow with Laura's current situation. She wondered when Alastair had had the chance to listen to the radio that day. Perhaps it'd been on in one of the farmhouses he'd visited?

But then it dawned on her that he didn't mean that all, and she gasped in surprise.

'Were you— goodness me, you were on the telephone to the prime minister!'

'Oh heavens, no. They wouldn't give *me* the coveted direct line.' He chuckled. 'No, Mr Wyngate dragged me along to the War Office to discuss the sabotage. The tea was terrible.'

'Wait, you actually met him *in person*?' Laura was even more amazed. Churchill was the most famous person in the country at that moment. One of the most famous on earth. And even he knew about what was happening in Bramble Heath. 'And now you're sitting next to me in this ordinary little bedroom. You've had quite a day. What does Mr C think about the network of traitors, then? Or would I need to sign those papers first before you can tell me that... if at all?'

'The PM's opinion of them is precisely the same as ours,' Alastair replied. 'We must take them very seriously indeed. Now we know how widespread this effort to sabotage our farms is, their days are numbered. And you were the first person to find hard evidence of poison, Laura; without that, all we had was conjecture.'

'The test tube that told all,' Laura said. She felt rather pleased with herself that she'd had the foresight to test the spilt feed. 'I was lucky, really, that I managed to run the test early enough. Cyanide's volatile, it doesn't hang around too long. I'm so glad I was able to help.'

And together, they were going to put a stop to the sabotage. Whoever had attacked Laura earlier had no idea just how far things had gone. Their days were numbered; they had to be.

Laura shifted in the bed, getting comfortable. She was

feeling sleepy now. 'We ought to get some sleep, I suppose. I'm feeling tired now, but not that weird, dizzy sort of tiredness I felt earlier. I better wish you goodnight before I drop off. Thanks for everything today, Alastair, you've been wonderful.'

She turned her head just a little, and her lips brushed against Alastair's cheek. She felt that urge again, to kiss him. Did he feel the same about her? She wasn't sure. But she gave him a gentle peck on the cheek anyway.

'Get some rest now,' Alastair murmured. 'And I'll see you in the morning.'

Laura took his hand, as if it was a signal that she wasn't going to let him go. 'And I'll see you too. Could I...?' She paused, wondering if it was a good idea. But she decided to go ahead anyway – maybe it was the bump on her head after all? 'Could I possibly ask for a goodnight kiss, Alastair?'

For a moment, Alastair looked at her, his gaze searching her face as though he didn't quite understand what she had asked. Then he tentatively touched his lips to Laura's and, very gently, kissed her.

Laura smiled against his lips, her heart light for the first time in so long – perhaps ever. As she gently kissed him back, she tightened her hand round his. When she broke away from his lips, she gazed back at him. It was as if they had stumbled into a new world.

'Goodnight, Alastair,' Laura whispered.

'Goodnight Laura.' He smiled. 'Sweet dreams.'

THIRTY-FIVE

Laura was woken by the insistent trill of her alarm clock. She wished she'd remembered to turn it off the night before, but she'd had other things on her mind.

As she opened her eyes, the main thing she had on her mind was right there in front of her: Alastair.

She remembered falling asleep with her head against his shoulder, but at some point in the night they had slipped into an embrace, Laura's head resting against Alastair's chest. Her legs were tangled in the bedclothes around his. She noticed his scent again, that spicy cologne.

She reached out to knock the alarm clock off the bedside table and it landed on the floor, silent at last.

'Sorry about the alarm clock,' she whispered. 'A rather rude awakening.'

'I fell asleep, sorry...' Alastair murmured, his voice sleepy with contentment and his eyes still closed. 'Did a terrible job of keeping an eye on you.'

'I'd say you did a pretty good one,' Laura assured him, as she glanced up at him. He looked slightly tousled from sleep, and she liked that. Thank goodness that he'd got some sleep at last.

'Do you know, I don't have a headache any more. I feel... restored.'

She realised it might not solely be down to having a good sleep. Because they'd kissed last night, hadn't they? Or had she dreamed it?

'You make a lovely pillow,' she quipped. She really wasn't sure what she should say. But she didn't feel awkward. This felt just right.

'It's quite a nice job,' he said, a smile in his voice. 'Better than the civil service.'

Laura kissed his cheek. That was what she was meant to do, wasn't it? 'Good morning, Commander. I suppose we ought to get up? I'd rather stay here, though.'

'Good morning, Miss Fellgate.' Alastair finally opened his eyes; when his gaze met hers, it glittered in the morning sun. 'How fares the bruise?'

She touched the plaster and could feel a bump under it, but she knew that was a good sign. She'd be worrying if there wasn't one. 'I'm almost back to normal, you know.' And this time, she pecked a kiss to his lips.

There was a sharp knock on the door downstairs, but Laura barely noticed it. It wouldn't be for her, after all; if anyone needed a vet at this time, their first port of call would be Mr Morgan's office instead. Besides, after her brush with death last night, surely she and Alastair had earned just a few minutes to themselves before they faced the day.

Footsteps thundered by as the toddlers ran downstairs.

'Woof-woof!' they heard one of them shout.

'Sorry about that,' Laura said, feeling that *definitely* required an explanation. 'The neighbour's dog has had puppies, and the boys are desperate for Iris to let them have one. So, we get regular dog impressions from them now. They're such funny little chaps.'

'Laura? Commander Seaton?' Iris called up the stairs. 'There's someone to see you. A Mr Wyngate.'

Laura gasped. What would Mr Wyngate do if he found them in bed together?

'Thank you, Mrs Pearson.' Alastair was the man from the Ministry again, with that polite, patrician commander's manner firmly back in place. He gave Laura a wide-eyed look, though, as if to say, *oops*. 'I shall be down to see him presently.'

There was a pause, and Iris shouted, 'Mr Wyngate says it's rather urgent, Commander.' Then she added, 'Tom, stop that!' Though that wasn't addressed to Alastair.

'Mr Wyngate did *not* say that,' barked a voice from the foot of the stairs. This time, Alastair *did* sit up, his arm round Laura. 'Mr Wyngate said *presently* had better mean in the next sixty seconds. We have business, Commander Seaton! Miss Fellgate, my commiserations on your bruises!'

Laura shook her head, then whispered to Alastair, 'Is he your boss?' She called down, 'Thank you, Mr Wyngate. I'm much better now!'

'He's Mr Churchill's boss,' Alastair deadpanned. 'Are you going to stay at home today or would you like to be there when I call on Mr Morgan?'

'I would come to see you call on Mr Morgan even if I was head-to-toe in a plaster cast and had to be wheeled in on my bed,' Laura told him, and gave him another peck on his lips. 'I do feel a lot more myself now, really. I want to see this. I need to.'

Alastair dotted a kiss to her lips in return and swung his legs down off the bed. 'Shall I call at Mr Morgan's at nine?' he asked. 'He and Mr Pullen have complained about me to the Minister for Agriculture; I doubt he'll be happy to see me.'

Laura nodded. 'Yes, he's usually about at nine, unless he's been called out. I'm so sorry they've complained. They've no right to. You've done your job, that's all. Honestly, and to think that bully Mr Pullen is in line for a knighthood.'

'They hand them out like confetti these days.' Alastair took his coat from the hook where he had hung it last night. Everything had shifted so much in one night; they had found the radio, something concrete at last, and Mr Churchill himself had listened to their concerns. And now, she and Alastair were more than just friends.

Laura's feeling of despair had passed: now, thanks to her determination, the tide had turned. She'd seen far too much: the fire that nearly killed Lottie, the ailing livestock; all disasters set in motion by someone who was supposed to be on *their* side. This was no time for anyone to turn traitor, not when young women like Martha could be cut down just trying to do their job.

'I'll follow you down soon, I'll just get ready,' Laura said, getting off the bed. But she didn't feel dizzy or in pain any more. She felt prepared, ready for action. Whatever that might be.

She gave Alastair one last kiss on his lips. And another; now they'd had one kiss, they didn't seem to be able to stop. 'Good luck with Mr Wyngate,' she whispered.

'His bark's worse than his bite.' He opened the door. 'Sometimes.'

Laura had witnessed horrors in Coventry, she had endured the terror and had seen the carnage and the grief. She couldn't stop the enemy planes from flying in, but she had the chance now to stop the enemy within. And even if they came after her, with poisons or fire, Laura would fight them. She would go on until she fell, if that's what it took.

THIRTY-SIX

Once Laura had washed, dressed and checked the plaster covering the bump on her head, she went downstairs to the kitchen. The boys were no longer rushing about pretending to be dogs, but were quiet, staring in fascination at their visitor. Iris was too. They'd clearly never met a man like Mr Wyngate before.

'Good morning,' Laura said to the Ministry man sitting at Iris's kitchen table with a cup of tea. She was surprised he was still there and hadn't already left with Alastair. 'Sorry I wasn't up and about when you arrived.'

Wyngate held up his hand to acknowledge her, but his attention was still on the children. He sat back in his chair and said, with the air of a conclusion, 'And *that* is why Mr Churchill always brings his dog along to cabinet meetings.'

The boys absorbed that information, before Sam turned to stare hopefully at Iris. 'Mr Churchill has a dog. Please, Mummy, can we?'

Wyngate turned and fixed Iris with an unblinking gaze. 'Mr Churchill has a dog,' he echoed.

'But who's going to take it for walks?' Iris asked them. 'Although I suppose at least we have a resident expert.'

She smiled at her lodger, which only made Laura feel guilty. She still hadn't told Iris she'd lost her job. But she had no intention of leaving Bramble Heath just yet. Not while the traitor was still out there, planning their next attack. The thought of leaving the village felt too painful to face right now, but at least she could put off the conversation for a little longer.

'You do,' Laura replied. 'And perhaps, without Bertie here, and with everything that's been going on lately, you might feel more secure with a dog? Having a pet is wonderful for children too.'

Sam and Tom nodded eagerly, and turned their pleading gazes on their mother.

'We'll see,' Iris replied, before turning to Laura. 'Your commander's gone to the pub to change, by the way.'

Laura nodded. But she wasn't sure why Wyngate hadn't gone with him. It struck Laura then that he was waiting to speak to *her*. She hoped it wasn't because she hadn't yet signed the paperwork.

'I take it you need to see me, Mr Wyngate?' she asked him.

Wyngate nodded and rose to his feet. 'Somewhere we can speak privately.' He turned to Iris and the boys and, to Laura's surprise, something in his manner softened. Just a little, but enough that she noticed it. 'Don't forget,' he said. 'Mr Churchill is all for dogs.' Then he looked back to Laura. 'Miss Fellgate, shall we?'

'Yes, of course,' Laura said. 'We can use the sitting room. It's this way.'

She led Wyngate from the kitchen to the sitting room at the front of the house, and gestured to one of the comfortable armchairs, with its neatly embroidered antimacassar and handmade cushion. He couldn't be used to rooms like this, simple but comfortable. Surely in London he lived in a world of art deco design, all sharp edges and shiny surfaces. At least, what had been spared from the bombings.

Once the door was closed she whispered, 'I'm sorry I haven't signed the papers yet. I really didn't feel very well yesterday, after...' She gestured to the bump on her head.

Wyngate sat, though he made no effort to remove the hat he was wearing. His gaze flickered up to her head and he said, 'It builds character.' He nodded to another armchair, indicating that she should sit. 'I need you to tell me everything you saw and heard last night before you were hit. *Everything*.'

Laura sat down. She tried to gather her thoughts, but it was so odd to be having this conversation with Iris's knitting bag sitting by her chair. She caught sight of the photo of Bertie, smiling like a film star in his army uniform, and swallowed. She had to do her best. Everything they could do to catch the traitor meant that Bertie might come home safely to Iris and their boys; that all those brave young men at the airbase would see their families too; and that Martha – poor Martha – who gave her life so tragically would not have died in vain.

'It was late. About nine, I think. I'd gone to the Goslings' farm on a call, and it took a while for my patient to stabilise,' Laura told him. She was sure he didn't need to know that, but it was helping her to remember what she'd seen and heard. 'I was driving back, and... this all happened in a split second, so bear with me... I saw movement. Obviously it was dark, so I couldn't see much, but I saw enough that I knew there was someone there, a person. They were on the other side of the gate, in the field. Moving away from the road, you see. So, then I drove to the nearest phone box and I rang Alastair. And while I was in the phone box I could see a light. Someone had lit a light, like a candle, because it was flickering, and it was coming from the old shepherd's hut. It's terribly dilapidated, but still offers a little shelter.'

As Laura knew from taking shelter there herself with Alastair, on the terrible night when she'd soothed him through the memories of his own tragedy and something precious had formed between them; a connection, a link, that Laura hoped would grow and never break. And while they had been sheltering, out there in the screaming dark, a Land Girl had made the ultimate sacrifice.

'I know I should've waited for Alastair, but I went over to look,' Laura admitted, returning to the night of her attack. She watched Wyngate's face, wondering if he was about to berate her for her recklessness. 'I just thought, I want this to end now, and if I can get to the hut and find the traitor I can stop them. No more animals will be harmed. The bomb had just hit, you see, and one of our Land Girls died when she tried to save livestock. I couldn't bear the thought that, after dear Martha's sacrifice, the traitor could kill more of the animals and keep attacking the farms. I couldn't let that happen.'

Wyngate watched her, saying nothing. Laura had once thought Alastair unreadable, but looking at this man she knew what unreadable really meant. His expression gave absolutely nothing away, nothing at all.

Then he nodded, a curt, single nod. 'Too many people wait before they act. I'm not one of them.' He blinked. 'And nor are you. You did the right thing.'

Laura smiled at him. She hadn't expected to find that she had anything in common with a man like Wyngate. But it appeared that she did after all.

'So, I crept through the field, as quietly as I could. But the grass is getting long... I suppose they must've heard me,' Laura reflected. 'I suppose I've watched too many films. I put my back to the wall and slid along to the door. And I peered inside. I saw the radio. I was so surprised, because I'd only been in there the day before, and I'd had no idea it was hidden under the straw in there. If only I'd known...'

She wondered if Wyngate needed an explanation for that. 'Got caught in the rain, you see. And there was nothing unusual about the place then. But last night there was. So I went into the hut, to look at the radio, and I heard a footstep and...' Laura felt embarrassed. What, exactly, had she achieved? 'And I don't remember anything more. Just the pain, and everything going dark.'

'And that's where Commander Seaton enters the picture.' Wyngate said, but she didn't feel as though there was anything judgemental in that, it was just a statement of fact. Wyngate reached into his coat and produced a bundle of stapled paper. He leaned out of his chair and offered it to her. 'Read. Sign. Tell nobody. All of this is going to go away, Miss Fellgate, because, if there *are* traitors operating within our shores, we don't want to tell anybody about it. And we must bring them down, fast.'

'Oh, but Mr Wyngate, I'm so sorry,' Laura replied, taking the paper. She felt rather guilty. 'It's all over the village already. We had to tell them, so that they'd be on their guard.'

'Not that,' he said. 'Radios. Other incidents of poisoning. Commander Seaton has already told you more than he should.' Wyngate watched her, though what he was seeing Laura could hardly guess. 'The cases in the region are isolated, so far as Bramble Heath knows. There is no wider, coordinated campaign to undermine the nation's farms. You understand?'

Laura nodded slowly. Now she understood. 'I see... It'll never reach the newspapers, or the radio, or the newsreels at the pictures. I understand.' She was about to start reading through the papers when she looked back up at Wyngate. 'But please don't punish Commander Seaton for telling me. He felt I ought to know, and I'm glad he did tell me too.'

'Commander Seaton isn't with Agriculture; he's in my section. A very capable man. He punishes himself too much already.' Wyngate clearly knew Alastair better than Laura had thought. 'I generally prefer to have the signature before we share information. But I *will* have the signature before I leave.' And he held out a silver pen.

Laura took it from him, noticing what looked like a crest on it. She recognised it. Wasn't that the royal crest?

But wherever Wyngate got his stationery from, it was no business of hers, and she settled down to read. The stern document told Laura, in more words than were perhaps necessary, that she simply needed to keep things secret. She wasn't to tell a soul about the network of traitors that was threatening the whole country from the inside.

She knew very well she could keep a secret, especially when it came down to the security of the realm, so once she reached the last page she signed. Then she passed the papers back to Wyngate.

'Here you are,' she told him. 'All *I* know is that someone's operating locally, a lone crank...' And she gave Wyngate a conspiratorial wink.

He blinked, then returned the wink, and slid the signed agreement into his pocket. As he did, Laura thought about the look that had passed between Sally and Alastair in the George and Dragon's cellar on the night of the air raid. Alastair didn't strike her as an aviation enthusiast, yet he knew the celebrity stunt pilot turned Attagirl somehow. Perhaps Sally'd had cause to sign a document like this one day, not that Laura would ever ask. Careless talk really could cost lives.

'You're about to be unemployed.' It was a statement, not a question.

Laura gasped. He knew, then – but of course he would; he seemed to know everything. 'Yes. My boss sacked me.'

'Something'll turn up, I expect.' He rose to his feet. 'I'll see myself out.' Wyngate strode to the door. Only as he reached it did he pause and turn back to look at her. He tapped his finger to his head, mirroring the place where Annie had applied the plaster to Laura's injury. 'Consider it a war wound, Miss Fellgate. For the greater good.' Then he swept through the door and was gone.

THIRTY-SEVEN

As Laura headed to work, she tried to tell herself it was just another day. But everything was different, in so many ways. She'd been so resigned to never falling in love, and yet her path had crossed with Alastair's and now she carried in her heart the warmth and promise of just that. But despite such expected happiness, she couldn't forget the shadow that hung over her, and over the whole of Bramble Heath, after Martha's terrible death, and with a traitor still on the loose who had thought nothing of starting fires and poisoning livestock, and even trying to crush her skull. And yet, they were getting closer to snaring them, Laura was sure. Hopefully, before anyone else – animal or human – in Bramble Heath could be harmed.

And she'd just signed a document that she could never tell anyone she'd even seen. She was glad that she had, though; her role in the investigation now felt more official.

When she arrived at the practice, Mrs Morgan was standing in the hallway holding a duster. But instead of being her usual busy self, buffing the plaques at the door and the pictures in the hall until they gleamed, she looked rather lost.

'There's gentlemen here to see my husband,' she whispered

as Laura arrived. She glanced at Laura's plaster but didn't remark on it. 'I've seen one of them here before, but not...' Her eyes grew large, no doubt as she thought of Wyngate. 'The other one.'

Laura wondered how he'd spoken to Mrs Morgan. He'd been kind to Iris and the boys, but she suspected he wouldn't have much truck with Mrs Morgan's pretensions.

She glanced over to the waiting room. The door was slightly ajar and she could just about see the shoulder of Alastair's overcoat through the gap. Her heart beat faster; this was the man who was going to confront her boss. But it was also the man she'd kissed; the man who had slept by her side all through the night.

'I'll go in and see them,' Laura whispered in reply. Without stopping to take off her coat, she went over to the waiting room door and knocked, before peering in. She smiled at them. 'Gentlemen?'

Wyngate, to her surprise, was settled back in a waiting room chair, his arms folded across his chest and his fedora tipped down over his face. He gave the impression that he was sleeping, but Laura wasn't so sure. Alastair, on the other hand, rocketed to his feet to greet her, sweeping his own hat from his head.

'Miss Fellgate.' His voice was polite but formal, his manner entirely that of a forces man stuck in a desk job; his eyes, however, betrayed his unmistakable affection. 'Good morning. I'm afraid Mr Morgan appears to be busy.'

'Ha!' Mr Wyngate barked from beneath his hat. He shouted, 'Mrs Morgan, any movement?'

Laura grinned at Alastair. She wished she could've embraced him and given him a kiss, but she tucked that thought away.

Mrs Morgan came bustling into the room. 'He *is* very busy, I'm afraid.'

'Is he with a patient?' Laura asked. 'I can take over.'

But she knew what the answer was, because Mrs Morgan's gaze swivelled towards the sitting room. 'He's... busy.'

'I'm sure he can find time to speak to these two very important government gentlemen, who have come all the way down from London to see him,' Laura told Mrs Morgan. 'Especially as he's in the sitting room.'

Mrs Morgan's mouth dropped open in a comically perfect circle.

So, I'm right, aren't I? What a surprise.

Wyngate slid his hat back on his head and narrowed his eyes. His expression was almost amused when he said, 'I don't wait for the king, and I don't wait for Mr Morgan.' Then he was on his feet and heading for the door at a clip. 'Sitting room, which way?'

Laura could see that Mrs Morgan was caught in a dilemma. This man had the ear of the king, or so he claimed, but at the same time Mr Morgan would've given her strict instructions that the two men from the Ministry were not to be allowed in.

'The king?' Mrs Morgan said, trying to block Wyngate's way. 'Please pass on my most sincere regards to him when you next meet him.' She dropped a curtsey. 'Only you mustn't disturb my husband. Really, you oughtn't to!'

'His Majesty would want you to tell me which way to the sitting room,' Wyngate told her, spinning on his heel. Yet his manner was somehow less stern now, as though he had sensed the briefest chink in her armour. It seemed to Laura as though he was rather enjoying this little sport. 'Or should I ask Miss Fellgate?'

'His Majesty...' Mrs Morgan said in a reverenced, hushed tone. 'Well, in that case...'

Laura gave Mrs Morgan an encouraging smile. Snob though Mrs Morgan was, she felt rather sorry for her being married to Mr Morgan. He ruled the roost, and his wife did whatever he said.

'The sitting room.' Wyngate leaned forward a little, the atmosphere suddenly conspiratorial when he whispered, 'Which way?'

'It's just through there,' Mrs Morgan whispered back, pointing to the sitting room door. Then she backed away, as if she was trying to make herself invisible. Wyngate reached into his coat, his gaze still fixed on her, and when he withdrew his hand he was holding the silver pen with which Laura had signed the agreement to keep the secret they shared.

'His Majesty's pen,' Wyngate said. Gone was the curt man from the Ministry, replaced by this seemingly benevolent character. 'He'd want you to have it.'

Mrs Morgan's eyes widened in amazement. She reached forward, then flinched back. 'His Majesty's? But... no, I couldn't...' But she reached towards it again and delicately took the pen. 'His Majesty's...'

Alastair met Laura's gaze and gave a hint of a smile. Then he placed his hand on the small of her back and shepherded her from the room in Mr Wyngate's wake. When the man from the Ministry reached the sitting room door, he threw it open and strode inside without so much as a pause, announcing, 'Mr Morgan, good morning!'

Mr Morgan reeled back in his armchair with a look of horror on his face. He quickly recovered, threw aside his newspaper and leapt to his feet.

'What in the blue blazes do you think you're doing, bursting into my sitting room like this? Get out!' he bellowed. Then he shook his fist at the wall and, even though his wife wasn't in the room, shouted, 'Mrs Morgan, I told you not to let them come in under any circumstances! Go on, get out!'

Laura looked at the angry, red-faced man, who had belittled her and doubted her, who had sacked her, and who treated his wife like a servant. She wasn't scared of him; she knew she was on the side of the angels. Even if they had come as civil servants in impeccably tailored suits.

In London, Churchill was demanding action, and it was high time her boss understood the reality of the situation. He couldn't be allowed to stand in the way any more. Because if he did, if he spread his scepticism around the village, the traitor might never be brought to justice. They needed everybody to believe that a criminal was at large, a criminal who was trying to undermine everything that the allies were fighting for. Morgan's disbelief couldn't be allowed to infect the community; everyone had to have their wits about them.

'Mr Morgan,' Wyngate said. 'You have placed yourself in a very difficult position and obstructed – wilfully or otherwise remains to be seen – a matter of national security.' He looked to Alastair. 'Commander Seaton?'

'What?' Mr Morgan interrupted in a splutter; his eyes narrowed with rage. 'How dare you barge in here and accuse me like this!'

Laura glanced at Alastair. He looked unmoved in the face of Morgan's anger, and Laura liked him all the more for it.

'Mr Morgan,' Alastair said, 'I have examined the records and I'm satisfied that Miss Fellgate brought her concerns to you. I'm also satisfied that those concerns merited further investigation. Yet you dismissed them as the ravings of a hysterical female, did you not, sir?'

Morgan was looking at Alastair like a boxer sizing up his opponent. Laura remembered the cruel words hurled at her by him and Pullen, and hoped she wouldn't be hearing them again today.

'I knew there was a problem,' Morgan claimed, raising his chin imperiously. 'I merely objected to the way in which Miss Fellgate went about things. Straight to the Ministry, and didn't stop to think about people like my excellent friend, Mr Pullen, local people – important people – people who would be better placed to help. That's a hysterical way to carry on, Miss Fell-gate. Besides, if we must talk about ravings, I know all about you, Commander! Invalided out of the navy, because you're not right in the head!' Morgan jabbed his finger against his scalp, eyes wide.

Laura wished she could grasp Alastair's hand to show him her support.

'There is a measure of truth in that,' Alastair said in a level tone. 'And yet, sir, only one of us appears at face value to have conspired to conceal a campaign of deliberate sabotage of the nation's war effort. I need not tell you which one of us that is.'

'It *is* a worrying story,' Wyngate agreed. 'Especially when we consider your efforts to silence Miss Fellgate by removing her from your practice. Commander Seaton's report contains the same obstructive name again and again. Mr. Charles. Morgan.'

Morgan flinched as Wyngate spoke each particle of his name. His manner changed; the rage was gone. He was stony instead. 'Conspired? That's a very strong word, sirs. You're accusing me of a want of patriotism. I wasn't obstructing – I was merely acting based on the facts available to me. But you're twisting it. You surely can't be suggesting that *I'm* the traitor? Or that I'm in league with them?'

Hadn't he behaved as if he was, though, Laura thought; shutting her up because she'd stood firm in her belief that some-thing was wrong?

'Swallow your damned pride, man!' Alastair suddenly snapped. 'I've come up against too many men like you; you can't see further than the end of the nose you turn up in the air.' This time it was he who jabbed his finger, pointing it accusingly at Morgan. 'Admit it! You were wrong. You ignored her because she's a woman and because the likes of you and your self-satisfied friends have had the run of the land for far too long. Gentlemen from the club, braying and mocking and clicking their gouty fingers

to bring people running.' He glared at Morgan, who seemed to
have been rendered silent. 'You're too blustering and incompetent
to sabotage anything other than your own reputation. Mr Morgan,
you wouldn't have lasted five minutes on my ship, but a year or two
serving your country might've been the making of you.'

Laura was astonished. She glanced at Alastair, wondering
where the mild-mannered civil servant with the dry sense of
humour had gone. *This* was the man who had commanded a
destroyer. And she liked it. Alastair had stood up for himself,
and for her, and for truth.

Wyngate nodded. 'And you'll rescind Miss Fellgate's firing,'
he added, suddenly cutting quite an amiable figure. 'Or I'll
requisition this practice for the Ministry and give it to her
myself.'

'What's your pleasure, *sir*?' Alastair asked.

'Requisition my...?' Morgan's ruddy cheeks turned pale.

Laura knew that Wyngate could do it, too – Heath Place
had been requisitioned by the RAF, and the two families who'd
lived there had to move out, their flight school shut down for the
duration. Countless country homes had been, whether they
were now HQs for the armed forces, hospitals or accommodation for evacuees. Morgan's Georgian gentleman's residence,
with its brass plaques by the door, its comfortable rooms and
expensive paintings, could be yanked from his grasp with one
flick of a pen.

'No... no, you can't do that,' Morgan said, his voice quiet, his
bluster gone. 'This was my father's house. And I built up my
business here. You cannot take it away, just because...' His gaze
fell on Laura. She sensed another insult coming her way, *hysterical female*, or *silly girl*. And yet Morgan looked down at his
well-polished brogues and shook his head. He looked back up at
Alastair and Wyngate, and said, 'Very well, then. I'll do as you
say.'

He looked to Laura again. There was something pathetic in his expression, like a cornered animal. And yet Laura couldn't find any pity in her heart for him.

'Miss Fellgate, I would be delighted if you would consider continuing in your employment here, on the terms on which you were originally hired,' Morgan said with obvious effort. He glanced at Alastair and Wyngate again, and, as if an unspoken demand had passed between them, he added, 'And I should be very grateful if you could find it in yourself to forgive me for my hasty decision to terminate your employment. You are a valued member of this practice. I have never had cause to complain about your conduct or your work. I think we would all agree that we are living through very difficult times, and that it has... erm... led to an error of judgement on my part. I... I am sorry, Miss Fellgate.'

Laura had never thought for a moment that he would change his mind. But he had. He'd just needed some persuading. And she'd certainly never thought that he would apologise. Perhaps this was a new version of Charles Morgan. Perhaps he'd never belittle her again.

'I accept your apology, Mr Morgan,' she said. She took a step forward and held out her hand. He took it, and the two of them shook. It wasn't a particularly firm or enthusiastic shake, but it was a handshake, nonetheless. 'And I would be very pleased to have my job back. I do enjoy working here, you know. It's what I've always wanted to do.'

Morgan swallowed. He looked taken aback to hear those words from Laura. 'I made a very big mistake, Miss Fellgate. I should have listened to you, but I let my ideas – my old-fashioned ideas, I admit – get in the way. I won't any longer, I promise you. Perhaps you would like to have a plaque of your own by the front door? I rather think it's time, don't you?'

'My own plaque?' Laura laughed with excitement. She

glanced at Wyngate and Alastair, then back to Morgan. 'I would love that. I really would!'

'And... I'm sure we might be able to come to an arrangement regarding an increase in your pay?' Morgan added. He was smiling now, as if he'd suddenly discovered the pleasure of being nice to other people.

'I wouldn't say no,' Laura replied. 'Of course I wouldn't. Thank you, Mr Morgan.'

'Don't mention it, my gi— I mean, Miss Fellgate,' Morgan replied.

Peace had broken out, it seemed.

'Thank you, Mr Morgan.' Alastair stepped forward and held out his hand to Morgan. The two men shook. 'I'm glad we've come to an accord.'

'Right. Commander Seaton and I have business elsewhere.' Wyngate gave one of his curt nods. 'Mr Morgan, a word of advice. Your son is serving in Europe, I believe. When he returns, I suggest you show him a little more compassion, should he need it, than you've shown Commander Seaton today. And perhaps extend that courtesy to your wife too; she works very hard.' He nodded towards Alastair. 'The commander holds a Distinguished Service Cross and two bars; you should afford him some respect.' He flicked his gaze to Laura. 'Please show us out, Miss Fellgate?'

Laura headed for the door, but she turned when Mr Morgan said, 'He's looking after dogs, you know. Those dashed clever ones that can detect bombs and mines. I hadn't thought — my goodness, what if he... I extend my apologies to you too, Commander Seaton. God willing my boy will return unharmed in body and mind. Perhaps I have been too hasty. If so, I apologise.'

'Thank you, Mr Morgan.' And Alastair was the gentle civil servant all over again as he bowed his head in acknowledgement. 'And your son has all of our gratitude.'

Wyngate opened the door ready to depart, and Mrs Morgan nearly fell into the room. She must've been listening to everything that was said, Laura realised.

'My compliments to the king,' Mrs Morgan said to Wyngate, with a bow. She held up the pen and leaned round the door to show it to her husband. 'This fellow knows the king, Charles! Look, look at this pen! It was his gift from the king, and now it's *his* gift to me!'

And Wyngate smiled. An actual smile, which he awarded to Mrs Morgan and Mrs Morgan alone, before he swept out of the sitting room and along the corridor with Laura and Alastair following in his wake. Only when he was out of earshot did he turn and tell them in a deadpan whisper, 'It was a toss-up between that and Hitler's pencil.'

Laura did her best to stifle her laughter. 'You've made her very happy, anyway, Mr Wyngate. Now I'm back in my job, I'd better get on. Thank you, both. Really.'

'Your coat's still dusty from where you fell,' Alastair told her kindly. Laura knew that Wyngate would have his suspicions about them now; he seemed to see through everything.

'Oh, I'll take a clothes brush to it, don't worry,' Laura said to him with a grin. He cared for her, and it made her feel all soft and warm inside. She started to unbutton it.

'Wait,' Wyngate suddenly said. He reached out and plucked something from the coat. It came away with a clump of muddied straw. 'What have we here?'

THIRTY-EIGHT

Laura had no idea. She stared at the straw held in Wyngate's fingers, wondering what on earth he could see. 'That must be from the hut. It's full of hay and straw. I always give my coat a good brush at the end of every day, you see, but yesterday it wasn't really on my to-do list.'

But Alastair had seen something of interest too. He exchanged a look with Wyngate, then asked Laura, 'Do you think many women would have cause to go into that shepherd's hut?'

Before she could reply, Wyngate shook his head. 'Not if the radio's been there long enough to get as dusty as it was. That's why our traitor chose it for a base, nobody goes there.'

'Gosh, they really took time to plan it, didn't they?' Laura observed. 'I *had* wondered if courting couples use it. But I'm sure I'd have overheard the Land Girls mentioning it, if that were the case. Besides, in the blackout, couples can get up to all sorts of things without having to slog up the hill to that draughty hut.'

Alastair cleared his throat, then told her, 'It's a blonde hair. Do you see it?'

And there it was, just as Alastair had said: a single long, blonde hair.

'Oh, yes! Yes, I do,' Laura replied. 'Goodness me, it's from the traitor, isn't it? I don't remember getting any mud on my coat at Goslings' farm; I'd taken it off and hung it up out of the way. But... a long hair? A woman's hair?'

'It's something, at least,' Wyngate murmured as he took out a neatly folded handkerchief. He carefully parcelled up the dried mud and straw, with the hair still caught on it, and slipped it into his pocket. 'Right, Commander, shall we?' Laura received a nod of acknowledgement. 'Miss Fellgate. Good job last night.'

'Thank you,' Laura said. She suspected that Wyngate didn't dish out praise very often. 'I'm glad I went and had a look, even though I got a sore head for my troubles. It's taken us a *little* closer, hasn't it?'

Her mind was whirling now. A long, blonde hair. Whose on earth could it be? Women with long blonde hair were everywhere, thanks to Veronica Lake.

He nodded and stepped out onto the path. 'Meet me at the car,' he told Alastair, then strode away. Laura was surprised he'd given them a moment alone; perhaps the curt man from the Ministry had a softer side after all.

Laura glanced over her shoulder, but Mrs Morgan wasn't lurking with her duster now. She smiled at Alastair and took his hand. 'You were wonderful back there,' she whispered. 'Commander Seaton on the high seas again.'

'Maybe he's correct... maybe I'm not right in the head,' he whispered in reply, but his words were tinged with humour. 'A sane man would've knocked him senseless for saying such a thing.'

'A gentleman wouldn't have,' Laura told him. 'And that's exactly what you are. I hope he's realised how wrong he's been. I doubt he'll ever say anything as unkind as that again. And I'm rather glad to have my job back, you know – I really am grateful.

And to think I'll have my own brass plaque by the door soon too.'

Alastair smiled. 'Would you like to join me for dinner at the George tonight?' He asked. 'On Ministry business, of course.'

'I'd love to – to discuss business, of course.' She gave Alastair a wink. Despite the threat of the traitor, and the daily perils of wartime, they had found each other, and there really was something special between them. 'I'll come and find you there later?'

'Seven o'clock?' Alastair suggested. 'I'm going to go up to Heath Place and see George later. In case he wants to talk to someone who's been through it themselves.'

'That's so kind of you, I'm sure he'll appreciate you thinking of him,' Laura replied, touched once again at how caring Alastair was. 'And I'll see you on the dot, Commander.'

Then, confident that Mr and Mrs Morgan wouldn't see, she rose up on her toes and placed a gentle kiss on Alastair's lips.

THIRTY-NINE

Laura's day at work was quite a revelation. Morgan was all smiles and didn't once refer to her as a *girl*. He was sympathetic to her injury and initially told her to take the day off, but Laura refused. She felt much better now. Even so, he insisted on going up to Goslings' farm to check on Petunia and her piglets himself, and came back with a glowing report. He congratulated Laura for the treatment she'd given the sow and surprised her by saying that the Land Girls had impressed him with their *sterling work*.

At lunchtime, he asked Laura's opinion on something he'd read about in a veterinary journal and listened to her reply with what seemed to be genuine interest. He seemed to have finally realised she was a professional as much as he was. That she knew her job, and that she knew the animals, and that she wasn't just a stopgap until he found a vet who happened to be a man.

It shouldn't have taken the threat of his practice being requisitioned, but men like Morgan were so dyed-in-the-wool that the fact this change had happened at all made Laura feel very pleased.

As if he was making up for his past failings, he offered to do everything, even the menial task of scrubbing down the examination table. This left Laura with time on her hands; time she spent in a happy daydream about Alastair. She remembered the scent of his cologne as she'd lain with her head against his chest, and the feeling that there was no place on earth she would rather be than in his strong arms.

The Bramble Heath traitor would be caught soon, Laura was sure. She wasn't frightened any more, not even after being attacked last night, because she wasn't facing this threat alone. The whole village was behind her, and Alastair was at her side. In London, even Churchill was waiting for updates. Whoever it was, their days were numbered.

They had found the radio, and there was that long blonde hair too. She imagined a man, walking out with his glamorous girl, then after kissing her goodnight off he went, into the farms and the fields around Bramble Heath, with fire and poison, a traitor to the country and a traitor to freedom. But little did he know that he'd left his calling card at the hut – a long blonde hair from his girl, caught on the fibres of his jacket, slipping off to land in the hay.

Only who on earth was it, this faceless figure in the shadows?

Once she'd finished for the day, Laura said her goodbyes and made her way home. Morgan even offered to give her a lift to Iris's front door, but she refused. She wanted to walk home and enjoy the spring weather.

The day was sunny and warm with the promise of summer, and Laura walked along the street towards Iris's cottage, her coat slung over her shoulder. She was so happy, she started to whistle.

Then up ahead, just outside Iris's house, she saw Nicola. Laura felt panic bubble in the pit of her stomach. There couldn't have been another poisoning already, could there?

But her fear only lasted a second. Because Nicola was surrounded by a group of evacuees. And in her arms – *is that a puppy?*

The eldest among the evacuees were tall and gangly, the youngest small enough to be carried by the others. They had scraped knees from their adventures, and like everyone else wore clothes that were much repaired. But there was always a sense of wonderment about them as they encountered more and more of countryside life. And the puppy had clearly drawn them to Nicola like a magnet. Not that dogs didn't exist in the cities they'd come from, but wasn't there something about new life that enchanted everyone, especially children?

'Evening, Nicola,' Laura said, as she came close to them. It had to be one of Iris's neighbour's puppies. 'What a handsome little puppy!'

The puppy had patches of brown, black and white fur and the tips of its ears folded over. Its large black nose quested the air, and its huge eyes gazed about at its audience. Laura had seen the puppies when they were first born, but hadn't seen them since they'd got bigger. Now she could see something that she hadn't noticed before.

There was something very familiar about the puppy, and she was reminded of another dog in the village. There was collie somewhere in the mix, but there was terrier too. And she knew just who was responsible for that.

Wilbur.

Laura tried to hide her chuckle. She'd have to have words with Freddy and Sally about that.

'Isn't she cute?' asked Peter, Freddy's brother. Which made him the puppy's great-uncle, Laura decided. 'She looks like Wilbur!'

'Aye, she does,' said Nicola, laughing, giving Laura a cheeky wink. 'Funny, that!'

'And she's ever so good with Winnie!' Of course, Sarah was

among the gaggle of children, her tortoiseshell kitten perched watchfully on her shoulder. 'And Winnie thinks she's all right too!'

Bill, one of the evacuees, stared in fascination at the puppy. He held his freckled face close to the little dog, and his grubby fingers were knitted in excitement. 'I wish I could have one too. She's a little smasher!'

'Are you taking her to Goslings' farm, Nicola? She'll have a wonderful life up there,' Laura said. 'All that space to run around in! Won't she have a lovely time?'

Nicola dipped her head and kissed the puppy's nose. 'We want to give Lottie something to take her mind off... well.' She didn't say any more with the children so happy, but she didn't need to. Martha would never now be far from Laura's thoughts, and she knew every villager in Bramble Heath would hold the brave Land Girl tightly in their hearts as long as they lived. 'You know, something to care for.'

Laura reached out to gently stroke the spotted fur. The puppy wouldn't bring Martha back, but it would be a companion for Lottie when she needed one most. 'That's a lovely idea, I'm sure it'll help her. There's something about new life, isn't there? Hope for the future.'

Nicola smiled. 'That's the shape of it,' she said gently. 'We're expecting lambs to come along tonight, so Lottie'll have plenty to think about what with this young 'un too. She's an honorary Land Girl, aren't you, pet?' And she scrubbed behind the little dog's ears before addressing the children. 'Right, yous! Tell her cheerio and I'll head home.'

The children chorused their farewells to the dog, waving merrily as Nicola lifted the pup's paw and returned the gesture.

'Do us a favour,' Nicola whispered to Laura. 'Tell the commander thanks for the note. Lottie said it meant a lot to her.' She gave Laura a gentle smile, then waved to the motley gang of children again and strolled away.

'We're all going up to the woods to play in the clubhouse,' Sarah informed Laura. 'What're you doing tonight, Laura? Something fun?'

'I'm going to have supper with my friend in the hat,' Laura replied, smiling at the thought that she would be with Alastair again very soon. 'So yes, I'm doing something fun. I doubt *you'd* think it's fun of course, especially if you're going to the clubhouse.'

The evacuees had built the clubhouse themselves, a much-needed place of their own while they were so far from home. It hadn't been long before the local kids joined them, but it was always seen as the evacuees' place first and foremost.

'Take care, won't you?' Laura told her. She knew only too well who was prowling about the village. With any luck the traitor would keep away from the clubhouse, as they clearly didn't want to be caught. But still, Laura couldn't help but worry about Sarah and the evacuees, out there without any adults to keep them safe. 'Make sure you're home before it gets dark.'

'We always are!' Sarah assured her. 'And Winnie likes your mate in the titfer, because he helped her out when she was lost,' And Winnie, as though agreeing, gave a low purr.

'I'll let him know,' Laura said with a smile. 'He's a very kind man. And a very brave one too.'

Laura said goodbye to Sarah, then she went into the house, where Iris was waiting for her.

'My goodness, Laura!' Iris exclaimed. 'I couldn't say anything earlier, but gosh, the circles you do move in. That Mr Wyngate is a lovely man, isn't he? He's got something of a Hollywood leading man about him, that one! But I know you only have eyes for your commander!'

Laura couldn't help but smile at her. 'Shall I let you into a little secret?'

Iris nodded keenly. 'Oh, please! Do! I've spent all day

thinking about the way the commander looks at you. Gazes at you, really. He's falling in love with you, Laura!'

'Well... he's kissed me,' Laura replied, and Iris bounced on her toes with excitement. 'And I've kissed him.'

'I knew it! I knew it.' Iris flung her arms round Laura and hugged her. 'I knew you'd find a boyfriend one day. You're a pretty thing, you are!'

'I'm going to meet him for supper,' Laura told her.

'Let me choose your outfit,' Iris said, and grasped Laura's hand. 'And I'll comb your hair so that plaster's not so noticeable. You'll be the belle of the ball! Well, the belle of the George and Dragon at any rate!'

FORTY

Laura arrived at the George and Dragon just before seven. Iris had chosen for her a pretty dress with a print of blue flowers on it, a very different outfit to the severe skirt suit she'd worn when she'd met Alastair there last time. The pub was busy with the usual customers, the old farmers and the pilots. The atmosphere was a little subdued though; Martha's death was raw. And there was shock too, that death had come to one of Bramble Heath's civilians. Losing the young men from the airbase had come to be a grimly accepted fact of the war, but so far the rest of the village had been unscathed. That was, until the night Martha had run out into the blackout, her sense of duty overriding her instinct to protect herself.

The Land Girls were nowhere to be seen. Not only were they dealing with losing their friend, but it was lambing time now and they were needed on the farms more than ever.

She waved when she saw Alastair. It heartened her to see that he no longer sat on his own but was instead at the bar, chatting amiably to Henry and a couple of the men from Heath Place. There was one unoccupied table in the corner and on it were a pint and a half. It was the table she and Alastair were to share, Laura surmised.

'Hello, Commander!' Laura called. 'Hope you had a good day.' She wanted to give him a kiss hello, but she wasn't sure how Alastair would feel. Although now Iris had been let in on their secret, it wouldn't be long before everyone in the village knew that she and Alastair were a couple.

'Miss Fellgate.' Alastair beamed as he crossed the bar to meet her. She liked the Ministry man in the smart suits, and the Royal Navy officer who had laid waste to Mr Morgan's pretensions. But this was her favourite version of Commander Seaton: casual and smiling, his gaze only for her. And at the bar, a few of the pilots seemed to have noticed too. 'Good evening.'

'Oi,' murmured Chalky, nudging his mate. 'It's true what they say about the navy, then!'

'A girl in every port,' his friend Jack replied, as he thumbed the tobacco in the bowl of his pipe. 'Lucky devils!'

Laura felt a flash of embarrassment, but it was soon gone; they were only teasing, and, knowing Alastair's sense of humour, she was sure he wouldn't mind either. She smiled at him. She wasn't used to this, to dating. It had been so long.

'Only the one port,' Alastair assured Laura, before pecking a brief kiss to her cheek. The airmen mustered themselves to give a cheer, seizing the chance for a little bit of silliness in the midst of their sorrow. In Bramble Heath, everyone knew everyone else's business; Alastair might wear a wedding ring, but now Iris knew he was a widower, so it was likely everyone else did too. A married man would hardly be kissing a single girl so openly, after all. Not here, at least.

She returned his kiss with one on his cheek. She could smell his cologne again. 'It's lovely to see you,' she said, as butterflies danced in her stomach. 'I know it's not been very long, but... by the way, I've got a message for you. I bumped into Nicola earlier

– she's got one of my neighbour's puppies to give to Lottie! And she said to tell you that Lottie says thank you for the note. It meant a lot to her.'

'She'll feel very alone at the moment,' he said. 'That's why I went up to see George too. The poor fellow's bearing up, but it's a long road. I just wanted them to know that people understand. Nobody's ever truly alone.'

Laura rested her hand on Alastair's arm for a moment. 'You're such a sweet man. That was such a lovely thing to do for them.' And she wondered whether anyone had done the same for him.

'I hope Mr Morgan's been a gentleman.' Alastair took Laura's arm and politely escorted her to their table. 'I've spent the day asking after backfiring cars. There's no shortage of them, I'm afraid.'

'What rotten luck.' Laura sighed. 'But yes, Mr Morgan has completely changed. He's actually been rather pleasant. He even asked my opinion on something and listened! It's quite extraordinary. I feel as though I should buy Wyngate a new pen, though.' And she gave Alastair a wink.

But Alastair shook his head. 'He's probably got Stalin's feather quill tucked into his hatband.'

Laura chuckled as they took their seats. She loved Alastair's sense of humour, but having met Wyngate, even briefly, she suspected he might not be wrong.

Ted and his wife brought out plates of food for them, stew and dumplings made from local produce. It wasn't tea at the Ritz, but Laura didn't care. She was a farm girl at heart, and she knew Alastair was a farm boy too, despite his years at sea. Hearty country fare was the most exquisite royal banquet to them.

They chatted and got to know even more about each other, the layers peeling back. Laura couldn't remember having a nicer time, and it made the dates she'd been on in the past look flimsy by comparison.

The more she knew about Alastair, the more she liked him. She cared about him a great deal and, even though they hadn't known each other long, it felt as if she'd known him for ever.

The evening drew on, and Laura knew they'd have to go their separate ways again soon. She would miss sharing her bed with him tonight; it'd feel empty without him.

'Last orders!' Ted shouted and rang the bell.

'Would you like another one?' Laura asked, pointing to Alastair's pint. 'Or a wee nip of whisky for a nightcap?'

'Let's try the whisky,' Alastair decided as the telephone behind the bar began to ring. He rose to his feet. 'Makes a change from rum.'

Ted answered the phone as the bar became suddenly busier and his wife fielded their customers. He looked over his shoulder, scanning the pub, then his gaze settled on Laura.

'Miss Fellgate, it's that Nicola up at Goslings' on the blower,' he called. 'Says Mr Morgan's already out on a call, and would you go up as soon as you can.'

Laura's heart plummeted. *Not again.*

'She says it's one of the ewes, she's a first-timer that's got into strife with lambing,' Ted added.

'Tell her I'll be there as soon as I can,' Laura said, relieved that the traitor hadn't struck again... yet, anyway. She turned to Alastair and kissed his cheek. 'It's been such a lovely evening, Alastair, but I must dash.'

'Duty calls?' Alastair asked. 'I'll come along too if you like.'

'Oh, would you?' Laura smiled at him. She knew he loved being on the farms. 'After last night, I'd appreciate having you around. You're my honorary bodyguard now!'

While she was teasing, there was fear behind her words. Because going out to the farm meant heading into the lanes again, to the place where she had been so cowardly attacked.

The blonde hair might be a clue but, like a needle spinning on a compass, it hadn't settled to point at anyone yet. But Laura had to do her job, serving the farmers and their livestock, because the nation depended on them. Even if that meant crossing the path of the traitor out there in the dark. It was a risk that Laura was willing to take.

FORTY-ONE

They hurried back to the practice so that Laura could collect her car. The boot was full of kit that was essential to deal with lambing.

'I love this time of year,' Laura admitted, as she drove them through the dark, evening lanes towards Goslings' farm. She tried to focus on the long night of lambing ahead, but every shadow threatened to make her jump. 'The lambs keep everyone on their toes, but a field full of spring lambs bouncing about is one of the loveliest sights you can see. It'll give the Land Girls something to celebrate after... after losing their friend.'

'There's barely a moment to even think on a farm in lambing season. New life... it'll help,' Alastair said gently. 'How's Petunia? Feeling better?'

'Yes, she's doing very well, and so are her piglets,' Laura told him. 'I still can't believe Morgan insisted on going to check on her and had nothing but praise to give when he got back, for me *and* the Land Girls. I think you and Wyngate gave him a shock, and it was exactly what was needed to get him to change his ways.'

Out of the corner of her eye, she saw Alastair allow himself a little smile of satisfaction.

'We lifted fingerprints from the radio,' he told her in a hushed voice, as though they might be overheard. 'With fair luck, they'll be on file. I hope so.'

'You *did*?' Laura glanced away from the road to Alastair just for a second. 'That's wonderful news. And with that blonde hair we found too, it can't be long now before we have a name!' She felt hopeful. They were definitely closing in on the traitor now. They had to be.

But what did that mean for Bramble Heath, the friendly little village that had welcomed refugees and evacuees and pilots into its heart? The village that had welcomed her as warmly as if she'd grown up here. It was almost impossible to imagine that somewhere in this perfect corner of England there lurked a traitor, someone who would put the food supply of their countrymen at risk. Someone who would go as far as setting fire to a farm, endangering the lives not only of livestock but also of the farmers and the brave Land Girls and innocent young evacuees who lived with them. But there was a traitor somewhere among them, someone who knew the place well enough to have stayed out of sight all this time, someone who wouldn't stand out as a stranger in their midst.

They were on higher land now, above the village. Its streets were laid out below them, the moonlight catching features here and there of the cottages and shops.

'Someone down there is a traitor, Alastair,' Laura said with a shiver. 'Someone I've passed in the street. Someone I've said good morning to. I could've treated their dog or their cat, without having any idea that they want to harm England, that they were capable of poisoning livestock, setting fires to farms, attacking people, all in the name of the Nazis.'

He nodded, thoughtful. 'Somebody local... but somebody who has to drive all the same?' He might've been thinking aloud, as he answered his own question almost immediately. 'So they can carry the feed, but...' From the corner of her eye, Laura saw her passenger shake his head. 'The hut's in an excellent area for this sort of business. Undisturbed... secluded enough for cover, high enough to ensure an excellent reception on the radio. The problem we have now is *they* know *we* know. They're going to lie low.'

'And we won't be able to catch them. They'll wait until we feel secure again, then strike with something else?' Laura shook her head. 'Or go to another village and sabotage the home front there? Oh, how horrible. But we might have fingerprints, and there's the hair too. It's not entirely hopeless, is it?'

'Not at all. We'll find them.' And there was a real resolve in Alastair's words, a determination to win at any cost. Laura wondered what he'd do when the war was won, this man who had lived three lives already. Would he go back to Yorkshire, or even put out to sea? She couldn't see him sitting behind a Ministry desk all his life, and London held no comforts for him now. 'And we have their frequency, which should shut them down for a little while at least. It's something, Laura, when before last night we had nothing.'

'Yes, we're definitely further forward than we were,' Laura said confidently. 'And I wonder, maybe one of these other traitors elsewhere in the country – the ones I don't know about at all, of course – could leave a clue that dovetails with what we've found here, and everything ends up being tied up nicely... unless that only happens in films?'

Alastair smiled and shook his head. 'Films only, I'm afraid.' He gave a long sigh. 'Won't it be nice to drive these lanes on a spring night without worrying about air raids and traitors? One day...'

'Oh, I know.' Laura sighed nostalgically. 'We could actually really enjoy this beautiful country then, and not have to worry about it being brought down by attacks from all sides and from within.'

Laura turned the car into the lane that led up to the Goslings' farm. They were passing the very spot where she'd leapt out of the car to examine her first poisoned cow. If it hadn't been so dark, she was sure she would've seen the tyre tracks where she'd pulled to a sudden halt.

'Will you stay in Bramble Heath after the war?' Alastair asked.

'Maybe, if there's a job for me here,' Laura replied. She wished she could picture the village without tape on the windows and government posters on the walls, or without the bustling airbase. 'It is a lovely place. But once Mr Morgan's son is back, I'm not sure there will be anything for me to do. We'll have to see. And what will you do, Alastair? Will you go back to Yorkshire and the pig farm?'

He shook his head. 'My brother's worked that farm all his life; it'll be his when the time comes,' he replied placidly. 'Vicky and I always planned for a farm of our own. And not just pigs either.' He glanced at Laura and gave a smile. 'But definitely a farm. Somewhere.'

'There might be one around here that takes your fancy,' Laura told him. With a grin, she added, 'And I promise you'd get mates rates if you need a vet!'

She parked the car near the barn where she knew the ewes were kept. Even before she got out of the car, the baas of the sheep filled the air. Laura's wasn't the only vehicle either. She recognised the Parkers' old jalopy, even Farmer Bryant's trap, though the pony that pulled it would be munching a snack safely in the barn by now. No matter what the traitor tried to do, Bramble Heath and its friends would always pull together.

'Here's the maternity ward,' Laura told Alastair, not that he wouldn't have realised. 'And everyone comes to help!'

He nodded as Nicola emerged from the barn at the sound of

the engine. Seeing her visitors, she waved a welcoming hand and trotted towards the car.

Laura climbed out. The pretty dress that Iris had chosen felt rather ridiculous now. 'What's up? Ted said it's one of the young ewes with her first lamb?'

'Aye, it's triplets,' Nicola told her. 'Are you wanting some scruffs? You don't want to spoil your frock.'

And she glanced towards Alastair as he emerged from the car, clearly putting two and two together. Her gaze dropped to his left hand, where he wore the gold wedding band, then settled on Laura again.

'I've got some clothes in the car,' Laura replied, hoping Nicola wasn't judging her. But what else would she think, seeing Laura in a frock and a wedding band on Alastair's finger? Perhaps Iris hadn't spread the word that Alastair was a widower as quickly as Laura might have expected. 'I didn't have time to nip home and change, but I've come prepared.'

'You can change in my room,' Nicola told her. Then it was Alastair's turn to receive his instructions. 'Whatever Laura needs, mate, you all right to cart it along to the barn while she gets out of her glad rags?'

Alastair responded with a nod. 'I'm the assistant,' he confirmed.

'Canny.' Nicola smiled. 'It's doing us all good, keeping busy.'

Laura smiled gently. She knew Nicola was thinking about Martha; it was unavoidable that the loss would be on their minds.

She went over to the boot and took out the canvas rucksack with her change of clothes in it, and her wellingtons.

'Could you take my vet bag, please?' she asked Alastair with a smile. 'And we'll need some rope too.'

She was ordering about a man from the Ministry and the former commander of a destroyer. He deserved a kiss, but she couldn't give one to him yet, or Nicola's eyebrows would shoot off her head.

Alastair had grown up on a farm, so he didn't need too much instruction. Laura knew she could leave him to gather what she needed while she headed off to Nicola's room above the farm store to change into something a little more worka-day. They trudged across the yard, still slick from the previous night's rain, and away from the bustle of the lambing barn.

'Was it his wife what he lost?' Nicola asked as they walked. 'That's what the note to Lottie was about?'

'Yes, it was,' Laura replied in a whisper. 'She was killed in the Blitz. So, he knows what it's like to lose the person you love.'

'Too much of it about. Martha might not've been here long, but she was one of the family. We all miss her, it hasn't really sunk in yet that she's gone.' Nicola sighed, shaking her head. 'Lottie's been down to the barn to help, but she's back up in her room for a bit now with her little pup. I told her to come down whenever she's ready; she needs her rest.' She glanced up at a window, which Laura surmised must be Lottie's room. 'Mine's second on the left, top of the steps. I'll see you back at the barn, veterinary.'

'Right you are, Nicola,' Laura said. 'I'm glad Lottie's been down to help. It'll do her good to be around people, even for a little while.'

Laura went into the house and found herself thinking of her home back in the Cotswolds, with the huge kitchen and large wooden table, the stone flagging on the floors and the bunches of herbs hung from the ceiling. As she carried on, into the hallway and up the stairs, a dreadful thought struck her.

Had the traitor hit Oxfordshire too? Had her family had to suffer attacks and losses like the farmers around Bramble Heath, or worse? And what about Alastair's family in Yorkshire, who made their living from a farm as well?

But we're going to stop you. You're not going to harm anyone else.

She got to Nicola's bedroom, a neat, comfortable little room, and changed into some thick, old trousers and a short-sleeved blouse. Male vets could strip to the waist, but Laura wouldn't. She slipped a cardigan on over the top, and she was ready.

Then a door creaked open, and she saw someone watching her through the crack.

Lottie.

Her face was grey with woe, her eyes red-rimmed from crying.

Laura stilled. 'Oh, Lottie, I'm so sorry about what's happened.' Lottie nodded without saying a word in reply. 'When I've finished here with the sheep, I could take a look at your puppy if you like?'

Lottie smiled. For a moment she was silent, as if she was finding the words. 'Thanks, veterinary. I'll bring her down later.'

It felt significant somehow, that Lottie was willing to come down and join everyone else instead of hiding herself away with her grief. Not that Laura wanted to rush her, but if she felt ready to spend even a small amount of time with the other Land Girls then that had to be positive. And maybe being around her friends would help her.

'Great,' Laura said. 'You take care now.'

And Lottie slowly closed the door.

Having come face-to-face with Lottie's pain, Laura fought against the memories of Coventry again; she'd seen too many people grieving. And out there, the traitor lurked, someone who would willingly ruin even more lives. No, Laura wouldn't stand for that. She wouldn't let them win.

FORTY-TWO

Laura saw Alastair waiting for her by the door to the barn, carrying everything she needed to help the struggling ewe.

'Poor Lottie,' she whispered to him as she took her vet bag. 'I think she might come down in a bit, when she's ready. I can't begin to imagine how she feels, though. But she knows she's surrounded by friends, and that has got to help her right now.'

'I saw George earlier,' Alastair said, glancing up at Lottie's window. 'Poor fellow's beside himself. I just wanted him to know that I was here to listen, if he wanted to talk. I know it's not much, but...' He shook his head sadly. 'He's lost so many friends, all the RAF lads have. This bloody war...'

Alastair would know more than most how George was feeling, both men having lost the women they loved. 'It can't have ever crossed his mind that he'd lose his girlfriend. Working out here in the countryside, even if the farm's near an airbase, you'd think she'd be as safe as anyone can be during this war.'

But there were unseen dangers everywhere, whether it was a bomb that fell from an enemy plane, or a fire started by a traitor. But despite the risks Laura, and everyone on the farm, had jobs to do, and Laura knew all too well what a long, hard job lambing was, although the rewards made it more than worth-while. They would carry on, doing their bit for the war effort.

Laura heard an engine approach and looked up to see Joan arriving in her van. It was odd to see her making deliveries so late. She parked up and hopped down from the vehicle.

'Evening, everyone!' Joan greeted them, looking from Laura to Alastair. 'I heard they're busy with the lambing, so I've come to help.'

Laura smiled. That was one of the things she loved about the countryside, how everyone lent a helping hand.

'An extra pair of hands will be more than welcome, I'm sure,' Laura told her. 'Especially after losing poor Martha.'

Joan's expression was grave. 'Wasn't that a terrible thing? Such rotten bad luck.' She glanced up at the sky, as if she expected another plane to pass, another bomb to fall. 'If only this dratted war was over...'

Alastair greeted the new arrival with a gentle smile and said, 'We'll get there. If everyone pulls together like the people in these parts do, we'll soon have the Nazis on the run.'

Joan gave a decisive nod of agreement, then headed off into the barn.

'It's so good to see everyone doing their bit,' Laura remarked. 'Even when things are so difficult and sad.'

With a quick glance around the empty farmyard, Alastair dotted a kiss to Laura's cheek.

'Come on, veterinary,' he teased. 'Time to put you to work.'

FORTY-THREE

Lambing season was in full swing at the Goslings' farm. Although it was dark outside, bedtime long past, the barn was buzzing with activity in the light cast by the lanterns. Pens had been set up, some with mothers and their youngsters, and others with pregnant ewes who were waiting for their time. The mothers were contented and happy, licking their lambs or standing patiently as the lambs suckled. They had got through the difficult part, but the mothers-to-be were more nervous, even as the Land Girls kept a watchful eye on them. Laura could understand why; the barn was full of noise and scents, of new life, and of life hovering on the cusp of death.

In one pen, the Parker sisters sat either side of a ewe who had just given birth. The sheep looked rather stunned, until the lamb was presented to her and she lowered her head to sniff. In another pen, Frances sounded like a midwife as she knelt beside a ewe.

'That's it!' she encouraged. 'You're doing really well! Keep pushing, girl, you're nearly there!'

But it was another pen that Laura was heading to, where she could see Alastair and Mrs Gosling peering into the pen, their expressions full of concern, as Joan sat cross-legged beside the patient. Like some of the Land Girls, she'd rolled up her sleeves and tied her hair beneath a headscarf to keep it out of the way. Unlike them, though, she was turning a little bit green at the scenes unfolding around her.

In the middle of the pen, a ewe lay on her side. Laura could see that her waters had broken, soaking the straw in the pen. Two legs poked out from behind her, but it was clear she was struggling. Her belly was huge; she evidently was carrying more than one lamb, and Laura's heart sank. There could be a devil of a tangle inside her, and the clock was ticking.

'Poor girl. Has everything stopped?' Laura asked, as she peeled off her cardigan.

Joan looked up and nodded as Shona hurried over to join them with Nicola.

'She's just been laying there,' Joan said, her eyes wide. She didn't look as though she'd ever seen anything quite like it. 'I didn't think— the poor thing!'

'Come on, pet,' said Nicola. Joan scrambled to her feet and Shona helped her to climb over the rail of the pen. 'Go and fetch yourself a cuppa. We'll soon have her right.'

Joan's lip trembled as Shona rubbed her back. She looked to Laura and said, 'I hope you can save them.'

'All right!' Nicola clapped her hands together. 'Let's make some space for the veterinary to get in. C'mon, folks, leave her to work.'

Laura climbed into the pen, her mind whirring with what she needed to do. In her mind, she saw a cascade of diagrams from her veterinary textbooks, and journal articles floating page by page, with all the latest methods for dealing with just such an emergency. Following fast came her own memories from the farm she'd grown up on, when she was allowed to stay up well past her bedtime to help with the lambing.

She'd seen so many cases like this before, but she knew that each and every one of them was different.

'I'll need a bucket of warm water, soap and a towel, please,' she said, and she knelt down behind the sheep.

'That one came from a bunch of triplets herself,' Mrs Gosling told her. 'I'm not surprised she's popping at the seams with lambs. Anyway, we're prepared, here you go veterinary.'

She was always "veterinary" at times like this, and afterwards, once the cup of tea arrived, she was Laura. Mrs Gosling passed her the bucket and she soaped her arms, ready.

Laura gently pressed the sheep's sides, trying to work out what was going on. Elbows and knees poked against the sheep from the inside. Then she gently slipped her hand inside the sheep, closing her eyes so that she could concentrate on what she could feel.

First one lamb, whose front feet had already entered the world. Behind it, another, whose head was turned, leaning against its sibling's back, its legs tangled with still another lamb, which was further inside. All three were alive, their heartbeats insistent against Laura's hand, as if they were telling her how much they wanted to live.

And all the time as she felt her way inside, the ewe's contractions continued, squeezing against her lambs and against Laura, but they were faint, as if she was giving up.

Laura tried to not think too much about the fact that if she was giving birth she wouldn't have wanted someone doing this to her. But what else could they do? The sheep let out a plaintive bleat of complaint.

'I'm sorry, it's not comfortable for you at all, is it?' Laura said gently. Then she told her audience, 'There's three lambs in there, all twisted together. I'll get the first one out, then perhaps it'll get things going again – but I'll wait with her, of course, in case it seizes up. We don't want the last two getting stuck as well.'

She looked up at Alastair. What on earth must she look like, kneeling in the soaking hay, blood trailing up her bare arm? It wasn't much of a date. But he'd grown up on a farm. He'd understand better than most.

He met her gaze and she saw affection in his eyes and something she barely ever saw from Mr Morgan or indeed any other man: respect. 'Anything your assistant can do?' Alastair asked.

Laura nodded. She was so glad he'd come with her; he was just the sort of person she wanted to work alongside. 'I'm going to tie a rope round the first lamb's legs. I'll need to keep my arm inside, so you'll need to pull – if you don't mind?' She added with a smile, 'An old sailor like you must've had a lot of practice at tug o' war. Except these are lambs – and they're tough as old boots!'

Alastair began to unbutton his shirt, revealing a pristine white undershirt beneath. It wouldn't stay pristine for long.

'Hoisting the mainbrace?' he teased gently as he threw his shirt over the rail of the pen, then climbed into the pen and knelt beside Laura.

They were sitting very close, and for a moment the scent of his cologne overwhelmed the farmyard smells of straw and dung and blood. She wished she could've kissed him at that moment – even just a quick little peck. But she couldn't, not with everyone watching.

Laura gently tied a secure knot round the lamb's legs. It had to be tight enough not to slip, but not so tight that it would injure the creature. She passed the end of the rope to Alastair. His strong arms were just what was needed.

'I'm going back in,' Laura told him. She lay flat on the hard ground, the wet straw scratching against her. She slipped her arm inside again, checking to see if the unborn lambs had changed position. But they were stuck fast for now.

She pushed the second lamb's head gently from its resting place against its sibling's back, holding it away even as a cramp started up in her hand, then she looked over her shoulder at Alastair.

'Commander Seaton – pull!' she instructed. Alastair had already looped the rope several times round his elbow and, at her word, he tightened his grip on it and pulled.

Understandably, the ewe bleated in protest, but as Alastair pulled Laura felt the first lamb's body slide against her arm. It took only a moment for her to be able to let the second lamb's head drop back, and a slithery, very-much alive lamb entered the world.

Laura laughed with relief. 'Thank heavens for that!'

The sheep tiredly lifted her head, her nostrils twitching, and looked back to see her lamb. She fidgeted her front legs, as if she wanted to turn round.

'Quick, let's get that lamb up to her face,' Laura said. Her arm was still inside the ewe, so that she could guide out the last two without further tangles. The mother's contractions suddenly kicked in with full force, squeezing tightly against Laura's arm. 'Ouch! Oh – and the rope needs to come off the legs. We're back in business, everyone; I think these last two are going to shoot out!'

Alastair quickly untangled the rope from the lamb's legs and then, with careful tenderness, he scooped the newborn into his arms and presented it gently to the ewe.

Mother Nature stepped in, and the new mother enthusiastically licked her little one with reserves of energy that never ceased to surprise Laura. The lamb, who had been so still moments earlier, struggled to its feet. Laura watched, even as she separated the legs of the second lamb from its sibling, and her gaze settled on Alastair. Seeing the battle-scared commander, who'd fought through so much, beside the newborn lamb was one of the most touching sights she'd ever seen.

She saw Alastair let out a long breath of pure relief. For a moment he hung his head, then he lifted it again and looked back at Laura.

'It's one of the best things on earth, isn't it?' she said to him. After everything that'd had happened over the past few days, after the senseless poisonings and the tragic death of poor Martha, seeing new life held more wonder than ever for Laura. And for Alastair too, she knew.

'It is,' he replied. 'It really is.'

'I've brought you both a cup of tea,' Joan told them as she returned to the pen. 'For when you're done. Is she all right?'

'Thanks,' Laura told her. 'I'm really looking forward to a cuppa! She's doing well. One down, two to—'

Laura never got to finish her sentence. A strong contraction from the ewe forced the second lamb to emerge and Laura laughed as amniotic fluid gushed out with it, soaking her trousers.

'Commander Seaton, I don't suppose you'd do the honours with this one too, while I help out the last one?' Laura asked him. She could feel the third lamb's face, and received a nip on her finger for her troubles. 'It's lively!'

Nobby Bryant strode across to the pen with Farmer Gosling, dusting off his hands. 'Now then veterinary!' He gave Farmer Gosling a nudge as Alastair gathered up the second lamb and, with the same tenderness, brought it to its mother. 'She's not bad for a lass, this one. In it up to her elbow and not a word of complaint!'

'And drinks less of a man's brandy than old man Morgan!' Gosling told his fellow farmer, returning the nudge with one of his own. It was a rare word of respect from two of the village's most established men of the land, and it was something Laura had never expected to hear.

The ewe began to lick at the face of her second triplet and, just like its sibling, the little lamb stood on wobbly feet. The farmers and Joan looked on at the scene as Bryant said, 'Now then, Mr Ministry Man, this is *real* work, eh?'

'And cleaner than London,' Alastair deadpanned.

The Land Girls were peering over the pen now, even Frances, who must've finished delivering her own ewe without any trouble. Beside her, Laura saw another face, one she was very glad to see – Lottie's.

She still looked drawn and pale, but she was watching the two lambs as they stood beside their mother, nudging at her belly for milk. In her arms, she saw a bundle; the green of a Land Girl jumper and, poking out from it, the brown-and-white face of her puppy.

Laura didn't say anything, but gave Lottie an encouraging smile, and she was pleased beyond words to see her smile returned – just a tiny bit, but it was enough. Nicola came to join them at the pen, placing one protective hand on Lottie's shoulder as they watched.

The third lamb was a fighter and didn't need much help. Laura carefully guided it out as it wriggled its way to freedom and to life. She collected it up from the straw and went to sit beside Alastair as she presented the ewe with her lamb. Mother and child instantly bonded, Laura was pleased to see.

What a job that was. But it was always worth it, especially when it had such a happy result and she could watch the first moments in these innocent new lives.

She couldn't think of anyone she'd rather share this with than Alastair. He'd been so battered by life, so bruised and wrung out, but here in this chaotic barn was hope. It was a little messy, perhaps, but it was proof that sometimes endings could be happy ones.

'Cuppa before round two!' Nicola announced. She gave Laura and Alastair a respectful nod. 'You twos are a heck of a team.'

Laura washed in the bucket and passed Alastair the soap.

He'd got pretty covered too, but he didn't seem to care. There was something in his eyes, a twinkle that she'd seen for fleeting seconds, but now it was shining bright. He was in his element, enjoying every second, and Laura was beyond pleased to see it.

They had a hasty cup of tea, before another ewe got into trouble, and Laura and Alastair worked in tandem again to bring twin lambs safely into the world. It was turning into another late night, but Laura didn't mind. It was one of the best parts of the job, to help on evenings like this. And with all of them there, from the farmers, Lottie and the other Land Girls, to her brave Ministry man, she felt the spirit of Bramble Heath more strongly than ever before. The spirit of England itself: courage, hope, determination and community. Martha would have been proud of them all.

And this was why the traitor couldn't win. This village, and communities like it across England, must be protected at all costs.

FORTY-FOUR

It was quite a night for births at Goslings' farm, but eventually things quietened down. Laura checked over the newborns and their mothers and knelt with her stethoscope pressed against the mothers-to-be, trying to work out how many more twins and triplets might come.

She was exhausted and filthy, but beyond happy. She was in her element.

'Last wash in the bucket,' she said to Alastair with a wink, as Mrs Gosling brought them some fresh water and a clean towel. 'You're rather enjoying yourself, Commander, aren't you? Although after tonight, I think I'll have to call you Uncle Alastair! I'm sure the lambs do already.'

'I've missed farm life,' Alastair admitted as he drew the now far from pristine undershirt over his head and dropped it onto the straw. 'You were absolutely smashing, you know.'

'Just doing my job,' Laura told him as she lathered up. 'You were wonderful. All that pulling you were doing!'

She couldn't help her gaze wandering to his strong arms and his bare chest. If Alastair noticed, he didn't give any indication.

Instead, he took the soap from her and lathered his own hands
and the arms she'd been so busy admiring.

'It's going to be like this now for the next little while.' Laura
sighed. 'Just as well I've got lots of these blouses!'

She desperately wanted to tumble into a deep, hot bath, but
shortages meant it wasn't possible to do that every night of the
lambing season, unfortunately.

Lottie was standing by a pen, watching a new mother with
her twins as she held her puppy. A blue ribbon had been tied in
a bow on the dog's collar, and Laura realised that it was one of
Martha's ribbons that had once adorned her hair. Lottie wore a
gentle smile, and Laura knew that she was healing, although, as
Alastair had said, it would be a long road. As she looked at those
newborn siblings, was she thinking of the sister she had lost?
And yet, as the lambs bleated and took their awkward first steps,
Laura hoped that Lottie was comforted in some way; her sister's
death had been tragic, and yet there was still hope.

'I'm glad Lottie came down,' Laura whispered to Alastair as
he retrieved the shirt he'd taken off before helping to deliver the
lambs. 'There's something magical about lambing season, isn't
there? Maybe it helped her, even a little.'

Busy buttoning his shirt, Alastair looked over towards
Lottie. 'I hope so.'

Once Laura had washed as best she could, she went behind
some bales of hay to change out of her dirtied clothes and back
into the pretty dress she had been wearing earlier. She did what
she could to tidy her hair, but she suspected Alastair wouldn't
mind that she looked rather windswept.

As she came out from behind the hay, Alastair strolled
across the barn to join her.

'Ready for bed?' he asked. As soon as he'd said it, his expression told Laura that he'd just realised how that might sound to
her. He shrugged and teased, 'Once a sailor...'

Laura chuckled. 'Maybe you'd prefer a hammock in that case?'

Whatever Alastair might have said to that went unsaid, as Joan made her way across the barn towards the couple. She looked as exhausted as everyone else and still a little green around the gills. By now in her coat, and stifling a yawn, no doubt she was happy to finally be leaving.

'I don't know if this is important, but...' Joan glanced around, then dropped her voice to a whisper. 'I left my delivery up here until last because I knew they might want me to hang around and help. When I turned into the road up to the farm, I saw something that struck me as really odd.'

'Go on,' Alastair told her.

Joan brushed her hand over her headscarf, then fussed her fingers against her buttons again. Whatever had happened, it looked as though it had really unsettled her.

'There was a little delivery wagon, a bit like mine, parked on the verge,' she whispered. 'The driver had just got out and was faffing over by the fence where the trough is. When he saw me, though, he ran like the clappers back to the van and took off. It didn't feel right to me.'

Alastair's gaze darted over to Laura's. If Joan was right, she might've looked the traitor right in the face.

'Funny little bloke he was,' she went on. 'Wearing an eyepatch of all things.'

Despite the warmth of the barn, Laura shivered. *No, she must be wrong. She* must *be. It can't be Smudge. Oh, no, it* can't *be him!* She glanced at Alastair. Was he thinking the same thing? Smudge, of all people. What on earth could've happened to change the allegiance of a man who'd seemed so devoted to his commander, to his country? It must've all been an act. A deception. A betrayal so terrible, she could hardly bear it.

'An eyepatch.' Alastair was the man from the Ministry

again, utterly unreadable. But a muscle in his jaw tensed as Joan took a little bag from her pocket and held it out to him.

'I was sure he was mucking about with the troughs, so I scooped this out.' She put the bag in Alastair's palm. 'Look, it might be nothing, but...'

Alastair opened the bag and glanced inside. Then he nodded.

'Thank you,' he said. 'I suspect I may need to speak to you again.'

Joan nodded too. 'I'm always delivering around the village, but my name's Joan Hodgson. If you need to get in touch, I work at East Grinstead Agricultural Supplies.' She gave Laura an apologetic smile. 'Well, I hope that might be a bit of help. You did ever so well tonight, Laura. You get off to bed now; that's where I'll be soon enough.'

'Thanks, Joan,' Laura replied. 'I'm about to fall flat on my face if I'm honest! Bed's definitely where I want to be. Get home safe now, won't you?'

She tried to smile, but she couldn't. *Smudge?* He'd been delivering things to the veterinary practice for as long as Laura had worked there. Could he have been poisoning the packages he'd brought? Was this because he'd lost his eye serving his country, and now he was taking his twisted revenge?

'Drive safely, Miss Hodgson,' Alastair said, watching silently as Joan made her way out of the barn. Then he put the little paper bag into his pocket and said, 'I appreciate her keeping her eyes open, but we can rule Smudge out. He's a good man.'

'But who can it be?' Laura whispered. 'I don't want to believe it's Smudge either, but he's the only delivery driver I know of who wears an eyepatch. Could she... could she maybe have seen a shadow on the traitor's face and *thought* it was an eyepatch?'

But Alastair shook his head again, and Laura could only

hope his loyalty wasn't misplaced when he said, 'There's not a chance it's him. I'll have to speak to Wyngate, but I'll make sure he knows what I think.' He gave a nod, and it was clear there was no room for doubt in his mind. 'Smudge is one of the finest men I've ever known. Whoever left that poison she found, it wasn't him.'

Lottie, who had been gazing into the pen at the lambs, looked over at Alastair. Rather shyly, she came across the barn towards them.

'Hello, I just wanted to say thank you for the note, Commander.' Her voice was tired and tinged with sadness. 'It meant so much that you thought of me. It's been such a... a dreadful time.'

Alastair gave a gentle nod and replied, 'I hope it didn't seem presumptuous, but... I felt as though there was nobody else in the world when I lost my wife.' And Laura's heart went out to him again, just as it went out to Lottie. 'But you're not alone, Miss Morley. If you ever need someone to listen, someone who's been through this, think of me.'

'Thank you, that's so kind of you,' Lottie replied. She sniffed, before delving into her pocket and drawing out a hand-kerchief. 'Sorry, it comes and goes, doesn't it? You know, I just haven't properly slept since... since it happened. I managed to drift off a bit earlier, just after dinner, but I can't have been out for long before I woke with a start. Joan's van backfired and I was wide awake again.' She rolled her eyes. 'Thanks a lot, Joan!'

Joan's van backfired.

A thrill ran up Laura's spine at those words, and she turned to Alastair.

'Backfired?' Alastair's tone was filled with urgency. He looked from one woman to the other. 'Blonde?' he asked, as Nicola wandered over to join them. She looked to Lottie, then to Alastair and Laura, her expression questioning.

'She is,' Laura replied. 'Oh, heavens, she *is*! How could I have forgotten that? But we've been so busy all evening, and – she was wearing her hair under a scarf. If I'd seen it, maybe— Alastair, she drives around, she knows all the farms...'

Laura's tiredness disappeared. Her thoughts were spinning. Could it be Joan? That sweet-natured, friendly woman who had done her best to help them on the farm tonight? A villager known, well-liked and trusted by everyone at Bramble Heath? Could she really be the traitor, the one who'd crept through the lanes under cover of darkness, spreading fear, death and destruction?

Would Joan really betray her village, her country? But why?

Then Alastair, despite what they'd just heard, addressed Lottie in the same kind manner he had only a few minutes ago.

'You won't get over it,' he said. 'But you *will* get through it. Just don't shut yourself away. Believe me, loneliness is...' He shook his head and Laura wanted to embrace him, just as she had last night. 'Let your friends be friends.'

Nicola touched Lottie's arm and smiled. 'Aye,' she said. 'We're all sisters here.'

Lottie leaned against Nicola, resting her head on her shoulder. 'You've already been so kind to me, all of you. I don't know what I would've done without you, but I've hidden myself away because I just didn't know what to do. I won't now, I promise.'

The puppy was pawing Nicola's arm, and Lottie smiled. 'See, Blossom won't let me be on my own.'

Blossom; all those flowers that frothed on the branches in spring, promising the summer to come. Laura could see why Lottie had chosen the name. Despite the darkness that had enveloped her, Lottie hadn't entirely given up on hope.

'We all need a friend like Blossom.' Alastair smiled, glancing at Laura. 'Miss Fellgate, would you mind if I borrowed your car?'

He was going to go after Joan, wasn't he?

'Of course,' Laura replied, tension in her voice as she

thought of Joan out there, driving through the blackout, intent on God knows what. Because, if she had hidden her true self so expertly, then she really was capable of anything. 'But if you're going to do what I think you are, then *I'll* drive.'

Nicola furrowed her brow. 'I won't ask,' she decided. 'Come on, Lottie, little Blossom, time for sausage rolls and cocoa back at the farmhouse. Yous two sure you won't stay?'

Alastair nodded. 'I can't, I'm afraid. But I'm sure Lau—Miss Fellgate will. Could you telephone the Black Bull in East Grinstead and get a message to Mr Wyngate? Let him know we need him in Bramble Heath.'

'The bloke in the hat?' Nicola asked. 'I'll get to it.'

Laura shook her head. 'No, I'm coming with you. I'm not letting you go on your own.'

At that moment, the distant wail of the air-raid siren sounded down in the village. They should get to shelter, Laura knew. But wouldn't that mean Joan would get away and would have valuable time to cover her tracks?

'Laura, please,' Alastair implored. 'Stay here where it's safe. Please.'

'I know these roads, Alastair, I've driven around here in the dark countless times,' she told him, utterly determined. 'Besides, nowhere's safe until we catch the traitor.'

FORTY-FIVE

The rain was just spotting as Laura and Alastair ran to the car but, once they were inside and bowling down the lane, the raindrops drummed a noisy tattoo against the roof, adding to the cacophony from the sirens and the roar of the planes taking off from the airbase. Every sound urged them to get indoors, but there was no possibility of that, no matter how much Laura craved the safety of a basement or a cellar. Whatever it took, whatever dangers they must face, Laura and Alastair had to pursue their quarry.

Somewhere along these narrow lanes was Joan, a woman who had seemed so kind, so ordinary. But now it seemed that, under that unremarkable surface, a devious, murderous traitor lurked.

'Dreadful weather, and in an air raid as well,' Laura remarked to Alastair, as the windscreen wipers struggled back and forth. 'She's got a few minutes' head start on us, but she may well be heading for East Grinstead. We need to go this way.'

They had reached the top of the lane, and Laura turned right.

'What do you know about her?' Alastair asked, the words tight. 'I can't afford to get this wrong, Laura.' Then he murmured, almost to himself, 'I *know* it's her.'

'Not a great deal, really,' Laura said, steering around a large puddle that was spreading across the road. Water splashed up against the side of the car. 'She's from East Grinstead and has been a delivery driver ever since the beginning of the war. She knows the area better than me; she's driven from farm to farm around here for the last couple of years. She always seemed so pleasant and helpful, though, that's what I don't understand. You saw her tonight – would you expect the traitor who's been poisoning the cows, setting fires and doing their level best to bring down Bramble Heath to come and help with the lambing? But the clues certainly point her way...'

'Helping with the lambing gives her an excuse to be on the roads after blackout,' Alastair pointed out. 'And it makes her look innocent... it's a perfect smokescreen. "Joan *couldn't* be a traitor, she's always so ready to help out".'

'That's true...' Laura murmured. 'Helpful old Joan, doing her bit.' Her tone had turned bitter. What a slithering hypocrite that woman was.

They had passed Bramble Heath, the village shrouded in darkness, the cottages empty as everyone hurried to their shelters. The rain was falling heavily now, and the roads were slick with water. Laura drove as carefully as she could, but she knew – at least, she hoped – that Joan would be going slower. She had a bald tyre, after all, and that could be lethal in the rain if she tried to drive fast.

They reached a crossroads, the white of the painted-out signpost standing out like a sentinel in the night. And just ahead, Laura saw it. The dark bulk of a van.

'That's her, Alastair, it's got to be!' she told him excitedly. She could hear the engine too, and a sudden memory forced its way forward. When she had heard that engine late at night it had seemed familiar, though she hadn't been able to say why. And now she knew; it was Joan's van. She'd met her so often in the lanes and on the farms around Bramble Heath that the sound of the engine had blended into the background, much like the driver.

'Can you get in front of her?' Alastair asked urgently. 'Block her off so she has to stop.'

'I'll try,' Laura said, glancing at Alastair for a moment before focusing on the shiny surface of the road.

She sped up, water hissing against the wheels, closing in on the van. Joan must've heard the car coming behind, but she didn't accelerate. Laura took a chance, hoping against hope that no other vehicles would be coming in the opposite direction on such a dreadful night, and overtook.

Once she was ahead of Joan, she flipped open the window and stuck out her arm, waving at Joan to stop as she slowed down.

In the mirror, Laura could see the van slow and finally come to a halt. She sank back against the seat. 'This is it, Alastair. Be careful, though, won't you? We don't know what she's capable of.'

'If anything happens, get in touch with Wyngate through the War Office,' Alastair told her, yet she didn't want to entertain the notion of something happening that meant Alastair couldn't get in touch with Mr Wyngate himself. It wouldn't be fair, not after they'd come through so much. But she knew that Joan could be very dangerous indeed as soon as she knew they were on to her. A woman who would poison livestock, start lethal fires, strike people over their heads and leave them for dead... She could be capable of anything.

High above the little village of Bramble Heath the sky hummed with the sound of aircraft. But if Alastair felt afraid now, Laura detected no trace of it. There was only determination in his expression when he said, 'I *know* she's our traitor. We've got her now.'

Martha's face suddenly appeared before Laura, the young woman who'd died doing her duty, caught by a bomb out in the open during a raid. And now, she and Alastair were just as exposed as she had been. What if one of those planes passing overhead dropped a bomb on *them*? But they couldn't run now. Martha had died trying to save the livestock who she knew were so essential to the home front; the very animals that Joan had tried so hard to destroy.

FORTY-SIX

They got out of the car, Laura ignoring the deep puddles her feet sank into. The rain bounced off the surface of the road and soaked through her dress.

Joan flipped open her window and leaned out. 'Oh, Laura, Commander Seaton! What's up? Have you got a problem with your car?'

I've got a problem with you, Laura thought.

'Miss Hodgson,' Alastair said, polite as ever despite, or perhaps because of, his suspicions. There was a certain steeliness to him now, though, which Laura had first witnessed when he had finally put Mr Morgan in his place. 'Would you mind getting out of the van?'

'It's raining, Commander,' Joan replied. 'And I really should get going – I don't want to stop. There's an air raid, you know.'

Just as she spoke, Laura looked up at the sound of planes passing somewhere above the clouds overhead. She shivered, feeling exposed. *Are they ours, or are they the enemy?* Then she looked over at Joan. There, sitting in that van with her friendly, familiar smile, was one of the enemy.

Alastair approached the van as he told Joan, 'You've a bald

tyre; it's dangerous on these wet roads.' He took hold of the handle and opened the door. 'Why don't you let us drive you home?'

Joan winced at the rain, looking reluctant to get wet. But she climbed out anyway, and stood there, her arms folded. She left the engine running, evidently keen to get away. 'I know... I keep meaning to get it changed. But you don't need to drive me home, honestly.'

Laura watched Joan, seeking some proof that she was the traitor they sought, but there was none. She was still Joan, seemingly as innocent as ever, but her gaze had settled on Alastair and in that unblinking gaze... *that* was the proof Laura was seeking. There was something in it, a hint of malice that she couldn't conceal.

'Don't forget your keys.' Alastair turned to the cab of the van, ready to cut off the one avenue of escape still open to the traitor.

Suddenly, there was a flash in the darkness, and Laura only registered that it was the blade of a knife when it was too late.

Joan's arm flew out and came down on Alastair's shoulder, the knife slashing through his shirt and into his back.

'No!' Laura shouted, shocked to the core.

Joan shoved Alastair out of her way, into the road. She threw herself into the van, then slammed the door behind her and, with the gearbox roaring its complaint, threw the vehicle into reverse. As Laura ran to Alastair's side Joan's van was hurtling backward along the lane, but Laura's thoughts were all for Alastair.

'I'm all right,' Alastair gasped, scrambling to his feet.

Laura put her arm round him. 'You're not all right, she's just stabbed you!'

Suddenly, through the rain, the dark countryside lit up in a blaze of white. Joan had stopped the van and turned the lights on full, as good as painting a target for the bombers high above.

Then she hit the accelerator, and the van took off with its tell-tale thunderous backfire, heading straight towards Laura and Alastair.

'Quick!' Laura ran for the side of the road, dragging Alastair with her. The van passed by so close that Laura could have reached out and touched it, and it didn't stop even as it hit their car and rammed it out of the way, clearing the road so Joan could make her escape.

Laura stared in disbelief at the van hurtling away through the rain. Then she turned to Alastair. 'That maniac could've killed you – she could've killed both of us! Are you sure you're all right? I know I'm a vet but you must let me patch you up.'

'It'll wait!' Alastair said urgently. He took Laura's hand and began to turn for the car, revealing a slick of blood splashed across the back of his shirt. 'Come on!'

FORTY-SEVEN

Laura sped off down the lane after the traitor. Despite being rammed out of the way, her car didn't seem any the worse for wear, apart from a few dents.

Joan's headlights lit up the road, making her easy to spot and, with her heart pounding, Laura was soon hard on her heels.

That woman up ahead would've killed Alastair without a second thought. She had poisoned all those farm animals, leaving them to suffer, without blinking. She had set that terrible fire that had almost killed Lottie, just days before Martha had paid the greatest price for her country. And right now, Martha's loving boyfriend George and all the brave airmen of Bramble Heath were risking their lives to protect them all, while this woman, this traitor, was attacking them from within.

I'll stop you. I will.

The van backfired again as Joan followed a bend in the road and skidded in the rain before she regained control. Laura took the corner more carefully, the water gushing up against the car.

'I need to get in front of her again,' Laura said as she drove.

As if Joan had heard her, the van took a sudden turn,

forcing Laura to brake harshly in order to take the turn and follow her. She glanced quickly at Alastair; the last thing he needed at that moment was to be flung around inside the car. Despite his pallor, Laura sensed his determination. He wasn't going to give up now.

But how much blood was he losing? Was he really okay?

Alastair turned to look at Laura, gingerly shifting his shoulder against the car seat as he assured her, 'You don't need to worry about me.'

But Laura knew she would never stop worrying about him. Not while the Nazis and traitors like Joan threatened his life, and the lives of everyone and everything she loved.

Through the racket of the rain hammering on the car's roof and the hiss of water on the road, Laura heard planes overhead again. She hoped against hope that they weren't the enemy, but suddenly she heard it, cutting through the night, the high-pitched whistle of— no, it couldn't be.

Not again.

But the sound couldn't have been clearer, and Laura went cold: *That's a bomb.*

The whole world shook as the bomb struck one of the wheat fields that bordered the side of the road, drawn to them by the lights of Joan's van. The noise was phenomenal, a shuddering, thunderous *boom* as it hit the ground. In the road ahead Joan instinctively lurched the van away from the site of the impact, and the bald tyre on the rear axle caught the muddy edge of the road. Suddenly the vehicle was spinning on its axis, before it skidded across the rain-slicked surface and slammed into a farm gate.

Flames licked up from the field where the bomb had struck, igniting even the wet crop. There was no movement from inside the van.

'You don't think she's dead, do you?' Laura asked Alastair, shocked at the violence of what she'd just seen.

'She'd better bloody not be.' Alastair threw the door open and climbed out into the rain.

Laura followed him out of the car. The blood had spread across the back of his wet shirt, turning his back scarlet. She was desperate to clean up the wound and patch him up until she could get him to a hospital. She knew he needed to stop losing blood, and fast.

But they had to deal with Joan first.

The flames from the fire lit up the night, flickering against the van as if Laura was staring into hell. Joan was in the driving seat, staring ahead in a daze. Her scarf had fallen back from her head, revealing her blonde hair. Blood trickled down her cheek from a cut on her forehead.

For a horrible moment, Laura thought she was dead – then Joan's head turned slowly to face them and she glared through the window, her face a mask of such hatred that Laura gasped in horror.

'Could I have a length of that rope of yours?' Alastair asked Laura as he opened the door of the van. This time he was taking no chances as he took Joan's arm, and she stepped down from the van on shaking legs. The crash had knocked the stuffing out of her but that didn't mean she wasn't still dangerous. Laura knew that now.

'Of course,' Laura said, backing away towards her car. She couldn't take her eyes off Joan. The monster.

Laura took the rope from the boot. Bits of straw were stuck to it from the lambing, and the horrible contrast struck Laura: the rope that had helped to bring innocent life into the world would now bind a traitorous killer.

She hurried back with the rope.

'There's not just me, you know,' Joan said coolly. 'There's a storm blowing in.'

'More of a squall really,' Alastair replied, apparently as unruffled as ever.

Laura noticed that Alastair's injured shoulder was troubling him badly; he was holding Joan using his other arm.

'I'll tie her,' Laura said. Alastair nodded and brought Joan's hands behind her back. Only now, out of their captive's eyesight, did Laura see him allow himself a wince of discomfort.

Laura bound Joan's hands behind her back. She tried not to be harsh, but a memory hit her of Miss Pearson's farm, of Daisy, the cow who had lain with its head in her lap as Laura cried. Then, following swiftly on, was the face of Martha standing by the burning barn as she cried out for her trapped sister.

Martha, that poor girl.

'Ouch, too tight!' Joan complained, but Laura didn't care. Perhaps the rope was a little too tight round her wrists, but it was nothing compared to the suffering she had caused.

'It'll do,' Laura replied, without any sympathy.

'You want to watch him, Laura,' Joan warned as Alastair searched the pockets of her coat. He took out the knife first and handed it to Laura. The handle was sticky with his blood. 'Went a little bit doolally when we turned his wife to ashes. Probably still not quite all there.' She gave Alastair a bright smile and told him, 'There's not much we don't know, Commander.'

'Shut up,' Laura snapped, hot anger rising up inside her like lava. How dare she speak to Alastair like that? He was a hero, who had risked so much and suffered. A dirty turncoat like her had no right to say such things. 'The only person around here who's mad is *you*. Lottie almost died in that fire, you could have killed her, or anyone there. And twelve precious cows died on just one farm, and goodness knows how many others fell ill, because of you. And all for what? For that hateful man in Germany! You're a traitor – you're a traitor and I despise you!'

Alastair said nothing, his gaze meeting Joan's as he took a paper bag out of her coat and sniffed the contents.

'Cyanide, Miss Hodgson?' he asked. She shrugged one

shoulder as though to say *what of it?* and loathing pitched in Laura's stomach. 'For the ewes and the newborns?'

'There were too many folks around for me to use it.' Joan sighed. 'That's the problem with a village like this.'

Joan sounded so casual, and that made it worse for Laura. Much worse. She would've killed pregnant ewes, or ones whose lambs were suckling, and she wouldn't even have blinked. How anyone could've stepped into that barn, so full of new life, with death on their minds, was beyond Laura.

'That's the blessing of a village like this.' And Alastair was right. Bramble Heath was a place where people pulled together. It was a place where there was no room for the sort of hateful monster Joan had proven herself to be.

A large dark car entered the lane, its headlamps extinguished. Joan glanced towards it, then back to Alastair. She narrowed her eyes and twisted her lips into a cruel smile. When she spoke again, her words were drenched in malice.

'There's not only me, don't forget.'

FORTY-EIGHT

'Oh, we won't!' Wyngate slammed the door of his car and strode towards the trio, and Laura's heart filled with relief. Behind him, two uniformed soldiers were climbing out of the vehicle. 'And thanks to your radio, we'll be gathering your friends from across the country over the next day or so. Maybe we'll throw you a party. Or a wake.'

Laura shivered, and it wasn't just because the rain was still falling and she was soaked through. She knew what fate awaited traitors like Joan. There was a rope round her wrists now, but soon there would be one round her neck.

And yet Joan's eyes gleamed with pride, not fear. She was proud of what she had done; the death, the suffering, to her it was a job well done. She'd have done much more, committed even worse acts of treachery, given half the chance.

Wyngate put his hand on Joan's shoulder and glanced down at her bound wrists. He looked from Alastair to Laura and gave a nod that seemed almost impressed.

'Don't forget what I said!' Joan warned Laura as Wyngate led her towards his waiting car. 'He went mad! He'll probably go again one day.'

'Mad.' Alastair shook his head as he repeated the word. He drew in a long breath and Laura saw him swallow. Then, to her surprise he called, 'Mr Wyngate, just a minute.'

Wyngate paused and turned to watch as Alastair approached Joan. She smiled and asked, 'Are you going to hit me, Commander? Or shoot me?'

'Neither,' Alastair replied. 'Whatever you might think of me, know this. You failed, Miss Hodgson, because of the decent people in Bramble Heath. Villages like this are precisely why your sort *won't* win.' He gave Wyngate a nod. 'Take her away.'

And the soldiers took Joan's arms and led her to the car.

As they reached the vehicle, Wyngate opened the rear door and, to Laura's surprise, Sarah hopped out, her slippered feet landing with a splash on the road. The girl was wearing a pair of blue pyjamas and a dressing gown of red and blue stripes, which was fastened with a belt at her waist. From within the cosy garment, Winnie's glittering eyes peered out.

'I'll take Miss Hodgson,' said Wyngate sternly. 'You can take these two. Seems like a fair swap.'

'Sarah?' Laura gasped, trying to work out how a girl in her pyjamas could end up in Wyngate's vehicle. 'What on earth are you doing out so late?'

'Winnie got scared as we were running for the shelter and took off,' said the plucky evacuee as the cat lifted its head to rub against her chin. 'I managed to get hold of her but this one here' – she jerked her thumb towards Wyngate – 'nearly ran us down!'

Was there a flicker of amusement on his granite face? Laura was sure there was.

'A little girl and a cat in the middle of the road in a black-out?' He shook his head, watching as the car door closed on Joan. 'It'd never happen in London.'

Sarah looked back at the vehicle with wide eyes, realisation dawning as she gasped, 'Joan's never a blinking Nazi?'

And in reply, Mr Wyngate lifted one finger to his lips and whispered, 'State secret?'

'State secret,' Sarah replied, awestruck.

Laura let out a long sigh, as if she had been holding her breath the whole time that the traitor had been at large. But it was finally over. For Bramble Heath, at least. And perhaps, now that Joan was arrested, the whole ring of traitors would fall like dominoes.

'Good riddance,' Laura said.

The flames where the bomb had hit had died down a little, and the rain was easing off.

Across the village the mournful sound of the all-clear sang out and, from the airbase at Heath Place, the clang of a fire bell could be heard. Soon, the flames in the wheat field would be extinguished and the village would sleep safe and sound once more.

'Laura...' Alastair murmured weakly, watching the departing car as Mr Wyngate took Joan away, 'I think maybe I ought to see Nurse Russell.'

'Oh, Alastair, you should.' Laura nodded. 'Let me help you get back into the car.'

He'd be ready to drop now, Laura knew; his adrenaline would've given out. She slipped her arm round his waist but, before guiding him to the car, she rose up on her tiptoes and kissed his cheek.

'A kiss for the very brave Commander Seaton,' she told him gently.

'From the equally brave Miss Fellgate,' Alastair replied. He leaned against Laura, giving a gasp of pain. 'We got her, Laura. We bloody got her.'

'We did!' Laura said, as she helped Alastair to the car. 'We bloody did! Gosh... the next time the phone rings, I won't be thinking, *is it another poisoning?* And even though the bombs may still come, at least our Land Girls and farmers are safe from fires set by one of Bramble Heath's own. That nasty, vile woman.'

'Take that, Adolf!' Sarah announced with glee. 'Bramble Heath won't stand for it!'

Laura smiled at Sarah's joy. 'Exactly – we caught her in the end.'

Sarah opened the passenger door for Alastair and, as Laura helped him into the car, she recalled the evening before, when he'd helped *her*. He was a hero, and he didn't deserve to be called mad, to have his wife's tragic, pointless death mocked.

'I'm just so angry with her, Alastair,' Laura said. 'For what she's done, of course, but also for what she said tonight.'

'It doesn't mean anything.' Alastair climbed into the car. 'Not coming from someone like her.'

'People like her...' But Laura couldn't find the words. Not polite ones, anyway, and none that she could say in front of Sarah. She asked their unexpected passenger, 'Isn't Mrs Hubbard going to be worried about you?'

'I bet she will,' said Sarah. 'But I didn't want to leave Winnie. Martha didn't think twice when the cows needed her, did she?'

Alastair smiled and told the girl, 'We won't go far wrong with girls like you on our side.' Then he gave Laura a somewhat cheeky look and added, 'And you too, Miss Fellgate.'

'Well, I like to do my bit,' she replied with a wink. 'And it helps having chaps from the Ministry popping by too! Let's go and get you bandaged up, and drop Sarah off at home.'

She climbed into the driving seat as Sarah and Winnie settled in the back, and they set off. The car sounded a little more rattly than usual, but it wasn't surprising after the way Joan had rammed into it. Images from the evening hurtled through Laura's mind as if they were on a film strip – the chase, the rain, the planes, the knife, the blood, the bomb, the fire – but she pushed them away to concentrate on the drive, navigating the wet roads.

'She was so ordinary, that's what I don't understand,' Laura said after a short while, trying to understand how such a humdrum person could commit so many dreadful crimes. 'I thought traitors would stick out like sore thumbs.'

But they look just like the rest of us. And so do heroes.

Alastair shook his head. 'Life would be easier if they did.' He glanced towards Laura. 'Your letter started all this. We'd never have caught her if it wasn't for you – or at least it would have taken us a lot longer, and goodness knows what else she would have done. You should be very proud of that.'

'I just did what I thought was right,' Laura replied. It meant a lot to hear him say that, though, especially a man as brave as he was. A man who'd been attacked and who right now was in pain. But he hadn't given up the chase, and because of him, because of them, a traitor was heading for a prison cell. And Bramble Heath – indeed all of England – was just a little bit safer for it. 'We're nearly there, don't worry, we'll soon have you patched up.'

As they reached the village, Laura saw Mrs Hubbard standing on the path outside her cottage in her dressing gown, her hair bristling with pin curls. She looked beside herself with worry for the girl she'd taken on when she already had a house full of children. Clearly, her heart was big enough for everyone.

'Sorry!' Sarah was already saying as Laura pulled the car in outside the cottage and the girl opened the door and climbed down. 'I found Winnie, then Laura and Commander Seaton said I'd be safer sheltering with them than trying to get home.' She gave Mrs Hubbard a wide-eyed look and, somehow, so did Winnie; as they'd no doubt intended, Mrs Hubbard looked as though her heart would melt. 'We didn't mean no harm.'

And as Sarah had been told by Mr Wyngate, she had kept the secret of Joan's arrest.

'It's past your bedtime, young lady,' Mrs Hubbard said affectionately, then smiled with relief at Laura and Alastair. 'Thank you for taking care of her. Night!'

If only Mrs Hubbard knew what Sarah had witnessed. That had been quite an adventure for her; but the girl would never tell, Laura was sure.

Laura drove on. They arrived at the Russells' home, and she pulled up. 'This is becoming too much of a habit,' she said, hoping a little humour might help Alastair. 'They'll give us our own parking space at this rate.'

Someone inside the house must've heard the engine, as the front door opened and Henry appeared. He must've recognised them as he hurried down the path.

Laura got out of the car. 'Alastair's been attacked, Henry. Stabbed. Is Annie home?'

'Yes, she is,' Henry said, full of concern, and opened the passenger door for Alastair. 'Let me help you out, sir!'

'It's done, Constable.' Alastair sounded exhausted, as though the evening was finally catching up with him. 'Mr Wyngate has the traitor in custody.'

Henry must've seen the blood – it would've been hard to miss – and he carefully put his arm round Alastair's waist, levering him out of his seat.

'That is the best news I've heard all day. All week!' he admitted. 'But who on earth was it, Commander?'

'Since we've all signed the paperwork...' Alastair murmured. Then he said in a voice that was barely a whisper, 'Miss Joan Hodgson. I doubt it'll be made public, Constable.'

'Good heavens,' Henry whispered in reply.

Alastair winced and closed his eyes for a moment. He was in pain, Laura could see, even if he wasn't going to make a fuss over it. But someone needed to make a fuss of him. He wouldn't be alone any more.

He was a hero, and she would make sure he'd be looked after from now on. Just as she knew he would always look after her.

FORTY-NINE

Annie had made swift work of bandaging Alastair up, cleaning the wound and giving him a couple of stitches. Henry had stepped in with some brandy, as well as a clean shirt, while Laura sat beside him, holding his hand. She couldn't imagine how much it hurt, but at least Joan couldn't harm anyone else again. Alastair would still need to see the doctor at the airbase's sickbay the next day, but for now he was ready to go home to bed.

With a warning from Annie that Alastair couldn't be left alone overnight as he'd lost a fair amount of blood, Laura offered him her bed. It was a reversal of the night they'd spent together when he had been her guardian angel, watching over her. Now she'd do the same for him.

They got into the car and headed into the village, Laura driving carefully to avoid jolting Alastair about.

'I don't think my pyjamas will fit you,' she told him.

'I'll pick up what I need from the pub.' Alastair smiled. 'It's very kind of you to let me stay. You're sure your landlady won't object?'

'She won't at all,' Laura assured him. 'In fact, she'll posi-

tively encourage it. I didn't tell you, did I? From the first
moment I mentioned I was going to meet you in the pub, Iris
was convinced that we were dating. And she sounded very
pleased about it too.'

He chuckled and let his head rest back against the seat,
more relaxed now than Laura had seen him since the day they'd
met. Of course, he was probably just as shattered as she was, but
it was still nice to see the tension finally leave him.

'Mr Wyngate could give her a job with those powers of
observation,' he murmured.

'She says Mr Wyngate looks like a matinee idol.' Laura
giggled. 'What on earth would he make of that?'

She couldn't imagine he had any time for something as frivolous as film stars and Hollywood at all.

They arrived at the George and Dragon, and Laura helped
Alastair out of the car. She was so tired that her legs felt like
string, but she was determined to make sure Alastair passed the
night in as much comfort as he could.

Alastair had a guest key for a side door, and they headed
into the dark, empty pub. It was so odd to see it like this when it
was normally full of people.

The old wooden stairs creaked underfoot, and they reached
the landing. Laura had never been up here before, and she let
Alastair lead the way to his room. He walked carefully past
closed doors and unlocked the one that stood at the end of the
corridor, then stood back so Laura could go in first. Laura wasn't
sure why, but it felt as though being allowed into Alastair's
room was an act of true trust. He had been alone for too long
but had let her start to chip away at the wall that had contained
him. There'd be no more loneliness now.

The room was extremely neat, which didn't surprise Laura;
after all, it was the room of a man who had spent most of his life
in the military.

His suitcase was stowed on top of the wardrobe, his pyjamas

were folded tidily on his bed, and his toiletries were lined up on the side of the sink as if awaiting inspection by an officer.

But despite her first impressions, there was that scent of his cologne again, bringing with it an impression of spice and excitement.

And there, on the dresser, in a silver frame, was the photograph of a woman.

Laura knew who it was at once. *Vicky*.

She was frozen in time, beaming with joy, her light hair tousled by a breeze as she perched on a fence. And, poking their snouts between the wooden slats, were pigs.

Laura couldn't pretend she hadn't seen the photograph, and she sensed that Alastair had wanted her to see it, so that the two women could be introduced; at least, as far as fate had allowed.

'What a beautiful lady,' Laura whispered. 'You made her very happy, Alastair.'

'I hope so,' he said, settling his gaze on the wife he had lost. 'Because she certainly made me into a much happier man. A better man.' Alastair looked from the photograph to Laura. 'You and she would've got on. Forces of nature, each in your own way,'

Laura swallowed. Despite what was happening between her and Alastair now, she wished so much that Vicky had been spared, that he hadn't been forced to suffer. She took a step closer to the photograph and said, 'Hello, Vicky, pleased to meet you. I hope you don't mind, but I'll take good care, the *best* care of Alastair, I promise.'

Alastair kissed Laura's cheek. 'She'd tell you I need it.' He smiled. Then he began to gather what he needed for the evening.

Once he was packed, Laura took his bag for him and they went back down to the car. Laura had felt something change, as if Vicky had heard her, somehow. And as if she approved.

They arrived at Iris's cottage, and Laura helped Alastair into the house. Iris was still up, despite the late hour.

'I was worried,' she told Laura, then she saw Alastair's pallor. 'Oh, blimey, what's happened to you, Commander?'

'Lambing can be murder,' Alastair replied. 'But I'll live.'

'Those ewes really can kick, eh?' Iris tutted. *You'd be surprised*, Laura thought privately.

'Alastair needs to stay the night, if that's all right, Iris,' Laura told her. 'At Annie's request. He looked after me, so we're swapping roles. I hope you don't mind.'

Iris shook her head. 'Goodness me, no, I don't mind at all. You're more than welcome, Commander. You're a gentleman, and it's an honour to have you under my roof. Do you need anything? A hot-water bottle, perhaps?'

'Just a soft bed,' he assured Iris. 'It's very decent of you, Mrs Pearson. I'll contribute something for my board tonight, of course.'

Iris shook her head. 'No, you shan't! I won't hear of it. I won't take a penny from a chap like you. Go on, up to bed with you.'

Iris was, technically, a chaperone, but she had to be one of the world's worst. Laura helped Alastair up the stairs – they weren't wide enough for Iris to lend a hand too – and soon they were back in Laura's bedroom again.

'I bet you didn't think you'd see this place again so soon,' she said to Alastair, as she helped him to sit down on the bed. She gave him a gentle kiss on his cheek.

'But I'm very happy to,' Alastair replied with a smile. 'I think we'll both be glad of some company tonight.'

Laura left him to get ready for bed, then came back in, to find him settled under the covers in his pyjamas. She should have slept on top of the covers, as he had done yesterday, but she was so tired after that long, gruelling day that it didn't occur to her; she drew them back instead and slid in beside Alastair.

'Comfortable?' she asked him, although she knew that with a stab wound to the shoulder he couldn't be.

'Oddly enough, yes,' he said gently. 'I think it's the company that's the tonic.'

His words filled her heart with affection for him, and she took his hand before gently kissing him on the lips. 'I think it's only fair to tell you, Alastair, that I think I might be...' *Should I tell him? Oh, why not?* 'I think I'm falling for you.'

For a few moments Alastair didn't reply, but Laura saw the corners of his mouth curl into a smile. Then he lifted their linked fingers and kissed her hand. 'For me? A smart woman like you?'

'Of course!' Laura giggled. 'You've got brains, and you're ever so brave, and you're tough when you need to be, and adorable when you don't. You even know how to help deliver lambs, so really, I'd be a fool not to fall for you.'

But are you falling for me? Laura gazed into his eyes, and she was sure she saw something there. Something she'd never seen in the eyes of any other man before.

'It's very fortunate you said that.' Alastair leaned across and kissed her, his touch more tender than any she'd known. 'Because I'm falling for you too, Miss Fellgate. Hook, line and sinker.'

Alastair's words cut through Laura's tiredness. A thrill rushed through her body, as a whole new future, one she'd never allowed herself to imagine, opened up before her. *Love.* They were falling in love. The life Laura had thought she would live, fighting every battle alone, suddenly changed. Because maybe, just maybe, Alastair would be there, at her side.

She held his hand a little tighter, and kissed him on the lips again, this time lingering, enjoying. They had the rest of their lives ahead of them; there was no need to rush.

FIFTY

A week later, Laura and Alastair were sitting in the garden of the George and Dragon pub. She was enjoying some much-needed downtime between trips to the farms to help with lambing, and Alastair was by now over the worst of his injury. But somehow, perhaps thanks to Mr Wyngate, a magical order had come down from on high that he was to spend a month convalescing. And Alastair had taken that to mean a whole month in Bramble Heath.

Laura hadn't complained, and Alastair had decided that accompanying her on her rounds counted as part of his convalescence. He'd introduced a great many ewes to their lambs over the past few days and had even bottle-fed a lamb whose mother was struggling with her triplets.

On one of the other benches, Lottie and Nicola sat together with George, who raised his pint to Alastair, the man from the Ministry who had become his firm friend. They all looked tired, and a haunting sadness lay in the eyes of both George and Lottie. But even so, there was real happiness on their faces as Sally and Freddy came over to sit with them, and they watched Sarah chase Blossom and Wilbur around the garden. Now that the two dogs were together, Blossom's paternity was absolutely not in doubt; the similarity between them was striking. Even Winnie the cat was in on the action, travelling in the baggy pocket of Sarah's cardigan as she pelted this way and that around the beer garden with her friends.

But not everyone was relaxing – Laura heard a toot and saw Annie heading off up the high street on her motorbike. From the bench where he sat with some of the pilots who served under his command, Group Captain Chambers watched with a smile as his fiancée sped past.

Nicola put her arm round Lottie's shoulders and picked up her pint. 'To Martha!' she said, looking from Lottie to George. 'We won't ever forget her.'

'To my girl,' George replied, offering Lottie a gentle smile. 'She was one in a million.'

Lottie lifted her glass. She smiled wistfully and said, 'To Martha. I miss you.' Then she leaned against Nicola, resting her head on her friend's shoulder.

Poor George and Lottie. But they had friends; they had the support of everyone in Bramble Heath. They would get through this.

And Laura didn't feel as tormented as she once had by her memories of Coventry. She still thought about it, of course; the memories would never leave her. But the terror and the fear were fading in the face of her knowledge that, when a traitor had picked on Bramble Heath, she had stood up and stopped them.

Laura took a sip from her half pint. 'It's nice to have a breather,' she said to Alastair. 'But are you sure you're comfortable there, darling?'

She wasn't sure if Alastair was fed up with her fussing over him, but he was still healing from his wound, and she had promised Vicky she would look after him, so that was exactly what she planned to do.

'Probably too comfortable,' Alastair admitted contentedly. He certainly didn't seem tired of her attentions; in fact, the couple were virtually inseparable. Eventually he would go back to London, Laura knew, but the capital wasn't so far away, and the war couldn't last for ever. They'd see one another as much as they could, she was sure of it. 'But that's not a complaint.'

'I'm glad to hear it,' Laura replied, and pecked a kiss to his cheek. 'I'm so glad you're going to be here for a month. I just wish it could be longer, but that's very selfish of me, I know.'

'And weekends,' he assured her. 'And every other opportunity.'

Laura beamed at him. When she'd posted that letter off to the Ministry of Agriculture, she hadn't expected a reply, let alone... this.

She heard the throb of a powerful car engine, and looked up, wondering who was driving a vehicle like that through Bramble Heath. It had to be someone from the airbase, surely?

A sleek black car had stopped by the beer garden's fence, and Laura could make out the figure in the passenger seat. It was Iris's matinee idol back in the village, it seemed; chauffeured in a ministerial car, no less.

'Wyngate?' Laura whispered to Alastair. 'That's a fancy car and a half. Who else is there in the back seat with him?'

But other than a thick cloud of smoke emanating from the slight opening in one of the back windows, there were no clues. Laura didn't suppose she'd recognise them anyway; who knew what exalted circles Mr Wyngate travelled in?

The door opened and Wyngate climbed out of the car. He pointed one elegant finger at Alastair and Laura, then crooked it, no doubt to summon them to him. It wasn't very polite, but Laura got the impression that this was just how Mr Wyngate did business.

Laura rose to her feet and took Alastair's elbow to help him up.

'I wonder who Mr Wyngate's passenger is?' she whispered, mystified.

'I wouldn't like to guess,' he admitted. 'But I bet he's signed his paperwork.'

They met Wyngate at the gate to the beer garden, just a few feet from the car. He greeted them with a curt nod and said, 'Congratulations on the new job, Commander. I know you'll make a go of it.'

'New job?' Laura glanced at Alastair, confused. He hadn't mentioned a new job to her, but she could see he was just as flummoxed by Wyngate's words as she was. 'What do you mean, Mr Wyngate?'

'I haven't got—' Alastair began, but Wyngate simply cut him off by speaking over him. It was extraordinarily rude, but extraordinarily effective.

'I know a base of operations in East Grinstead isn't exactly the glamour assignment,' he said. 'But Agriculture – *actually* Agriculture this time – needs a good man on the ground to coordinate the national effort in these parts and keep the country fed and the crops watered. There was no better choice, Commander.' He gave a nod of approval. 'I trust you'll be able to find suitable accommodation in the area.'

East Grinstead?

Laura bounced on her toes with excitement. 'Oh, Alastair, you can live in Bramble Heath! I can't believe it! This is wonderful, so, so wonderful!' And she hugged him – carefully, to avoid his wounded shoulder. He wouldn't be going back to London. She wouldn't have to worry about him in that big city with the bombs raining down all the time, and she could see him almost every day.

'Mr Wyngate—' Alastair began, but his words were forgotten as he returned Laura's hug. It might not be terribly professional in front of the man from the Ministry, but she didn't care, and she had a feeling Alastair didn't either. This was where he belonged now: in Laura's arms.

'I hadn't heard anything,' Alastair finally told Wyngate, his arm still round Laura's waist as though to be sure not to lose her. 'But I'm happy to accept.'

Wyngate nodded. 'I've already accepted on your behalf.' He glanced over his shoulder to the car, where a fresh plume of smoke drifted up from the window. 'The other matter is... *concluded*. Our bird sang and we gathered up the whole nest.'

Laura knew what that meant. Despite Joan's pride in her horrendous deeds even when she was arrested, she had folded under questioning and named all her co-conspirators. Maybe even her handler too. Who knew how big that ring of traitors was? Joan might've saved her neck by giving up the other names, but Laura knew that it would be in exchange for a very long time behind bars instead.

'It's over,' Laura sighed. 'All over. Thank goodness! We can all sleep a little easier in our beds now.'

'Quite an uncomfortable bed in her case, for quite a long time,' Wyngate assured them. 'But given the alternative, it's amazing how even the most vicious traitors suddenly discover the error of their ways.'

Alastair nodded. 'Cowards are often like that,' he said. Then he offered his hand to Wyngate, who took it and shook. 'Thank you, Mr Wyngate, for letting us know. And for trusting me when a lot of people didn't.'

'*She* did.' Wyngate nodded towards Laura as he released Alastair's hand. 'Miss Fellgate, good job. Very good job indeed.'

Wyngate didn't seem to be the sort of person to fling praise about; it made his words mean even more to her.

'Just doing my duty,' Laura replied with a smile. 'But thank you, Mr Wyngate.'

A pony clip-clopped along the street, pulling the trap in

which Farmer Bryant and Farmer Gosling sat, heading for the pub and their nightly pint. Wyngate seemed to take their arrival as his signal to depart and, with a nod of farewell, he turned back to the car.

'Now then, veterinary, now then, sir!' called Farmer Bryant. 'All's well that ends well!'

'Good evening!' Alastair replied.

'Next time I need a lamb yanking, I'll know who to call on,' Bryant told Alastair as the trap carried the two farmers past the sleek ministerial car. 'I'll get you and Miss Veterinary here a pint in.'

'Thank you, Nobby, that's very kind of you,' Laura told Bryant.

From the beer garden there was a sudden streak of tortoise-shell lightning as Winnie the cat dashed across the grass and vaulted over the fence, with a laughing Sarah giving chase. The cat hopped up onto the car bonnet and Sarah dashed after her, shouting through her laughter, 'Winnie! Winnie!'

Behind Laura, the car window was lowered a little further and the unseen passenger asked in his unmistakable drawl, 'You called, young miss?'

Sarah shuddered to a halt, wide-eyed. Then she dropped into a curtsey and gasped, 'Blimey!'

Laura stared in amazement. It was Winston Churchill himself. Here, in Bramble Heath.

From his place in the passenger seat, Wyngate turned and whispered something to the prime minister. Churchill's gaze swept over Laura a moment before he said, 'Thank you, Commander, for helping us to resolve this most unpleasant situation.' Then he inclined his head towards Laura. 'And to you too, Miss Fellgate, our thanks for all that you have done to bring this dreadful conspiracy to light and, most importantly, to smother it.'

Laura swallowed. She was astonished. 'Thank you, sir.

You've said often enough this war is being fought on the home front too – we all have to do our bit, don't we? I was just doing what anyone in my shoes would've done.'

'Thank you, sir,' Alastair said respectfully. 'We simply did what was right.'

'Now, young miss, please retrieve your cat,' said Churchill benevolently to Sarah. She trotted to the bonnet and scooped up Winnie, who was happy to be deposited back into the girl's pocket. 'Good evening.'

'Cheerio, Mr C,' said Sarah with a smile, waving merrily at the car. 'And you too, Mr Wyngate.'

With that, Churchill rolled up the window as the stately vehicle pulled away with a purr of its powerful engine.

Still amazed, Laura watched it go, then she turned to Alastair. 'Did that really just happen? It did, didn't it? And oh, Alastair, you're staying!'

'You're stuck with me now.' Alastair slipped his arms round Laura's waist and embraced her. 'And I couldn't be happier.'

Laura hugged him back, this wonderful man who had suddenly come into her life and changed everything. A brave man who had suffered through so much and had survived, who had fought with her side by side against the Bramble Heath traitor. It had all happened so fast; but the truth was they had both waited a long time until their paths had finally crossed.

And thank goodness they had.

She gazed at him, the commander she was falling in love with. 'I can't think of anyone else I'd rather be stuck with! And there's nowhere else I'd rather us be than Bramble Heath, our little corner of England.'

EPILOGUE
1946

Laura leaned against the pen and the piglets rushed through the straw to see her, snuffling and oinking with excitement.

'Hello, little fellows, how are you?' she said, and smiled at Alastair as he came over to join her. 'They're in fine fettle, aren't they? And to think we thought we'd lose the whole litter when their mum got into trouble.'

'Well, we're very lucky on this farm, you see,' Alastair replied. He leaned on the pen beside her and put one arm round his wife's shoulders. 'We happen to have an absolutely splendid vet.'

'And we also happen to have a resident farmer who's a pig expert!' Laura chuckled and rested her head against his shoulder. 'By the way, those Soay sheep we asked about? The very, very rare ones? They've said yes! We're going to have our own little flock, and over time, of course, it'll grow.'

And Laura couldn't be happier about it. She had never expected to be one half of a thriving new farm – but then again, she had never expected to be one half of a married couple either.

But that was exactly what had happened and now, as the

country settled into peacetime at last, she and Alastair had found the idyll they had been seeking. Not too far from their beloved Bramble Heath and not too far from the coast that Alastair had always loved, the dreams of a farm they had nurtured during the war were coming true.

'Of course they said yes.' Alastair beamed at the news. 'That's because nobody can say no to you. You're irresistible.'

Laura snuggled against him. 'Well, I suppose you could say I'm persistent.'

But there was something else she needed to tell him, and she was sure he'd be very happy to hear it too.

'Talking of our own flock, Alastair, I have something to tell you... When I went to town earlier, I was actually going to see the doctor. You see, darling, I've got some very exciting news. I'm going to have a baby! We're going to have our own little family!'

'You're—' Suddenly, Alastair put his arms round Laura and embraced her with such enthusiasm that for a moment he swept her feet clean off the floor. 'Our very own flock!'

'Isn't it wonderful?' Laura sighed as she came back to earth. 'I love you so much, Alastair. I never thought I'd fall in love, then one day... we somehow found each other, in the middle of war, despite everything. And here we are.'

'Here we are,' Alastair echoed. 'Exactly where we were meant to be.' He kissed her and whispered playfully, 'I love you, veterinary. You make this farmer very happy indeed.'

They had faced pain and terror together, risked their lives for their country, and now this was their reward: love and happiness, and a farm and a family of their own.

Wherever life took them now, they'd take care of each other with all the love and courage they had. And in the end, that was all that mattered.

A LETTER FROM ELLIE CURZON

Dear Reader,

We want to say a huge thank you for choosing to read *The Wartime Vet*. If you enjoyed it, and want to keep up to date with all our latest releases, just sign up at the following link. Your email address will never be shared and you can unsubscribe at any time.

www.bookouture.com/ellie-curzon

Though Ellie Curzon is one name, it takes two authors to make her, and we both hope that you enjoyed *The Wartime Vet*. We were thrilled to salute the men and women who kept the home fires burning and the people and animals of Britain safe. We'd love you to sign up to our newsletter so you can be the first to find out the latest news about our series, *A Village at War*, as well as the folk of Bramble Heath, and even the unflappable man from the Ministry!

We would be very grateful if you could write a review. We'd love to hear what you think, and it makes such a difference helping new readers to discover one of our books for the first time.

We love hearing from our readers – you can get in touch through social media or our website.

Thanks,

Ellie

www.elliecurzon.co.uk

facebook.com/elliecurzonauthor
x.com/MadameGilflurt
goodreads.com/ellie_curzon

ACKNOWLEDGEMENTS

Huge thanks to the team at Bookouture, especially our editor Rhianna Louise, whose faultless guidance and enormous enthusiasm has really made *The Wartime Vet* all that it could be. Enormous amounts of love and thanks are always due to Rick and Gordon and, of course, Pippa and Vincent, who would prefer to avoid vets altogether.

Helen would like to thank Annelis for her stories about the animals on her smallholding, and Emmy for her tales of veterinary college. You've both helped to inspire this story!

Catherine's heartfelt gratitude goes out to her granddad Steve, who shared his great love of the British countryside with her – you never know what you might find. She still believes that distant light is Dick Turpin's camp!

And thank you to you, reader, for being the very best.

PUBLISHING TEAM

Turning a manuscript into a book requires the efforts of many people. The publishing team at Bookouture would like to acknowledge everyone who contributed to this publication.

Commercial
Lauren Morrissette
Jil Thielen
Imogen Allport

Cover design
Eileen Carey

Data and analysis
Mark Alder
Mohamed Bussuri

Editorial
Rhianna Louise
Lizzie Brien

Copyeditor
Jacqui Lewis

Proofreader
Elaini Caruso

Marketing
Alex Crow
Melanie Price
Occy Carr
Cíara Rosney

Operations and distribution
Marina Valles
Stephanie Straub

Production
Hannah Snetsinger
Mandy Kullar
Jen Shannon

Publicity
Kim Nash
Noelle Holten
Myrto Kalavrezou
Jess Readett
Sarah Hardy

Rights and contracts
Peta Nightingale
Richard King
Saidah Graham

Milton Keynes UK
Ingram Content Group UK Ltd.
UKHW012246290324
440241UK00004B/162

9 781837 909698